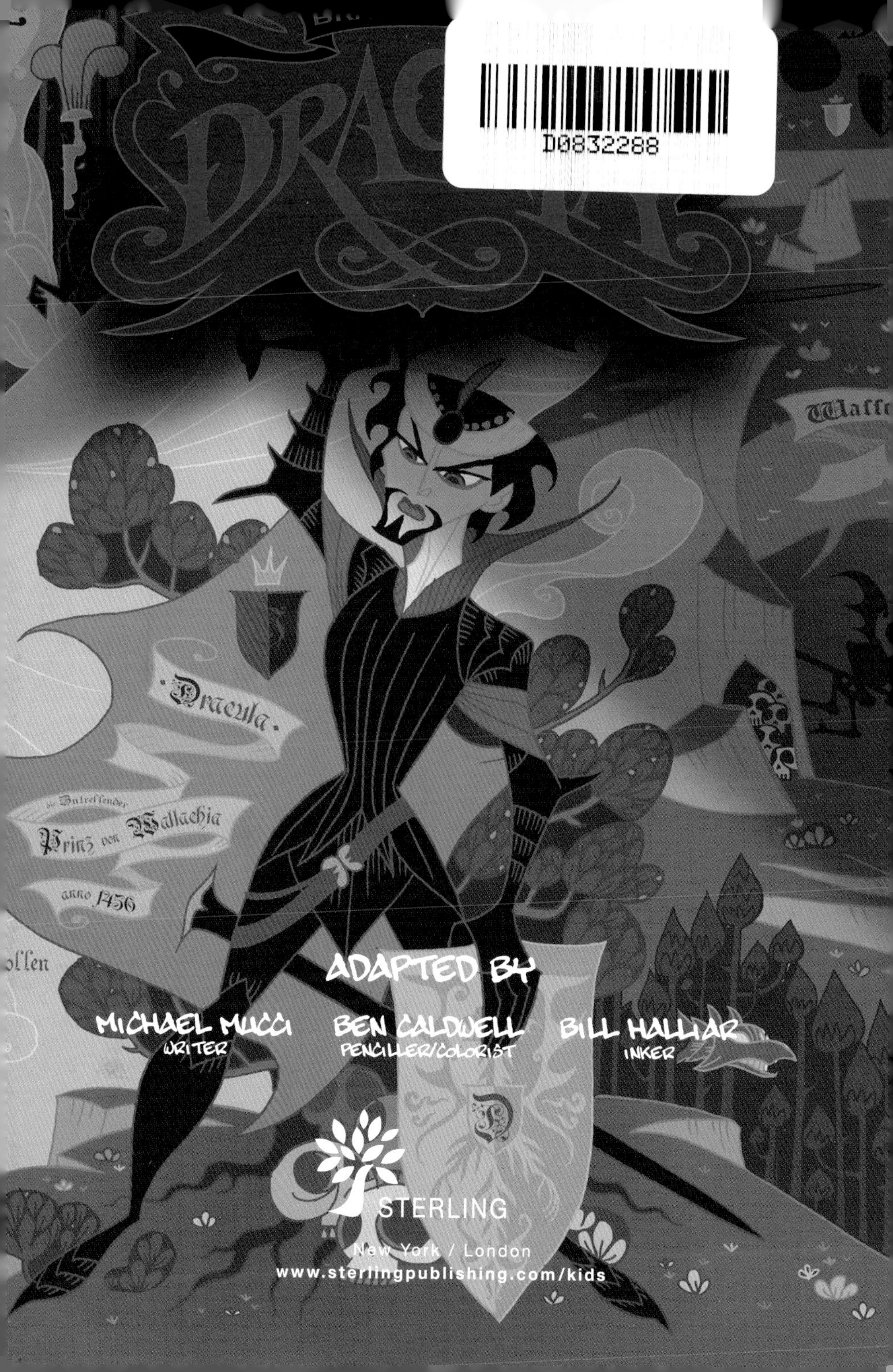
Dracula
die Butreffender
Prinz von Wallachia
anno 1456

ADAPTED BY
MICHAEL MUCCI
WRITER
BEN CALDWELL
PENCILLER/COLORIST
BILL HALLIAR
INKER

STERLING
New York / London
www.sterlingpublishing.com/kids

Y
DRA

FOR MY FOLKS,
WHO ALWAYS EMBRACED
THE IDEA OF MONSTERS
IN THE CLOSETS AND
TENTACLES UNDER
THE BEDS. I WILL BE
FOREVER GRATEFUL
- M. M.

FOR DAVID MOORE, WHO
TAUGHT ME TO LOVE
HISTORY.
- B. C.

Gift
6.95
10/08
DS

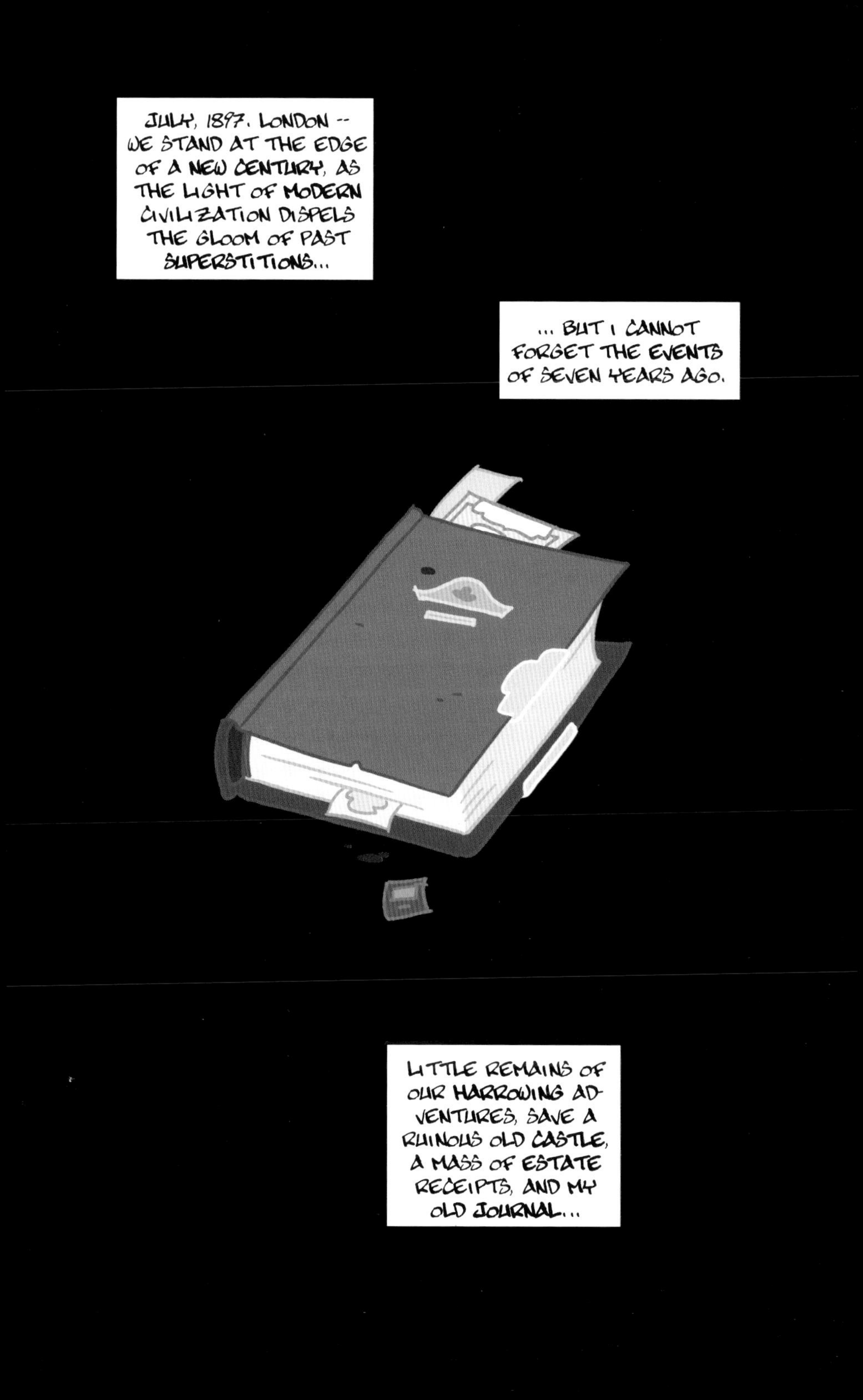
JULY, 1897. LONDON -- WE STAND AT THE EDGE OF A NEW CENTURY, AS THE LIGHT OF MODERN CIVILIZATION DISPELS THE GLOOM OF PAST SUPERSTITIONS...
... BUT I CANNOT FORGET THE EVENTS OF SEVEN YEARS AGO.
LITTLE REMAINS OF OUR HARROWING ADVENTURES, SAVE A RUINOUS OLD CASTLE, A MASS OF ESTATE RECEIPTS, AND MY OLD JOURNAL...

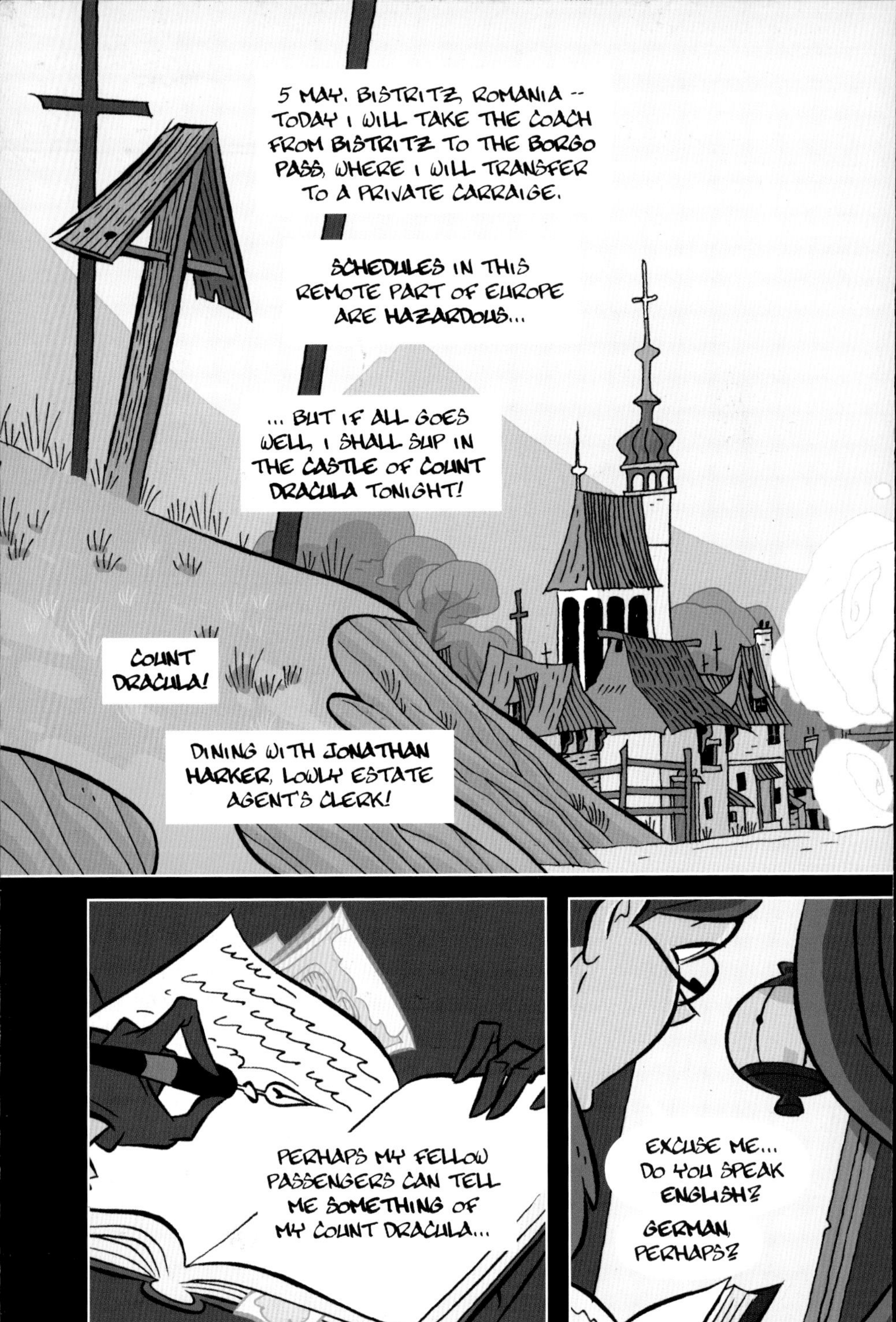
5 MAY. BISTRITZ, ROMANIA -- TODAY I WILL TAKE THE COACH FROM BISTRITZ TO THE BORGO PASS, WHERE I WILL TRANSFER TO A PRIVATE CARRAIGE.
SCHEDULES IN THIS REMOTE PART OF EUROPE ARE HAZARDOUS...
... BUT IF ALL GOES WELL, I SHALL SUP IN THE CASTLE OF COUNT DRACULA TONIGHT!
COUNT DRACULA!
DINING WITH JONATHAN HARKER, LOWLY ESTATE AGENT'S CLERK!
PERHAPS MY FELLOW PASSENGERS CAN TELL ME SOMETHING OF MY COUNT DRACULA...
EXCUSE ME... DO YOU SPEAK ENGLISH?
GERMAN, PERHAPS?

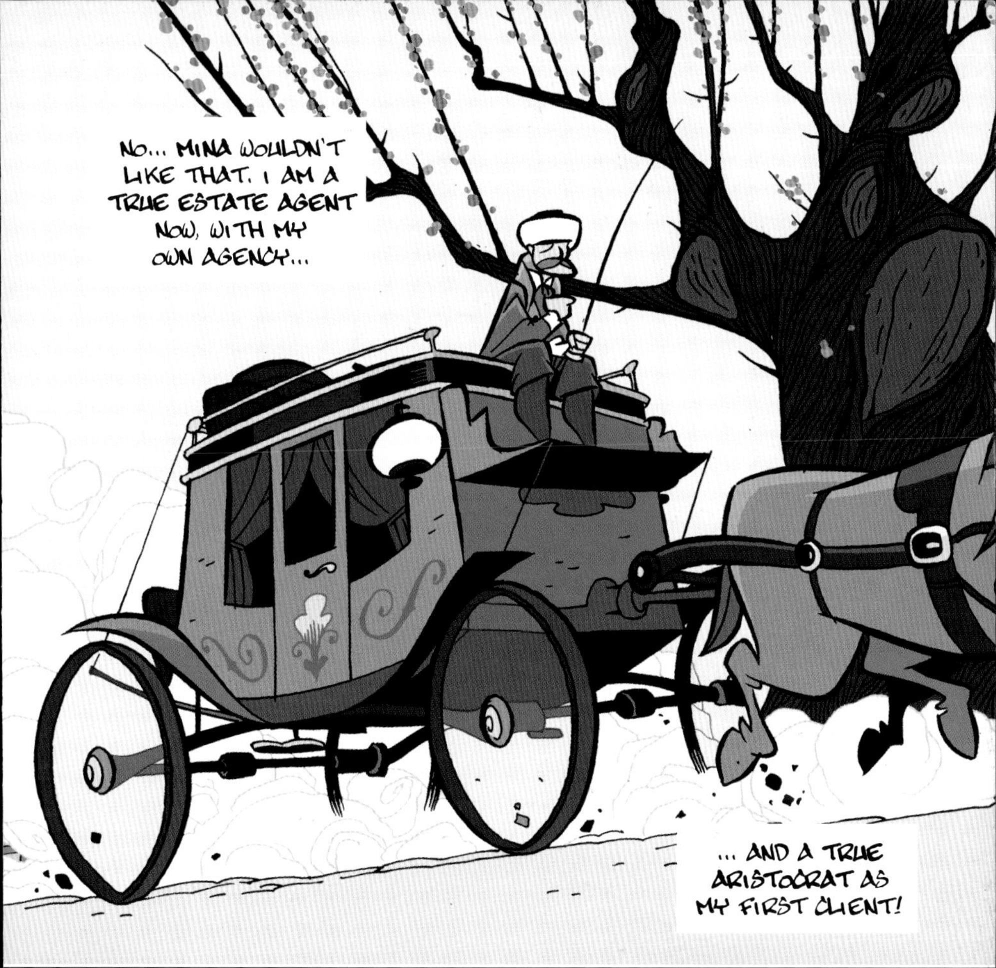
NO... MINA WOULDN'T LIKE THAT. I AM A TRUE ESTATE AGENT NOW, WITH MY OWN AGENCY...
... AND A TRUE ARISTOCRAT AS MY FIRST CLIENT!

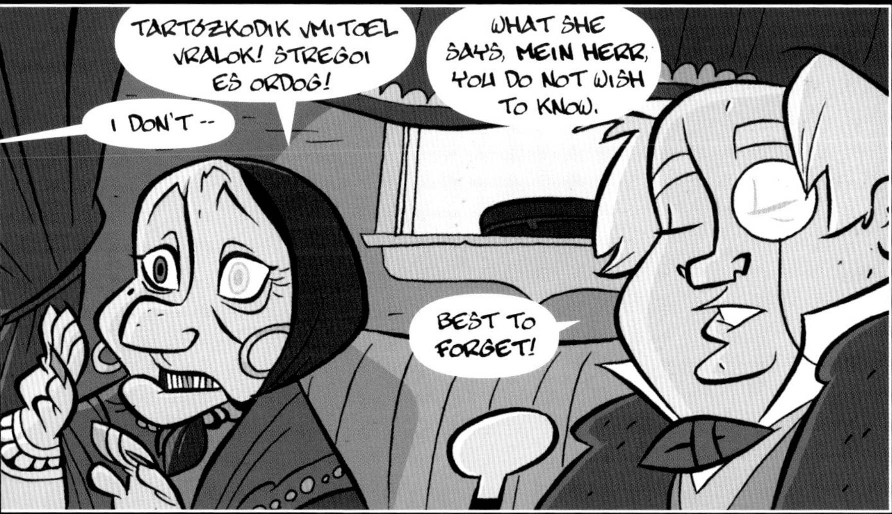
TARTÓZKODIK VMI TOEL VRALOK! STREGOI ES ORDOG!
I DON'T --
WHAT SHE SAYS, MEIN HERR, YOU DO NOT WISH TO KNOW.
BEST TO FORGET!

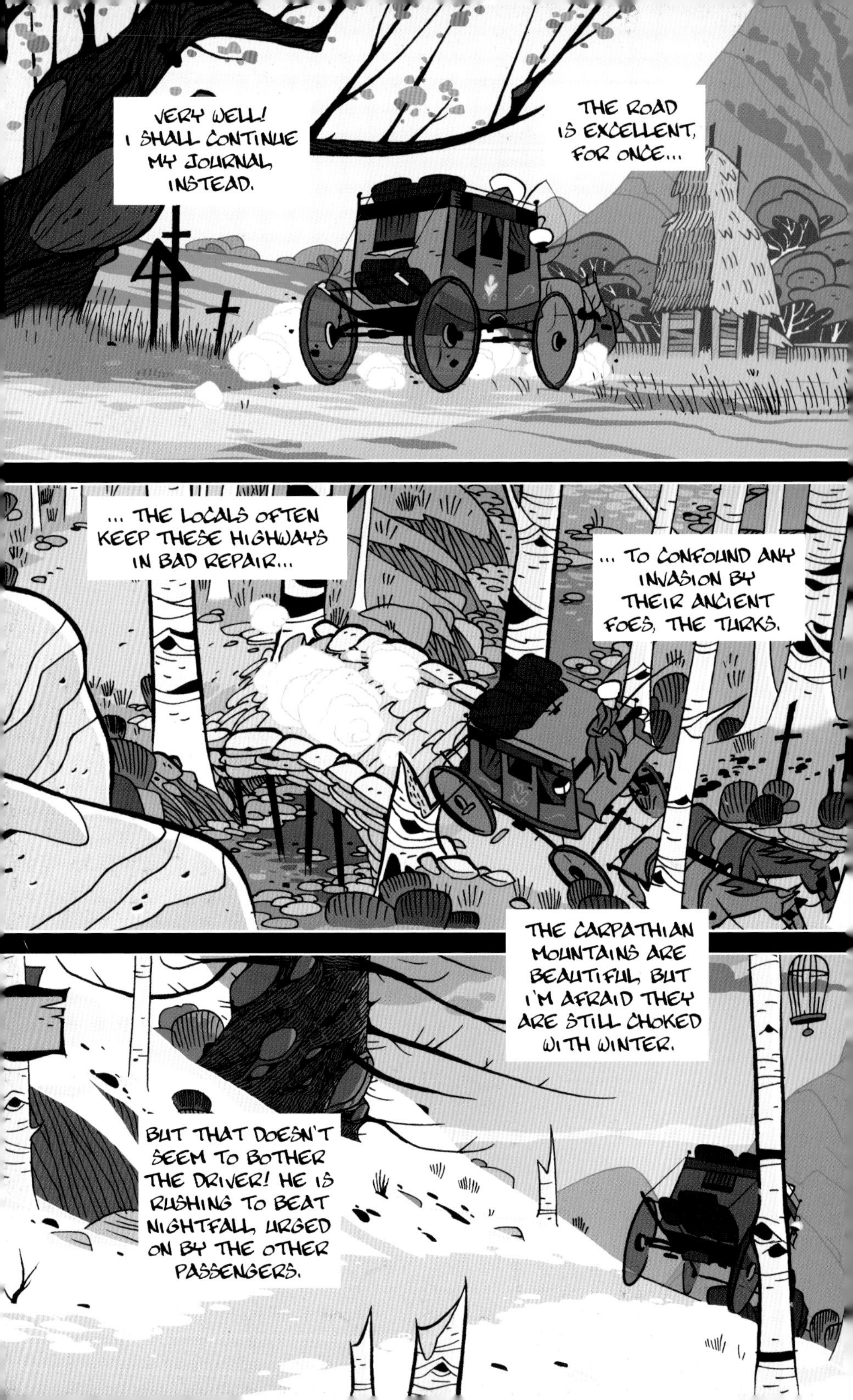
VERY WELL! I SHALL CONTINUE MY JOURNAL INSTEAD.
THE ROAD IS EXCELLENT, FOR ONCE...
... THE LOCALS OFTEN KEEP THESE HIGHWAYS IN BAD REPAIR...
... TO CONFOUND ANY INVASION BY THEIR ANCIENT FOES, THE TURKS.
THE CARPATHIAN MOUNTAINS ARE BEAUTIFUL, BUT I'M AFRAID THEY ARE STILL CHOKED WITH WINTER.
BUT THAT DOESN'T SEEM TO BOTHER THE DRIVER! HE IS RUSHING TO BEAT NIGHTFALL, URGED ON BY THE OTHER PASSENGERS.

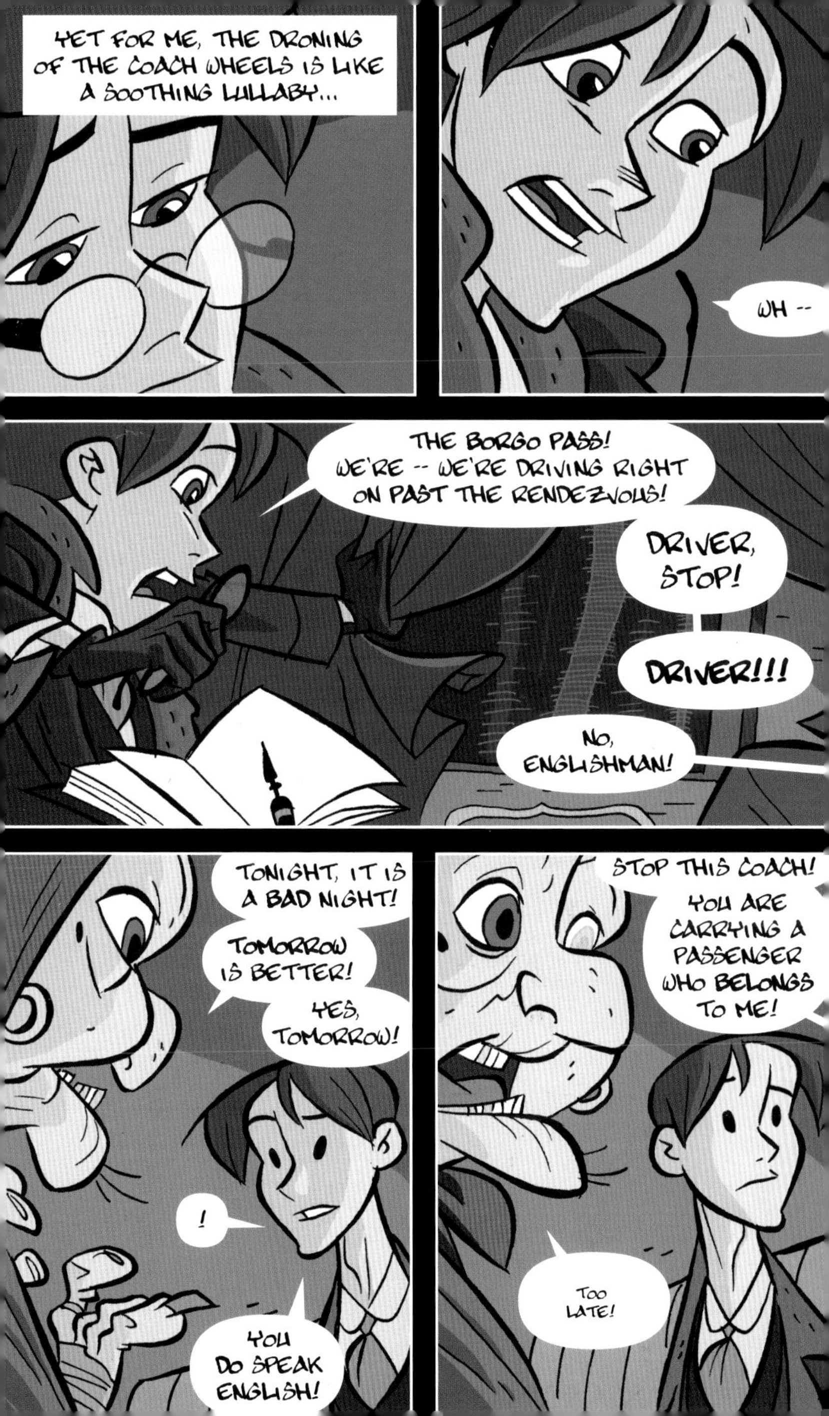
YET FOR ME, THE DRONING OF THE COACH WHEELS IS LIKE A SOOTHING LULLABY...
WH --
THE BORGO PASS! WE'RE -- WE'RE DRIVING RIGHT ON PAST THE RENDEZVOUS!
DRIVER, STOP!
DRIVER!!!
NO, ENGLISHMAN!
TONIGHT, IT IS A BAD NIGHT!
TOMORROW IS BETTER!
YES, TOMORROW!
!
YOU DO SPEAK ENGLISH!
STOP THIS COACH!
YOU ARE CARRYING A PASSENGER WHO BELONGS TO ME!
TOO LATE!

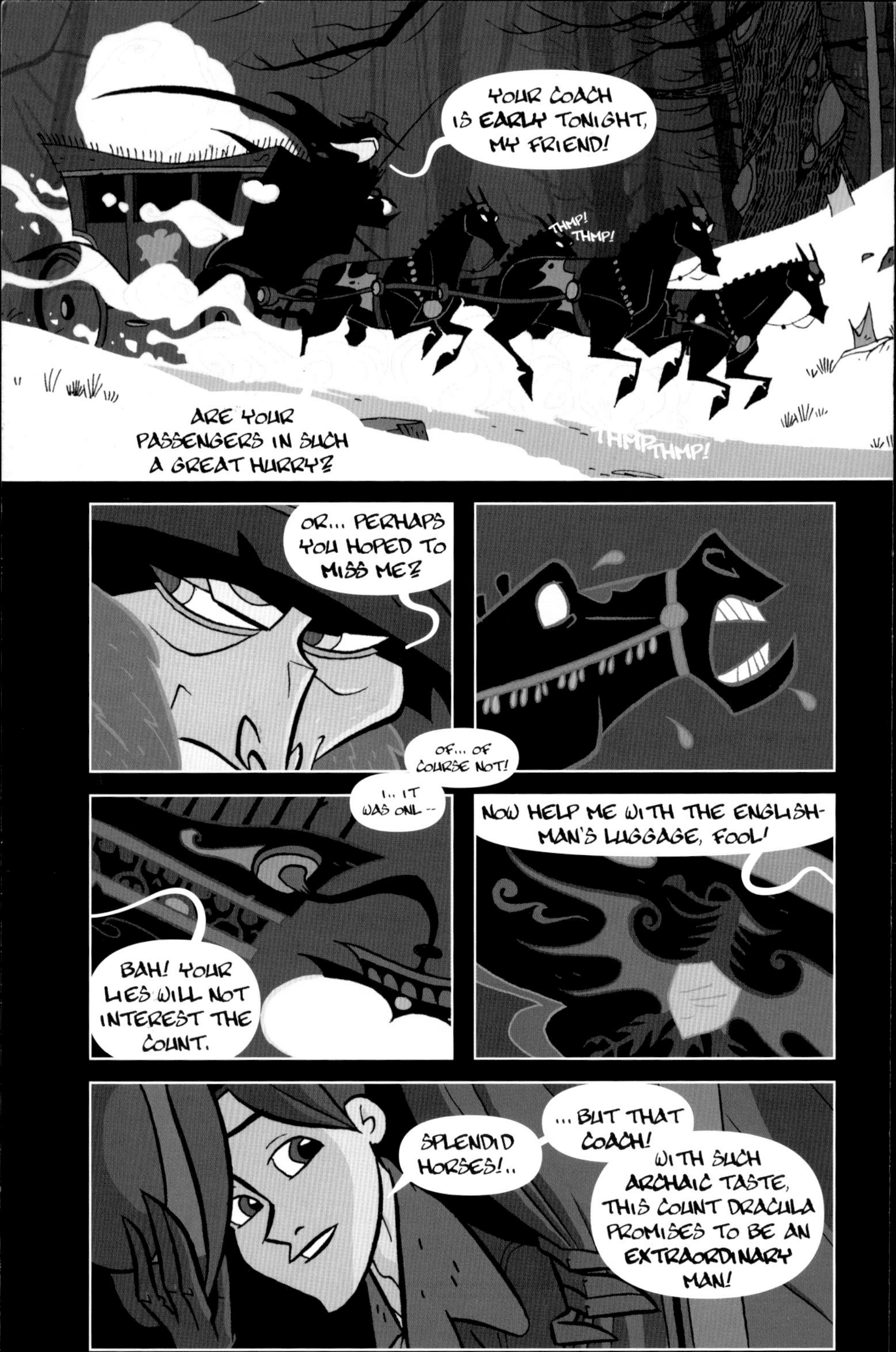
YOUR COACH IS EARLY TONIGHT, MY FRIEND!
THMP! THMP!
ARE YOUR PASSENGERS IN SUCH A GREAT HURRY?
THMP THMP!
OR... PERHAPS YOU HOPED TO MISS ME?
OF... OF COURSE NOT!
I.. IT WAS ONL --
BAH! YOUR LIES WILL NOT INTEREST THE COUNT.
NOW HELP ME WITH THE ENGLISH-MAN'S LUGGAGE, FOOL!
SPLENDID HORSES!..
... BUT THAT COACH!
WITH SUCH ARCHAIC TASTE, THIS COUNT DRACULA PROMISES TO BE AN EXTRAORDINARY MAN!

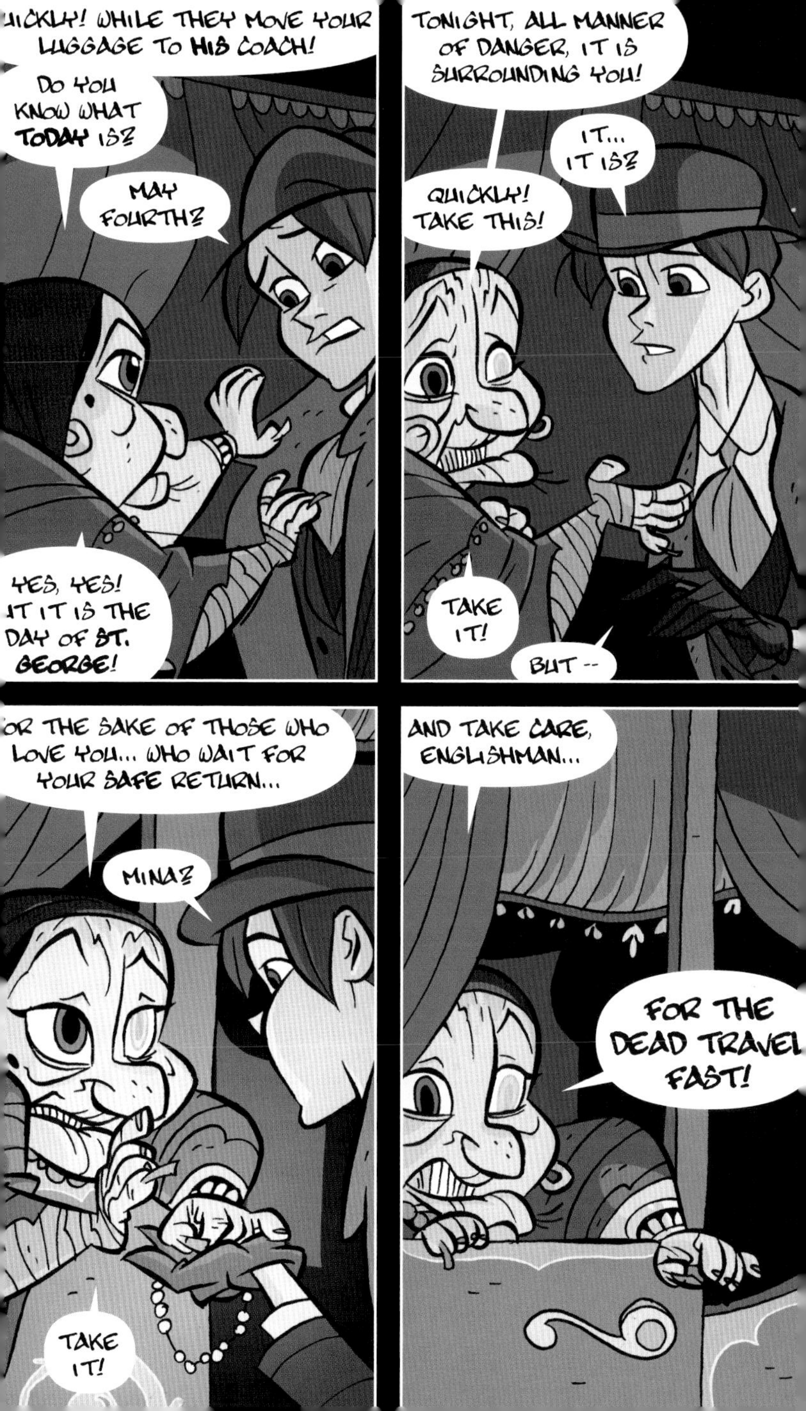
UICKLY! WHILE THEY MOVE YOUR LUGGAGE TO HIS COACH!
DO YOU KNOW WHAT TODAY IS?
MAY FOURTH?
YES, YES! IT IT IS THE DAY OF ST. GEORGE!
TONIGHT, ALL MANNER OF DANGER, IT IS SURROUNDING YOU!
IT... IT IS?
QUICKLY! TAKE THIS!
TAKE IT!
BUT --
OR THE SAKE OF THOSE WHO LOVE YOU... WHO WAIT FOR YOUR SAFE RETURN...
MINA?
TAKE IT!
AND TAKE CARE, ENGLISHMAN...
FOR THE DEAD TRAVEL FAST!

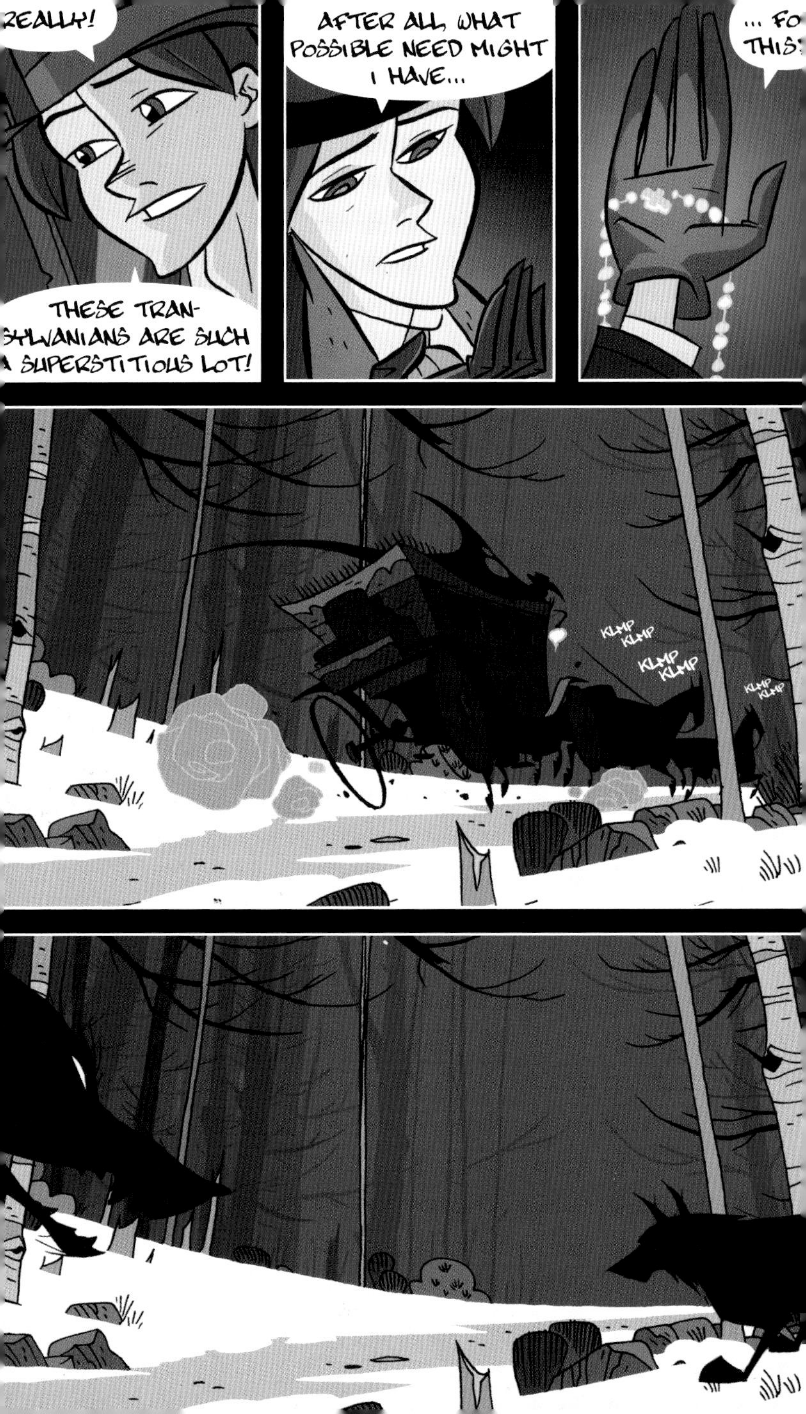

REALLY!
THESE TRAN-SYLVANIANS ARE SUCH A SUPERSTITIOUS LOT!
AFTER ALL, WHAT POSSIBLE NEED MIGHT I HAVE...
... FO THIS!
KLMP KLMP
KLMP KLMP
KLMP KLMP

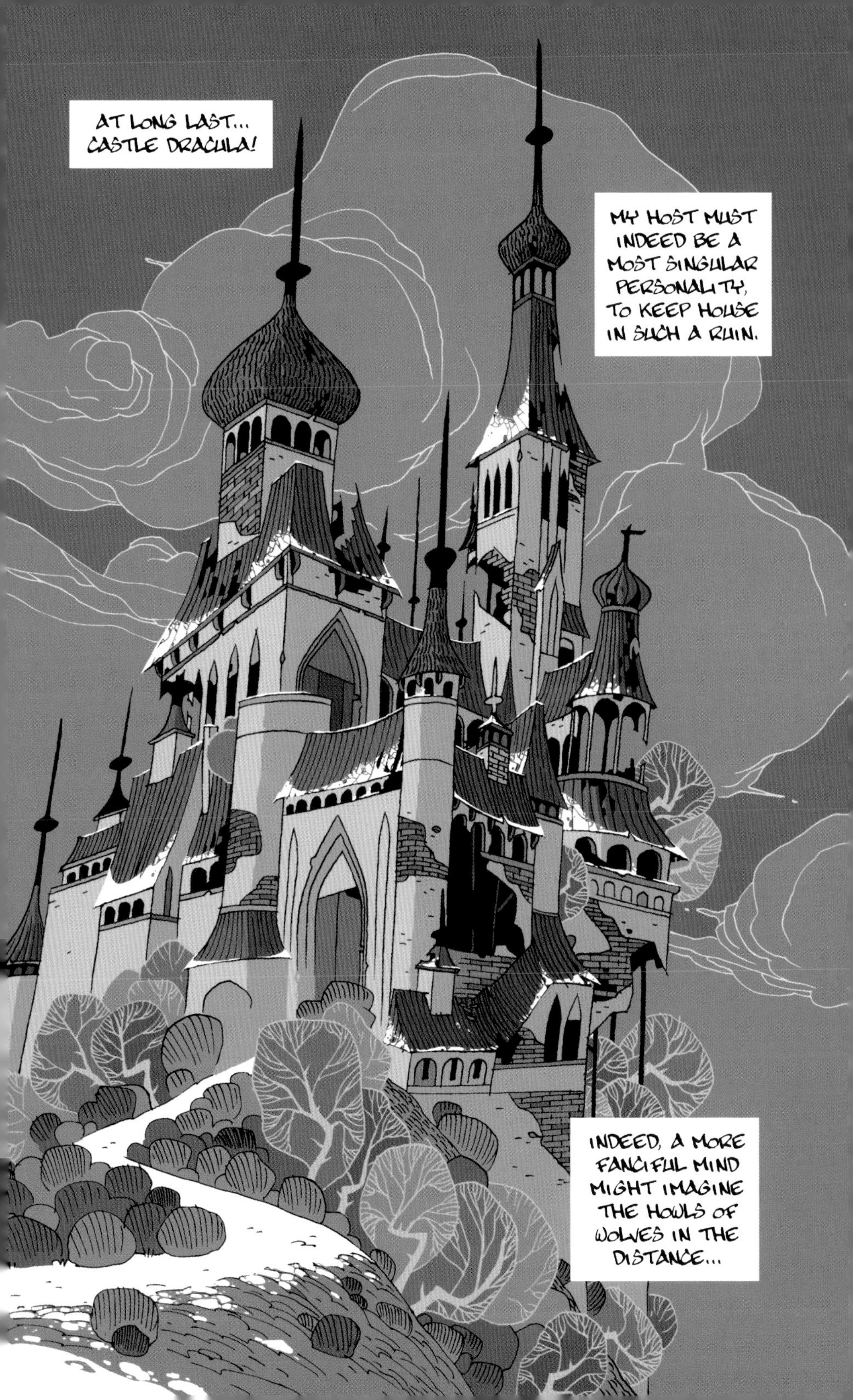
AT LONG LAST... CASTLE DRACULA!
MY HOST MUST INDEED BE A MOST SINGULAR PERSONALITY, TO KEEP HOUSE IN SUCH A RUIN.
INDEED, A MORE FANCIFUL MIND MIGHT IMAGINE THE HOWLS OF WOLVES IN THE DISTANCE...

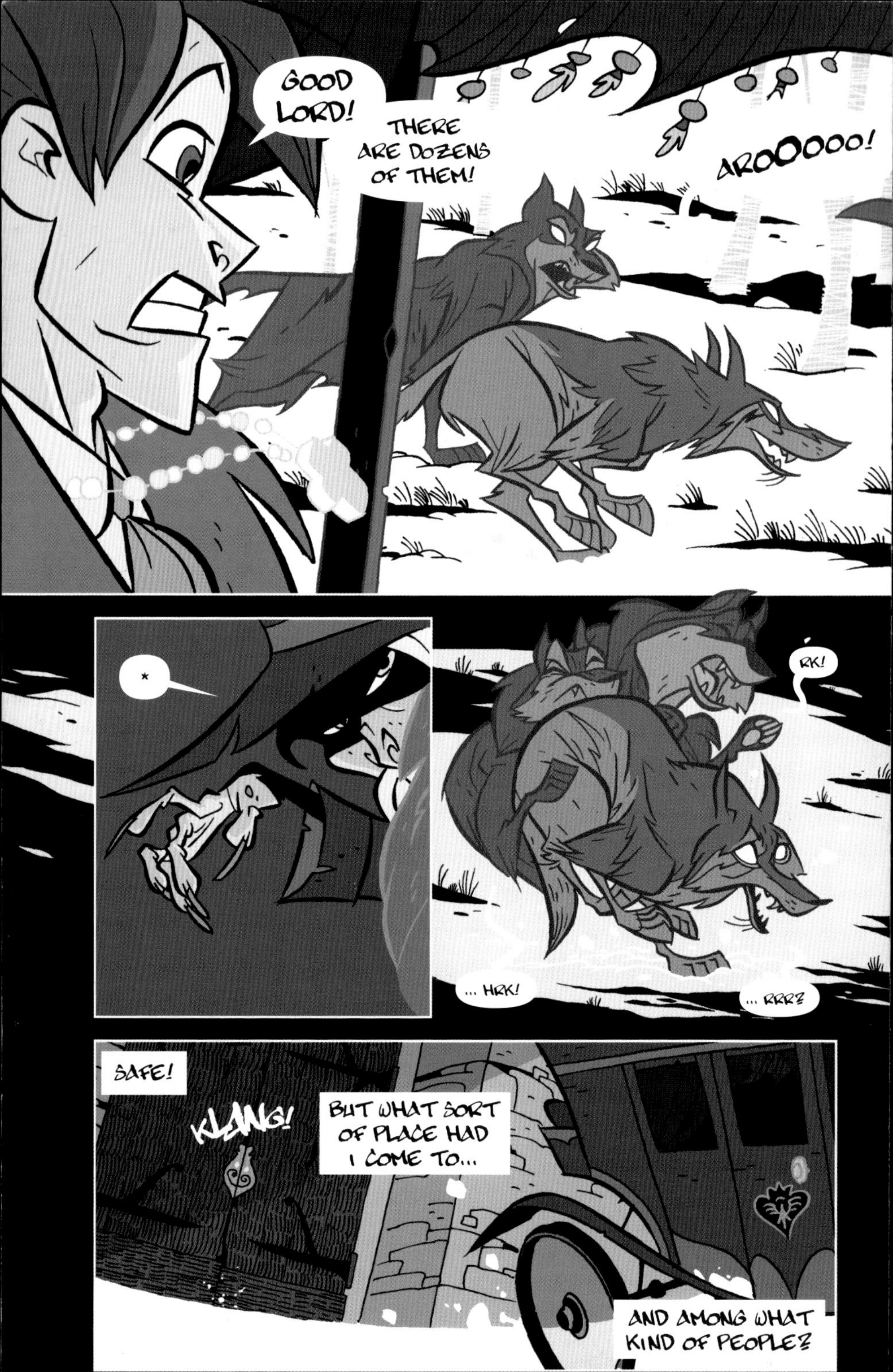
GOOD LORD!
THERE ARE DOZENS OF THEM!
AROOOOOO!
*
RK!
... HRK!
... RRR?
SAFE!
KLANG!
BUT WHAT SORT OF PLACE HAD I COME TO...
AND AMONG WHAT KIND OF PEOPLE?

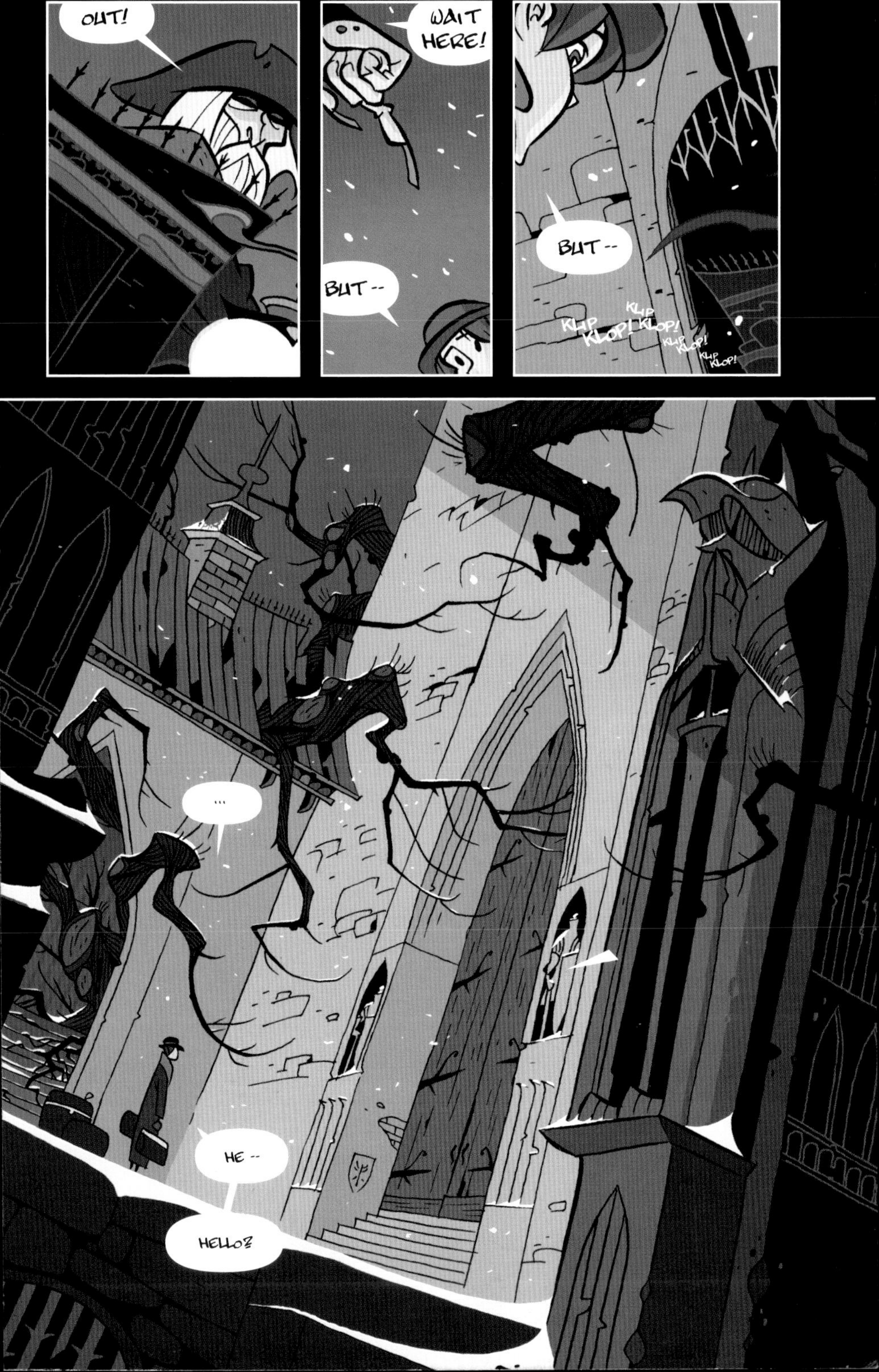
OUT!
WAIT HERE!
BUT --
BUT --
KLIP KLOP! KLIP KLOP! KLIP KLOP! KLIP KLOP!
...
HE --
HELLO?

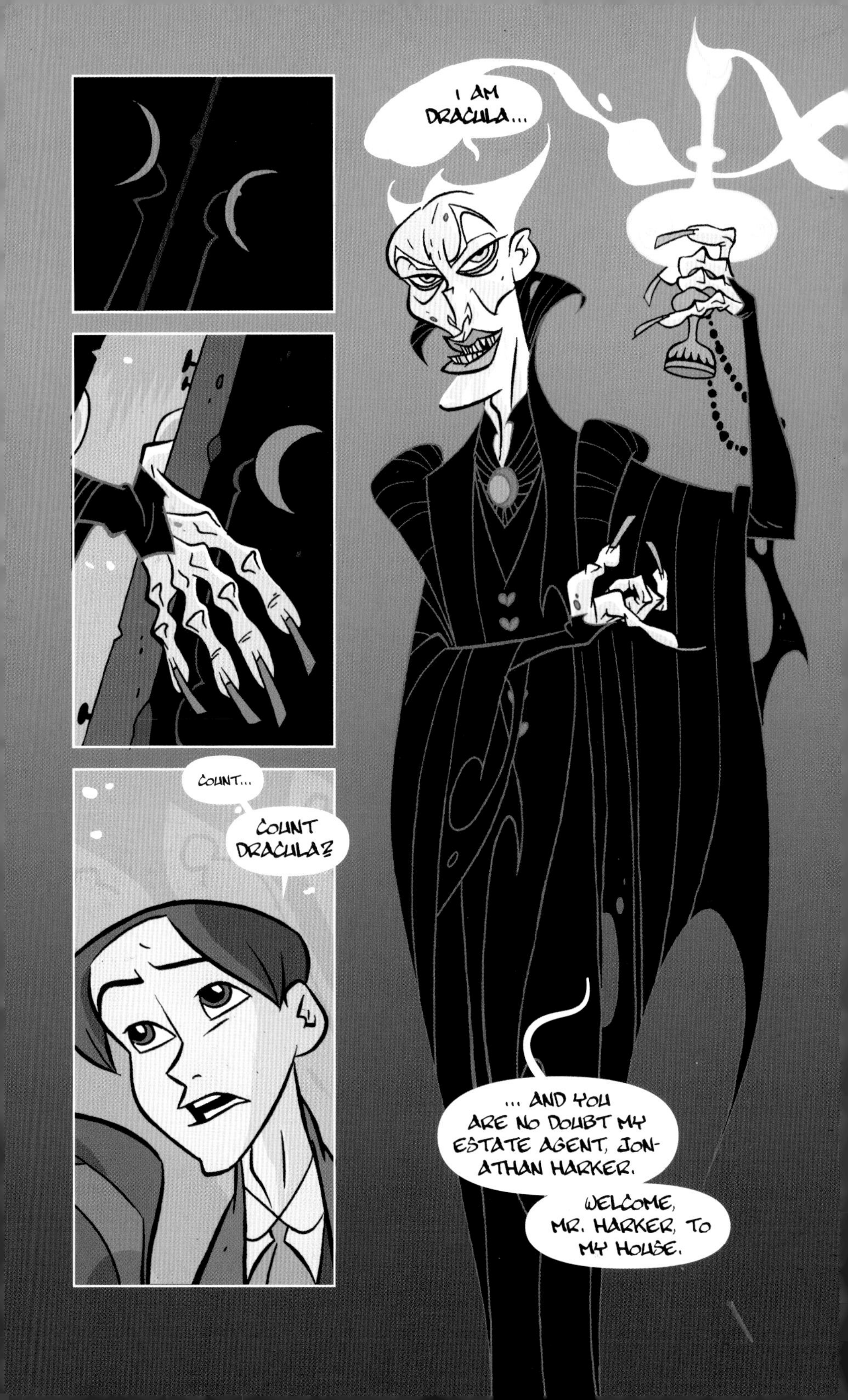

I AM DRACULA...
COUNT...
COUNT DRACULA?
... AND YOU ARE NO DOUBT MY ESTATE AGENT, JONATHAN HARKER.
WELCOME, MR. HARKER, TO MY HOUSE.

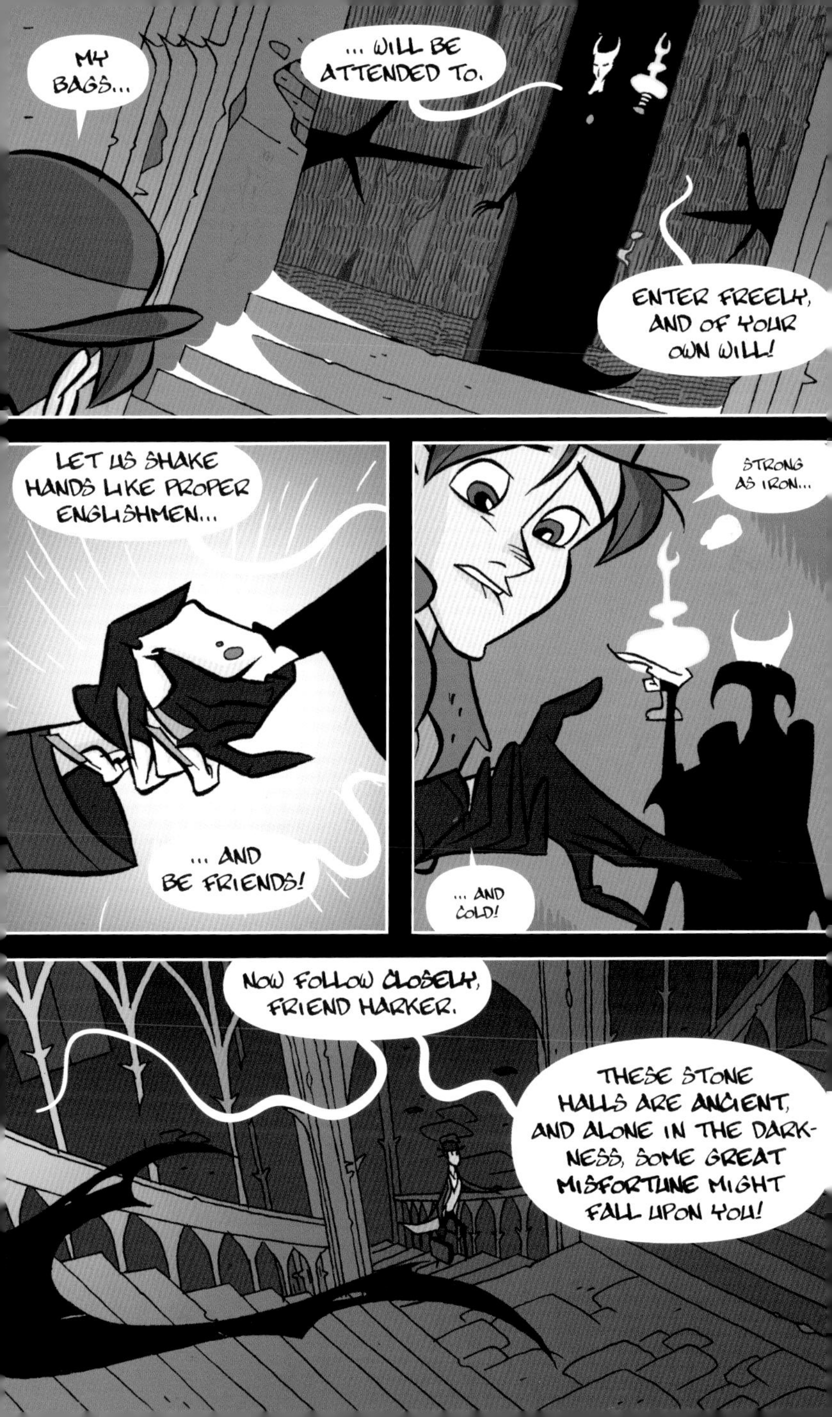
MY BAGS...
... WILL BE ATTENDED TO.
ENTER FREELY, AND OF YOUR OWN WILL!
LET US SHAKE HANDS LIKE PROPER ENGLISHMEN...
... AND BE FRIENDS!
STRONG AS IRON...
... AND COLD!
NOW FOLLOW CLOSELY, FRIEND HARKER.
THESE STONE HALLS ARE ANCIENT, AND ALONE IN THE DARKNESS, SOME GREAT MISFORTUNE MIGHT FALL UPON YOU!

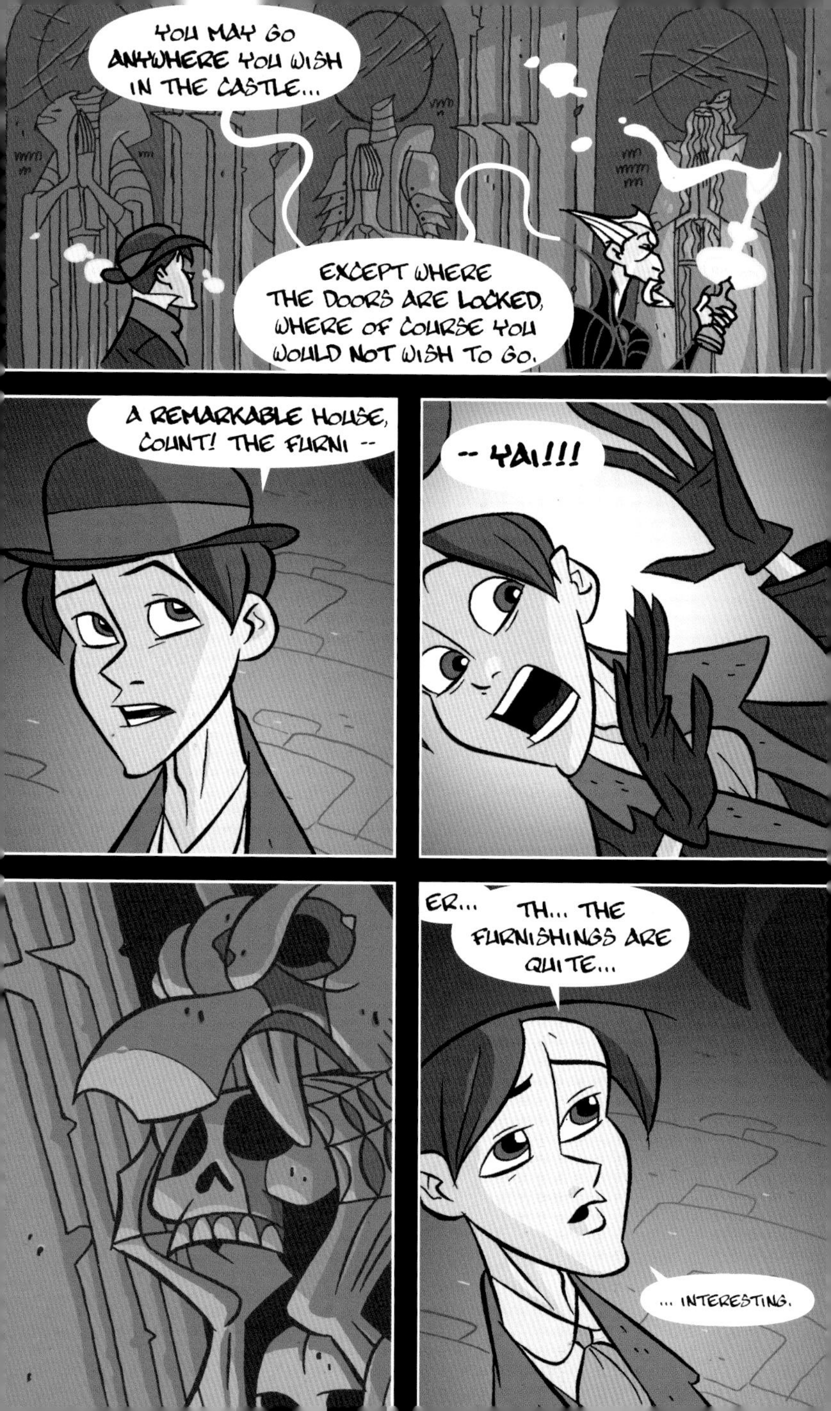
YOU MAY GO ANYWHERE YOU WISH IN THE CASTLE...
EXCEPT WHERE THE DOORS ARE LOCKED, WHERE OF COURSE YOU WOULD NOT WISH TO GO.
A REMARKABLE HOUSE, COUNT! THE FURNI --
-- YAI!!!
ER...
TH... THE FURNISHINGS ARE QUITE...
... INTERESTING.

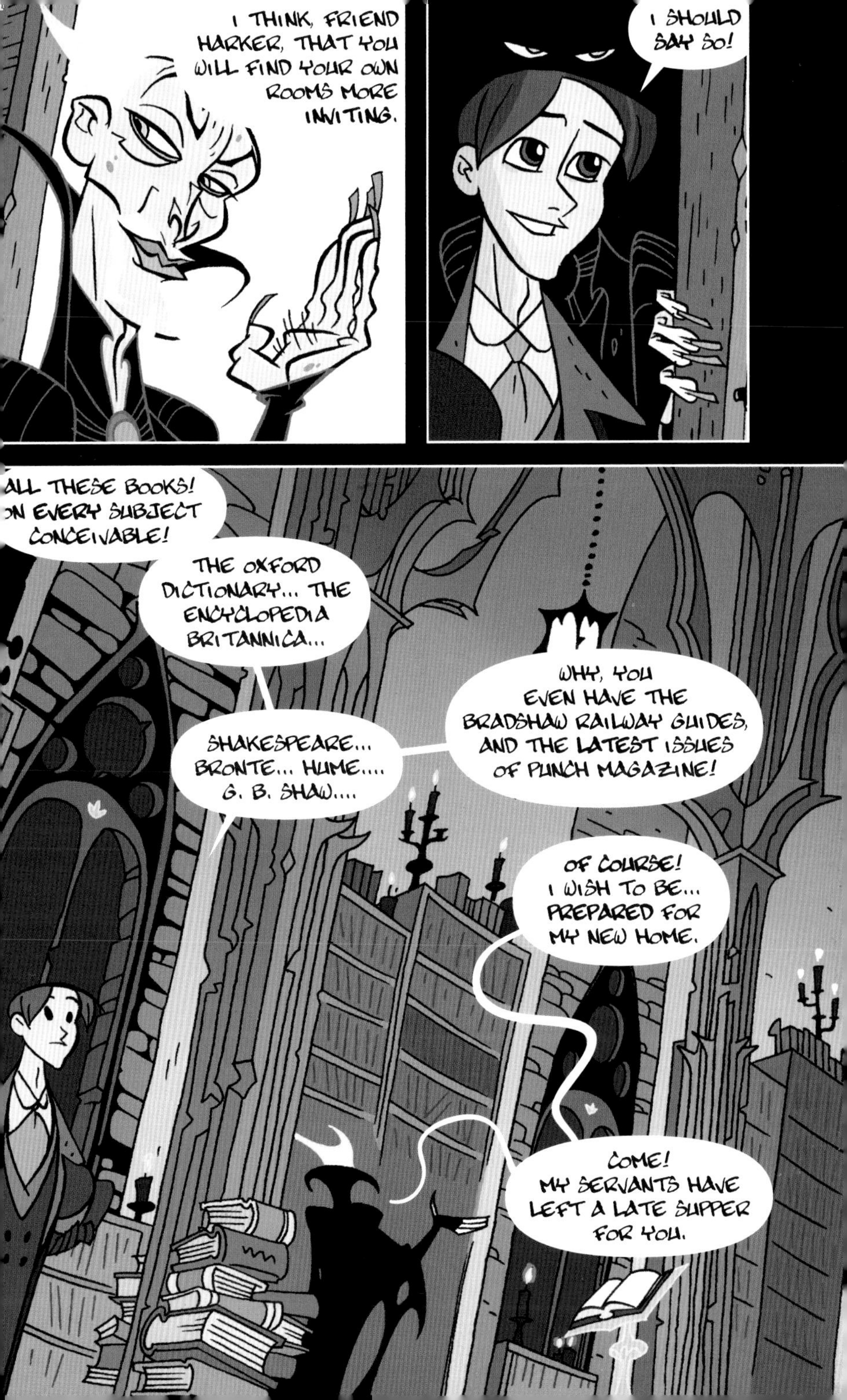
I THINK, FRIEND HARKER, THAT YOU WILL FIND YOUR OWN ROOMS MORE INVITING.
I SHOULD SAY SO!
ALL THESE BOOKS! ON EVERY SUBJECT CONCEIVABLE!
THE OXFORD DICTIONARY... THE ENCYCLOPEDIA BRITANNICA...
SHAKESPEARE... BRONTE... HUME.... G. B. SHAW....
WHY, YOU EVEN HAVE THE BRADSHAW RAILWAY GUIDES, AND THE LATEST ISSUES OF PUNCH MAGAZINE!
OF COURSE! I WISH TO BE... PREPARED FOR MY NEW HOME.
COME! MY SERVANTS HAVE LEFT A LATE SUPPER FOR YOU.

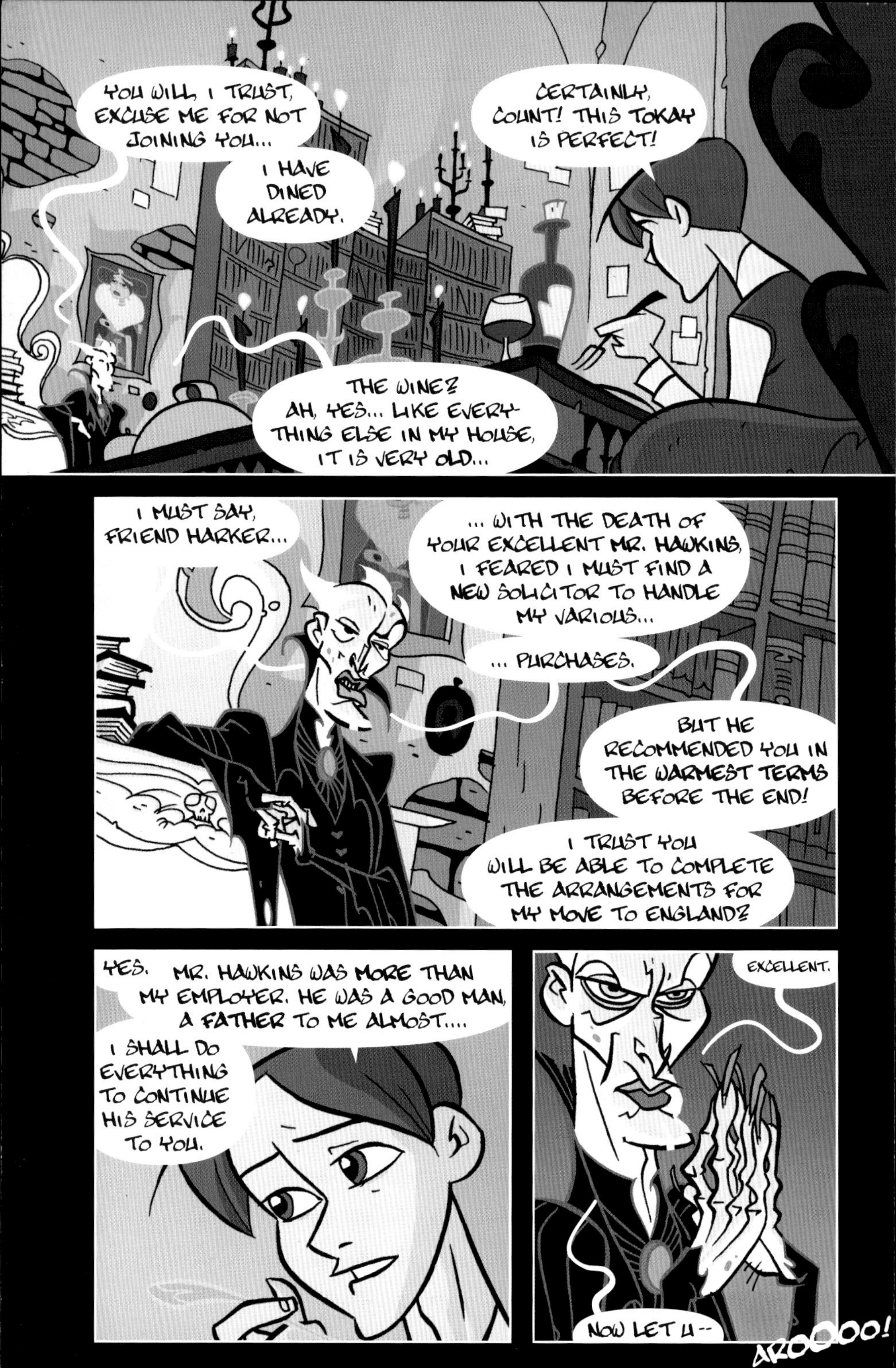
YOU WILL, I TRUST, EXCUSE ME FOR NOT JOINING YOU...
I HAVE DINED ALREADY.
CERTAINLY, COUNT! THIS TOKAY IS PERFECT!
THE WINE? AH, YES... LIKE EVERY-THING ELSE IN MY HOUSE, IT IS VERY OLD...
I MUST SAY, FRIEND HARKER...
... WITH THE DEATH OF YOUR EXCELLENT MR. HAWKINS, I FEARED I MUST FIND A NEW SOLICITOR TO HANDLE MY VARIOUS...
... PURCHASES.
BUT HE RECOMMENDED YOU IN THE WARMEST TERMS BEFORE THE END!
I TRUST YOU WILL BE ABLE TO COMPLETE THE ARRANGEMENTS FOR MY MOVE TO ENGLAND?
YES.
MR. HAWKINS WAS MORE THAN MY EMPLOYER. HE WAS A GOOD MAN, A FATHER TO ME ALMOST....
I SHALL DO EVERYTHING TO CONTINUE HIS SERVICE TO YOU.
EXCELLENT.
NOW LET U--
AROOOOO!

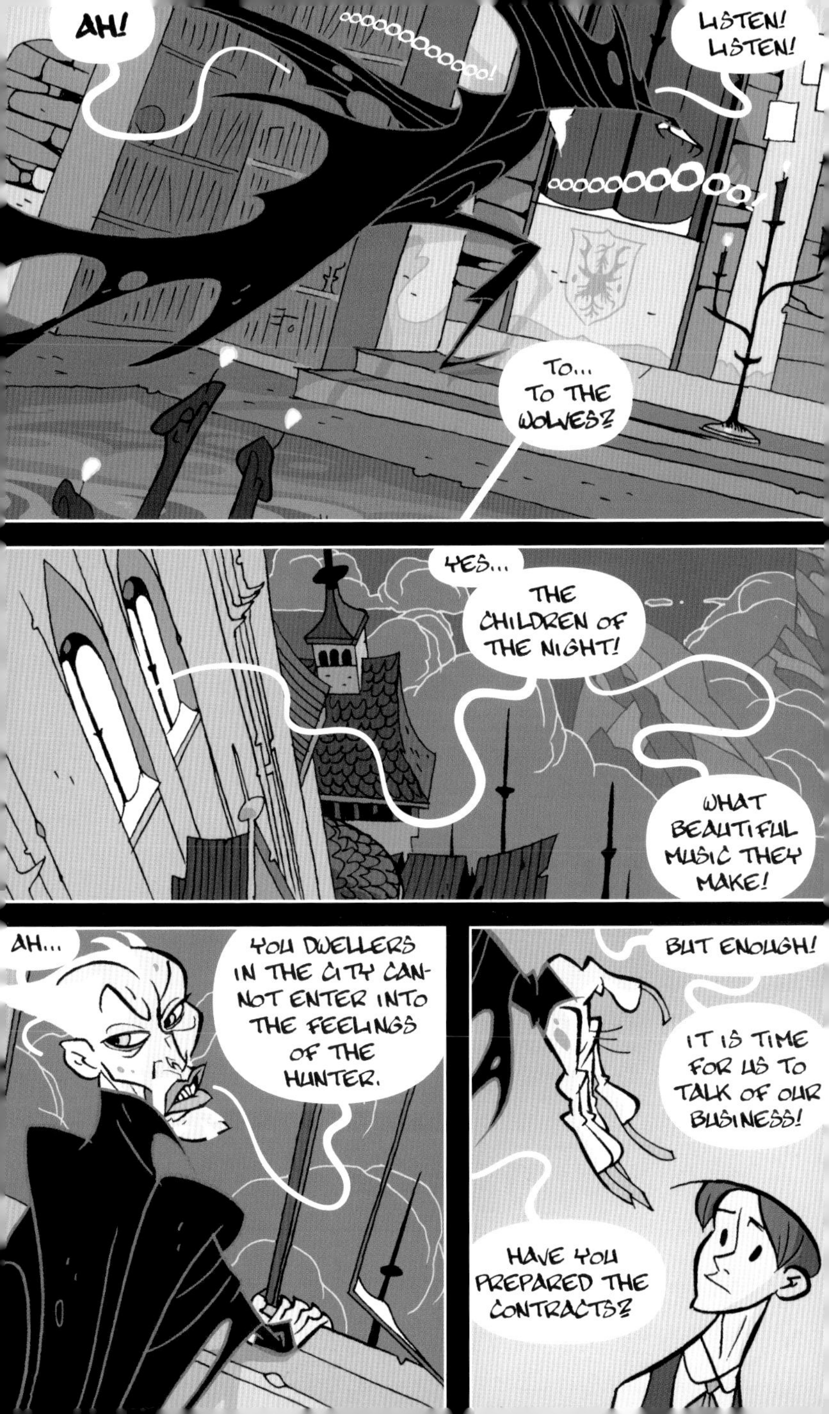
AH!
OOOOOOOOOOOOOoo!
LISTEN! LISTEN!
ooooooOOOOOOoo!
TO... TO THE WOLVES?
YES...
THE CHILDREN OF THE NIGHT!
WHAT BEAUTIFUL MUSIC THEY MAKE!
AH...
YOU DWELLERS IN THE CITY CAN-NOT ENTER INTO THE FEELINGS OF THE HUNTER.
BUT ENOUGH!
IT IS TIME FOR US TO TALK OF OUR BUSINESS!
HAVE YOU PREPARED THE CONTRACTS?

ONCE YOU HAVE SIGNED THESE PAPERS, COUNT, YOU WILL BE THE OWNER...

... OF TWENTY-THREE PROPERTIES THROUGHOUT LONDON AND YORKSHIRE!

INDEED.

AT YOUR REQUEST, I HAVE WORDED THESE CONTRACTS SO THAT YOU MAY USE DIFFERENT AGENTS FOR EACH PROPERTY...

... AND THUS KEEP YOUR AFFAIRS TO YOURSELF, IN THE MANNER OF MODERN BUSINESSMEN.

YOUR ARRANGEMENTS ARE THOROUGH AND EXCELLENT, FRIEND HARKER!

Yellow Book
Illustrated Quarterly
Volume I April 1894

I MUST SAY, YOUR NEW APARTMENT IN LONDON IS IN POOR CONDITION, BUT FENCHURCH IS A VERY ATTRACTIVE NEIGHBORHOOD, FULL OF LIFE!

LIFE? YES, THAT IS IMPORTANT...

Yellow Book
Illustrated Quarterly
Volume I April 1894

BUT COME, FRIEND HARKER! DAWN NEARS...

... YOU MUST SLEEP, AND KEEP WELL!

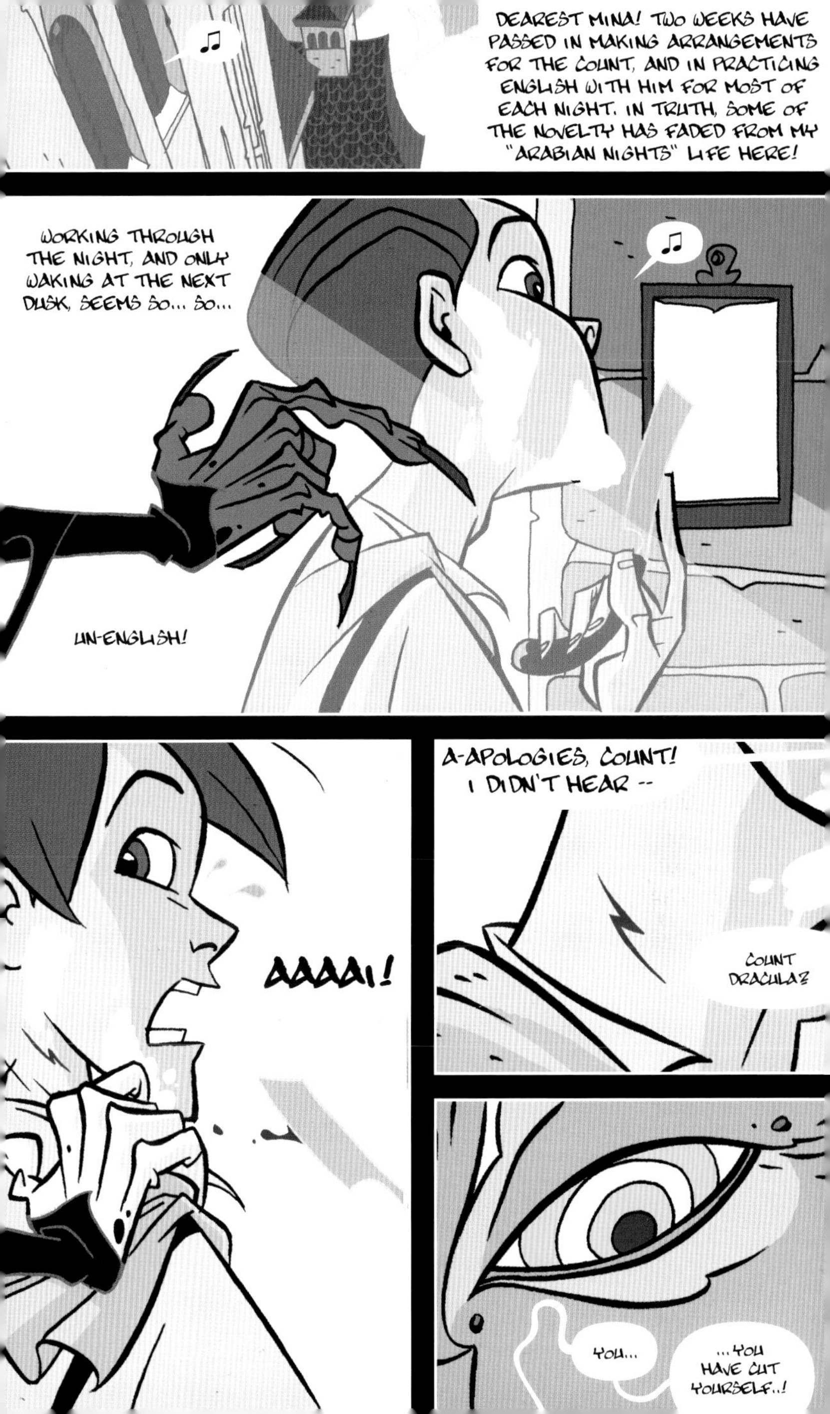
♫
DEAREST MINA! TWO WEEKS HAVE PASSED IN MAKING ARRANGEMENTS FOR THE COUNT, AND IN PRACTICING ENGLISH WITH HIM FOR MOST OF EACH NIGHT. IN TRUTH, SOME OF THE NOVELTY HAS FADED FROM MY "ARABIAN NIGHTS" LIFE HERE!
WORKING THROUGH THE NIGHT, AND ONLY WAKING AT THE NEXT DUSK, SEEMS SO... SO...
♫
UN-ENGLISH!
AAAAI!
A-APOLOGIES, COUNT! I DIDN'T HEAR --
COUNT DRACULA?
YOU...
...YOU HAVE CUT YOURSELF..!

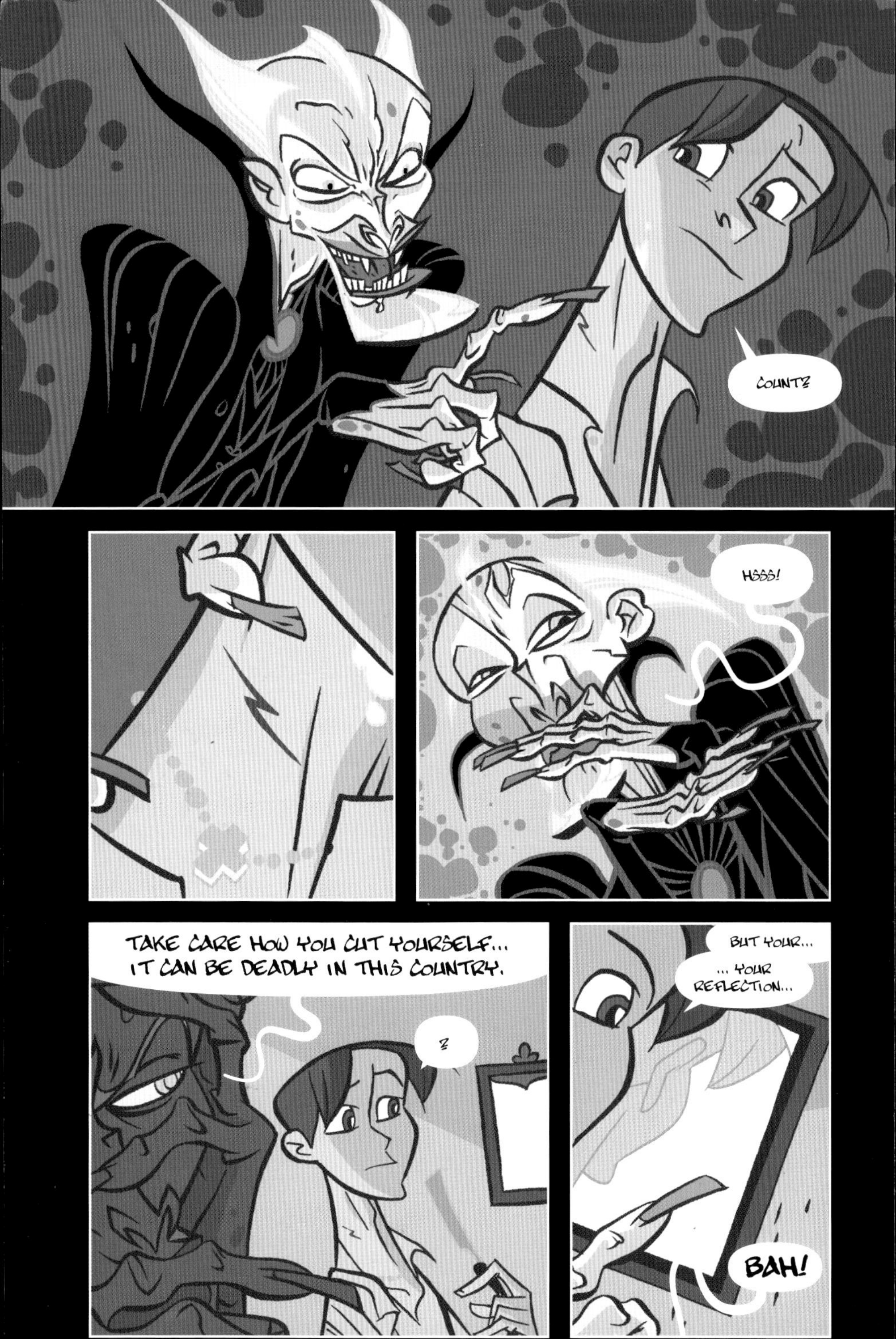
COUNT?
HSSS!
TAKE CARE HOW YOU CUT YOURSELF... IT CAN BE DEADLY IN THIS COUNTRY.
?
BUT YOUR...
... YOUR REFLECTION...
BAH!

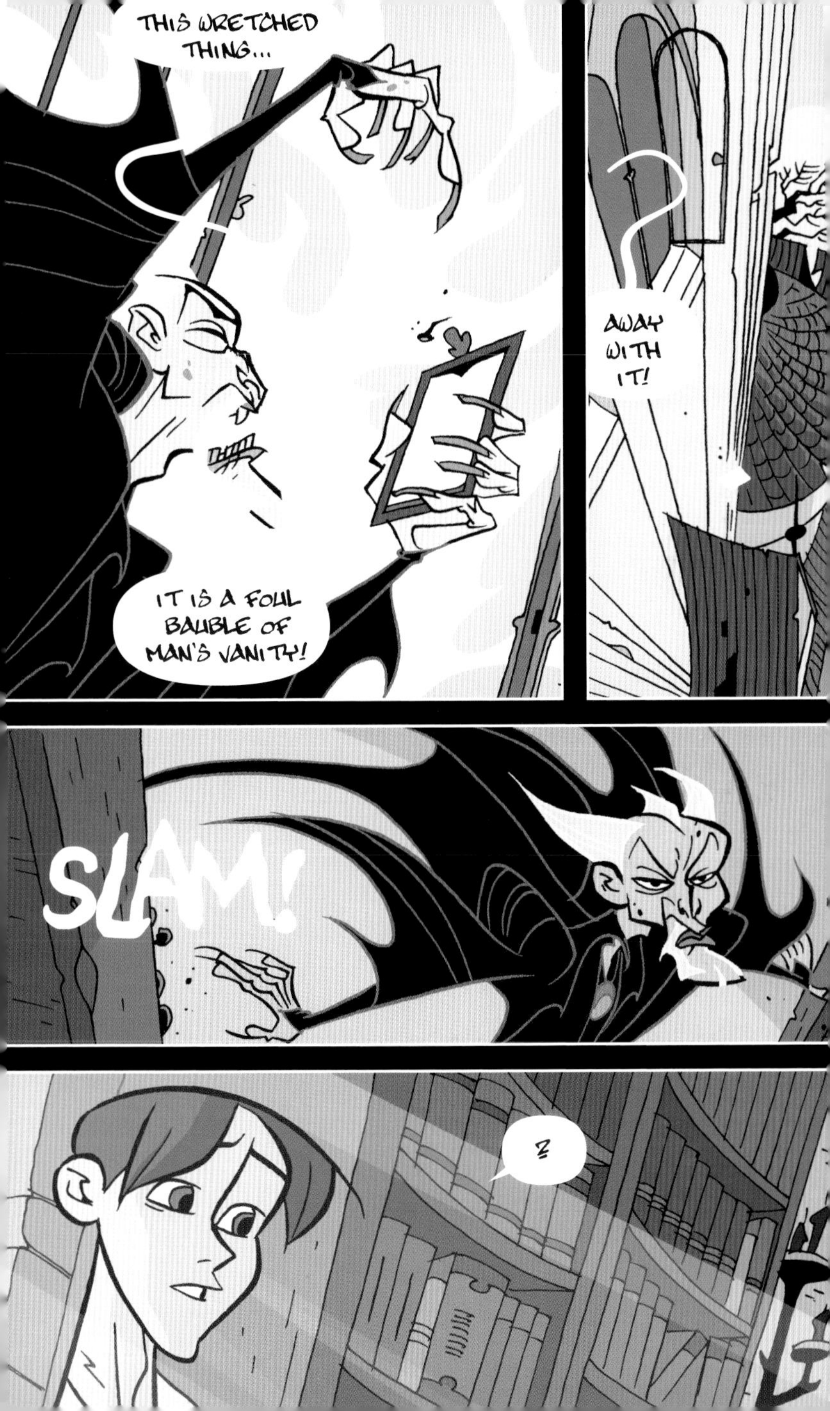
THIS WRETCHED THING...
IT IS A FOUL BAUBLE OF MAN'S VANITY!
AWAY WITH IT!
SLAM!
?

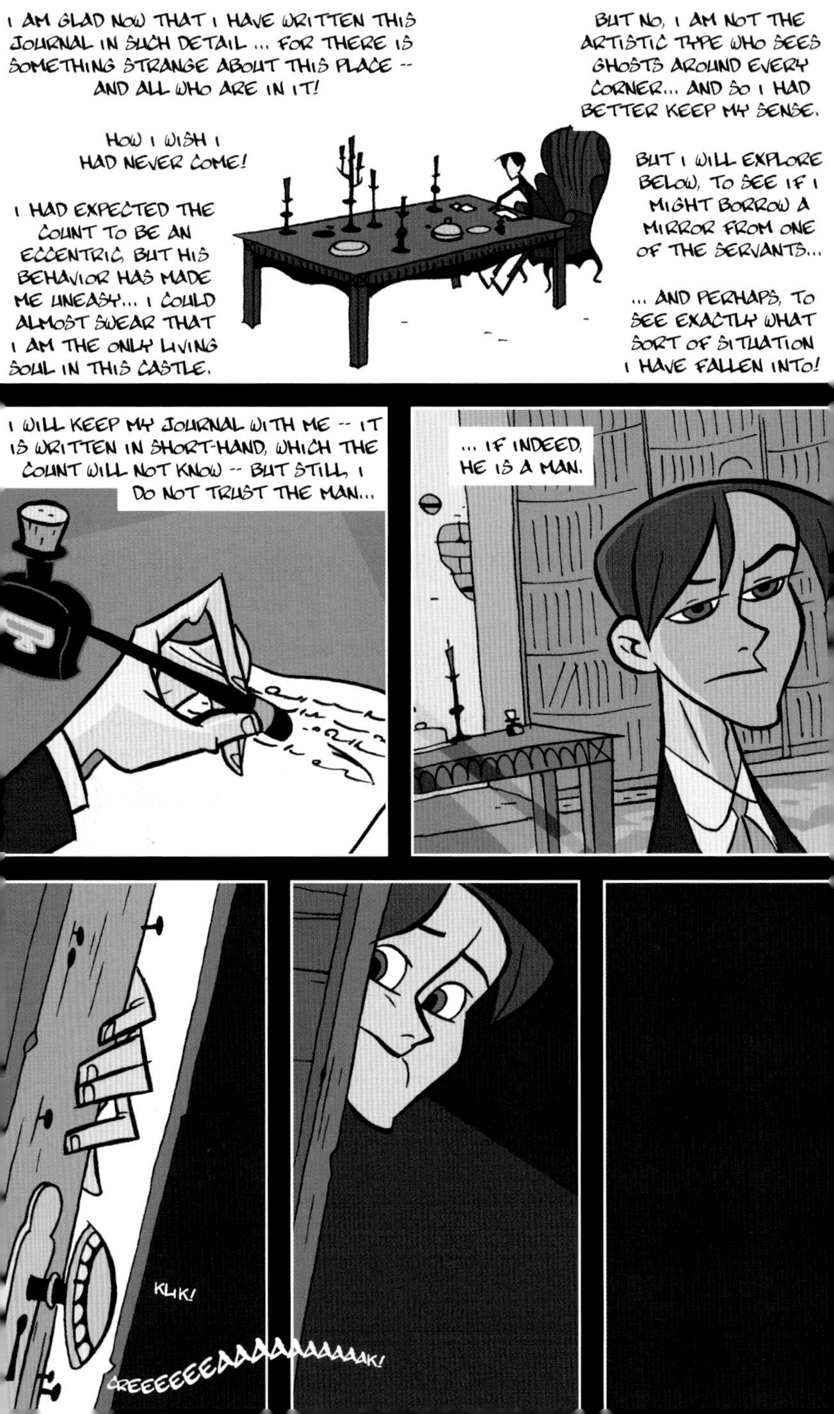
I AM GLAD NOW THAT I HAVE WRITTEN THIS JOURNAL IN SUCH DETAIL ... FOR THERE IS SOMETHING STRANGE ABOUT THIS PLACE -- AND ALL WHO ARE IN IT!
HOW I WISH I HAD NEVER COME!
I HAD EXPECTED THE COUNT TO BE AN ECCENTRIC, BUT HIS BEHAVIOR HAS MADE ME UNEASY... I COULD ALMOST SWEAR THAT I AM THE ONLY LIVING SOUL IN THIS CASTLE.
BUT NO, I AM NOT THE ARTISTIC TYPE WHO SEES GHOSTS AROUND EVERY CORNER... AND SO I HAD BETTER KEEP MY SENSE.
BUT I WILL EXPLORE BELOW, TO SEE IF I MIGHT BORROW A MIRROR FROM ONE OF THE SERVANTS...
... AND PERHAPS, TO SEE EXACTLY WHAT SORT OF SITUATION I HAVE FALLEN INTO!
I WILL KEEP MY JOURNAL WITH ME -- IT IS WRITTEN IN SHORT-HAND, WHICH THE COUNT WILL NOT KNOW -- BUT STILL, I DO NOT TRUST THE MAN...
... IF INDEED, HE IS A MAN.
KLIK!
CREEEEEEEAAAAAAAAAAAK!

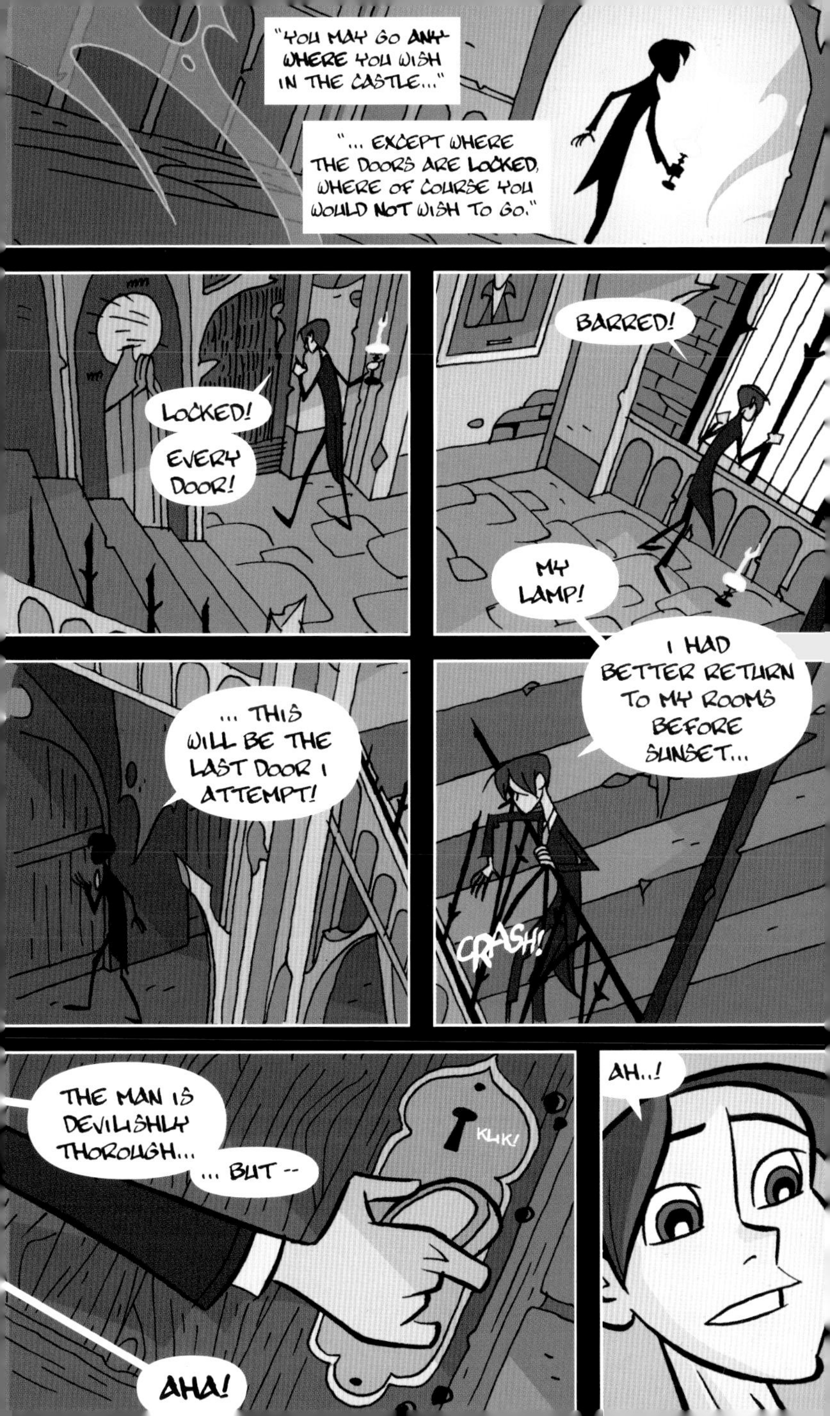
"YOU MAY GO ANYWHERE YOU WISH IN THE CASTLE..."
"... EXCEPT WHERE THE DOORS ARE LOCKED, WHERE OF COURSE YOU WOULD NOT WISH TO GO."
LOCKED!
EVERY DOOR!
BARRED!
MY LAMP!
I HAD BETTER RETURN TO MY ROOMS BEFORE SUNSET...
... THIS WILL BE THE LAST DOOR I ATTEMPT!
CRASH!
THE MAN IS DEVILISHLY THOROUGH...
... BUT --
KLIK!
AHA!
AH..!

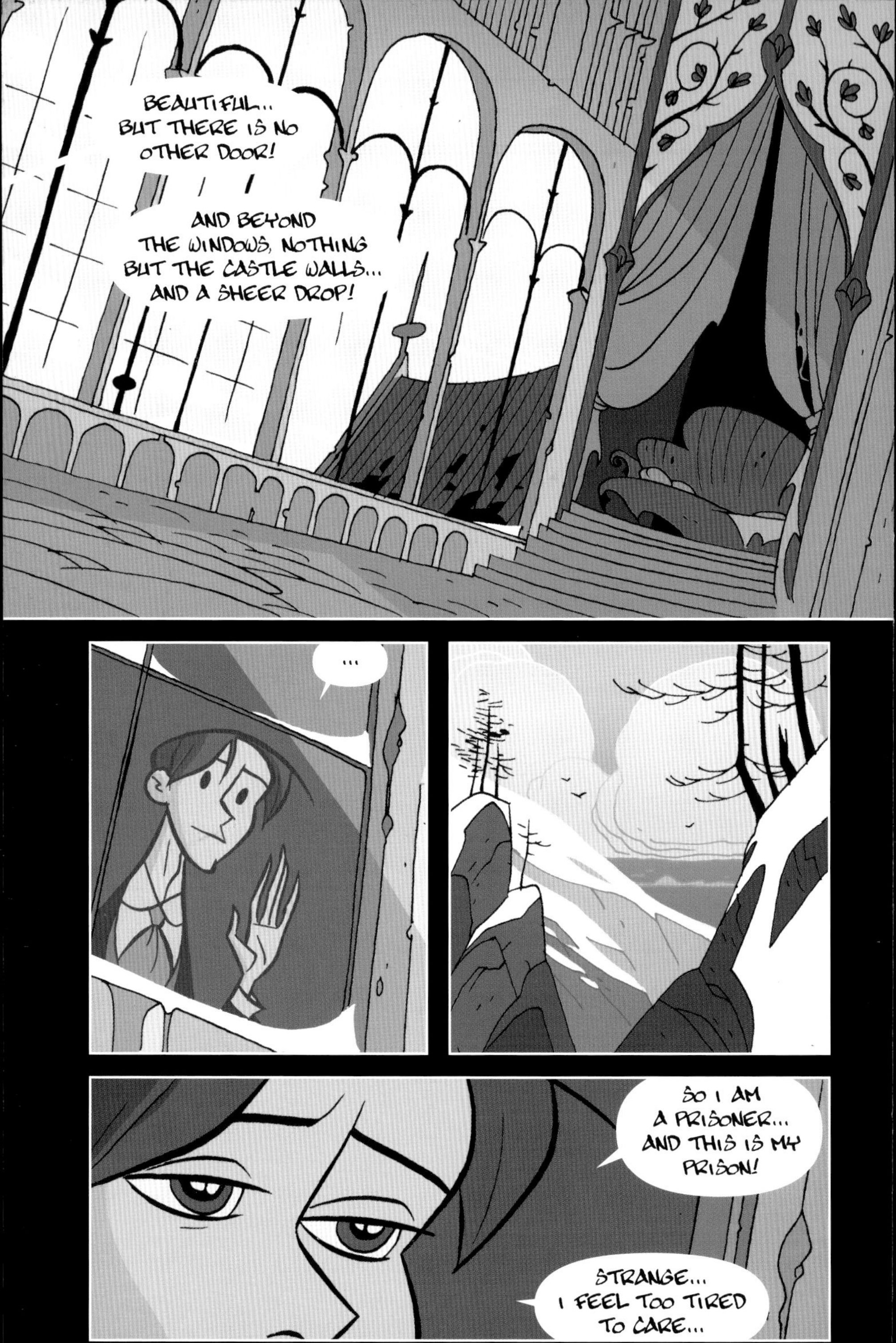
BEAUTIFUL... BUT THERE IS NO OTHER DOOR!
AND BEYOND THE WINDOWS, NOTHING BUT THE CASTLE WALLS... AND A SHEER DROP!
...
SO I AM A PRISONER... AND THIS IS MY PRISON!
STRANGE... I FEEL TOO TIRED TO CARE...

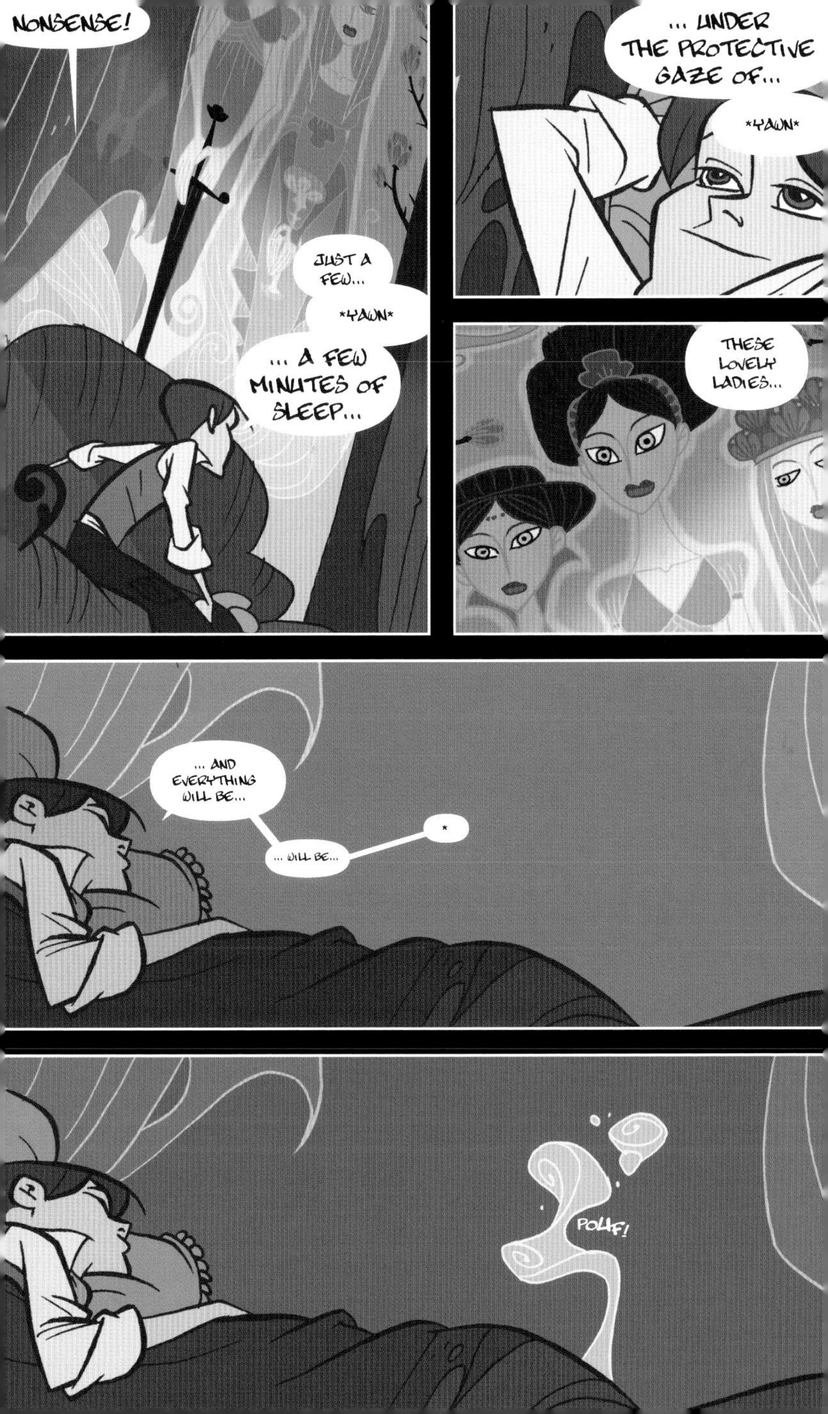
NONSENSE!
JUST A FEW...
YAWN
... A FEW MINUTES OF SLEEP...
... UNDER THE PROTECTIVE GAZE OF...
YAWN
THESE LOVELY LADIES...
... AND EVERYTHING WILL BE...
... WILL BE...
*
POUF!

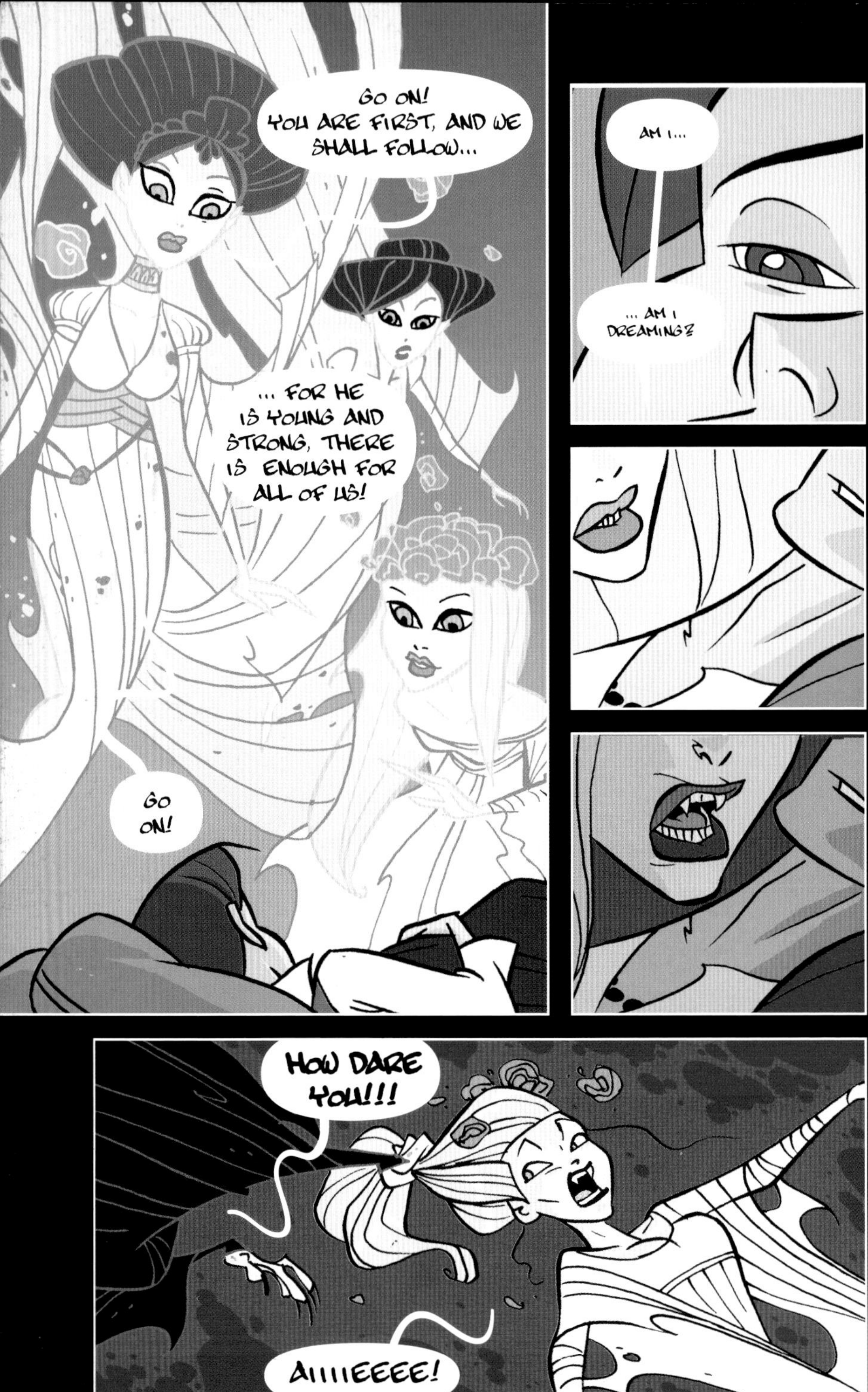
GO ON!
YOU ARE FIRST, AND WE SHALL FOLLOW...
... FOR HE IS YOUNG AND STRONG, THERE IS ENOUGH FOR ALL OF US!
GO ON!
AM I...
... AM I DREAMING?
HOW DARE YOU!!!
AIIIIEEEE!

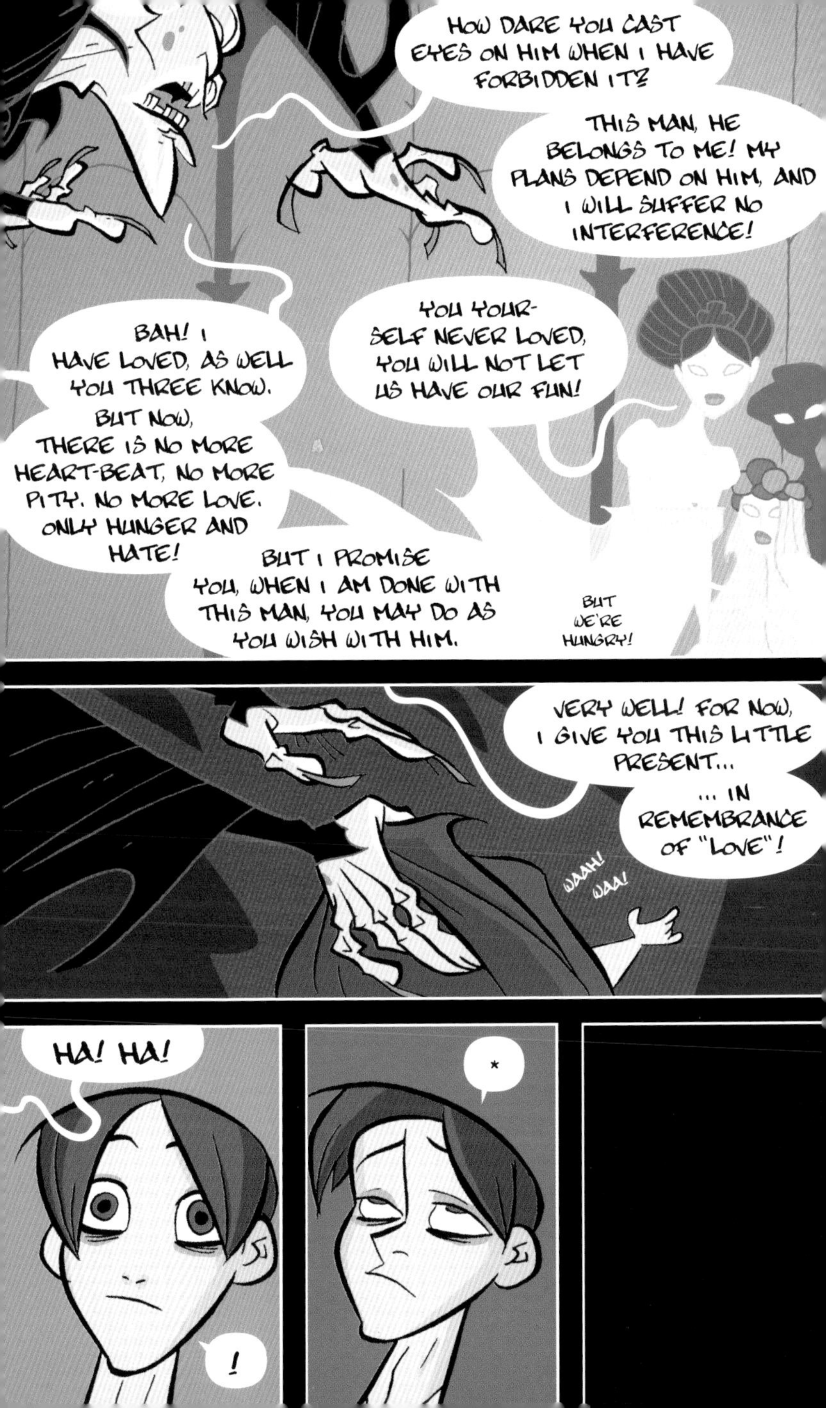
HOW DARE YOU CAST EYES ON HIM WHEN I HAVE FORBIDDEN IT?
THIS MAN, HE BELONGS TO ME! MY PLANS DEPEND ON HIM, AND I WILL SUFFER NO INTERFERENCE!
BAH! I HAVE LOVED, AS WELL YOU THREE KNOW.
YOU YOURSELF NEVER LOVED, YOU WILL NOT LET US HAVE OUR FUN!
BUT NOW, THERE IS NO MORE HEART-BEAT, NO MORE PITY. NO MORE LOVE. ONLY HUNGER AND HATE!
BUT I PROMISE YOU, WHEN I AM DONE WITH THIS MAN, YOU MAY DO AS YOU WISH WITH HIM.
BUT WE'RE HUNGRY!
VERY WELL! FOR NOW, I GIVE YOU THIS LITTLE PRESENT...
... IN REMEMBRANCE OF "LOVE"!
WAAH! WAA!
HA! HA!
!
*

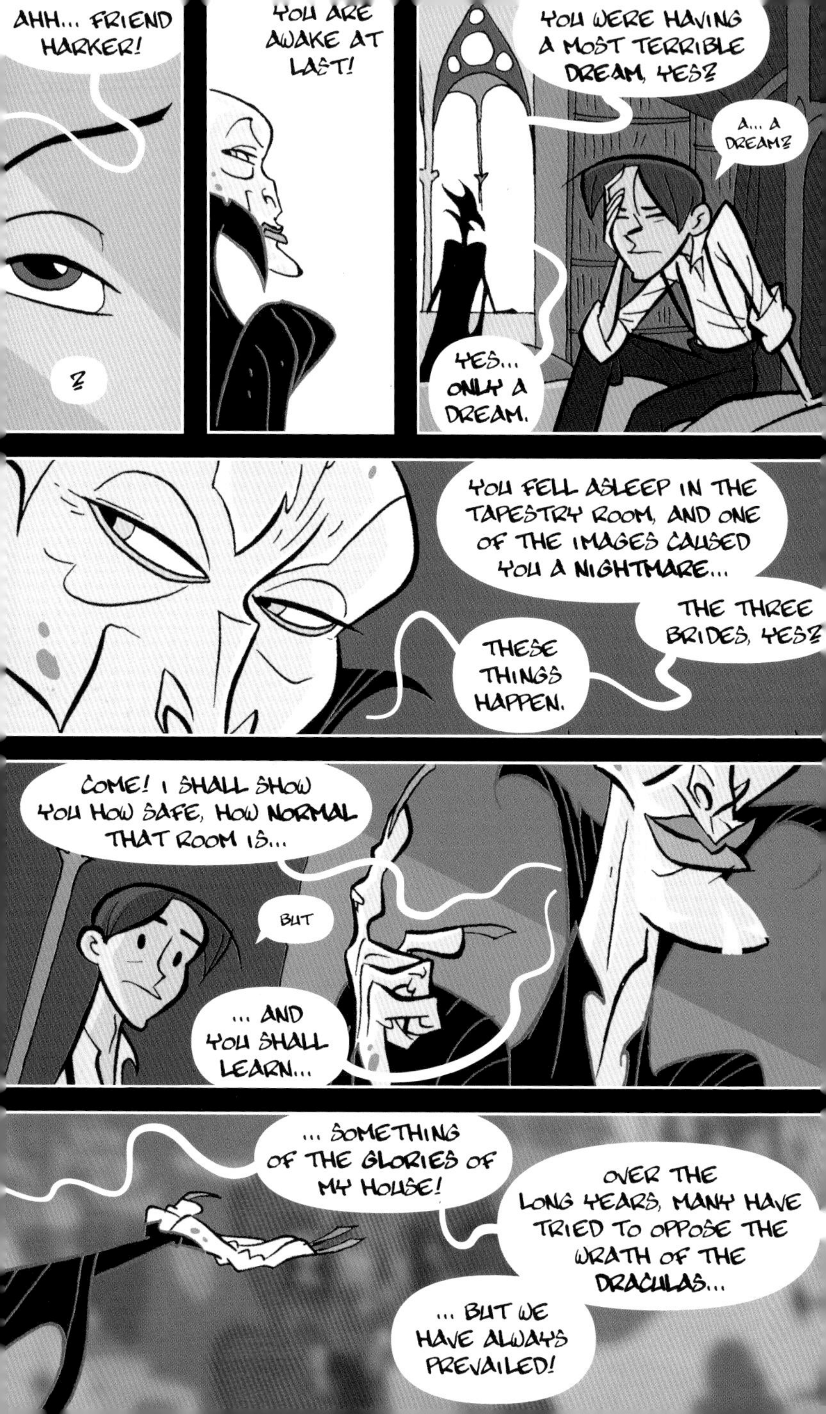
AHH... FRIEND HARKER!
?
YOU ARE AWAKE AT LAST!
YOU WERE HAVING A MOST TERRIBLE DREAM, YES?
A... A DREAM?
YES... ONLY A DREAM.
YOU FELL ASLEEP IN THE TAPESTRY ROOM, AND ONE OF THE IMAGES CAUSED YOU A NIGHTMARE...
THE THREE BRIDES, YES?
THESE THINGS HAPPEN.
COME! I SHALL SHOW YOU HOW SAFE, HOW NORMAL THAT ROOM IS...
BUT
... AND YOU SHALL LEARN...
... SOMETHING OF THE GLORIES OF MY HOUSE!
OVER THE LONG YEARS, MANY HAVE TRIED TO OPPOSE THE WRATH OF THE DRACULAS...
... BUT WE HAVE ALWAYS PREVAILED!

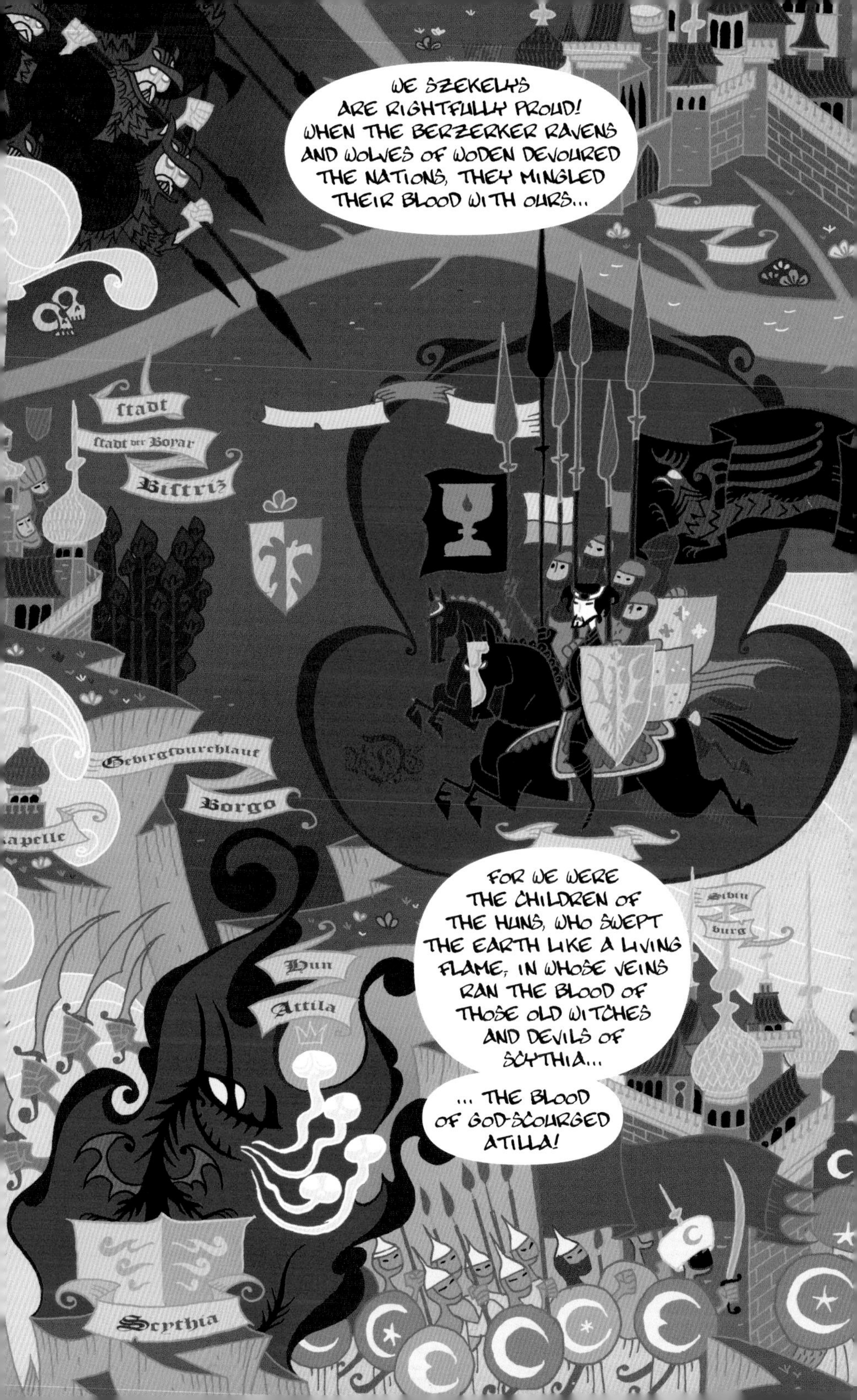
WE SZEKELYS ARE RIGHTFULLY PROUD! WHEN THE BERZERKER RAVENS AND WOLVES OF WODEN DEVOURED THE NATIONS, THEY MINGLED THEIR BLOOD WITH OURS...
stadt
stadt der Bojar
Bistriz
Gebirgsdurchlauf
Borgo
FOR WE WERE THE CHILDREN OF THE HUNS, WHO SWEPT THE EARTH LIKE A LIVING FLAME, IN WHOSE VEINS RAN THE BLOOD OF THOSE OLD WITCHES AND DEVILS OF SCYTHIA...
... THE BLOOD OF GOD-SCOURGED ATILLA!
Sibiu
burg
Hun
Attila
Scythia

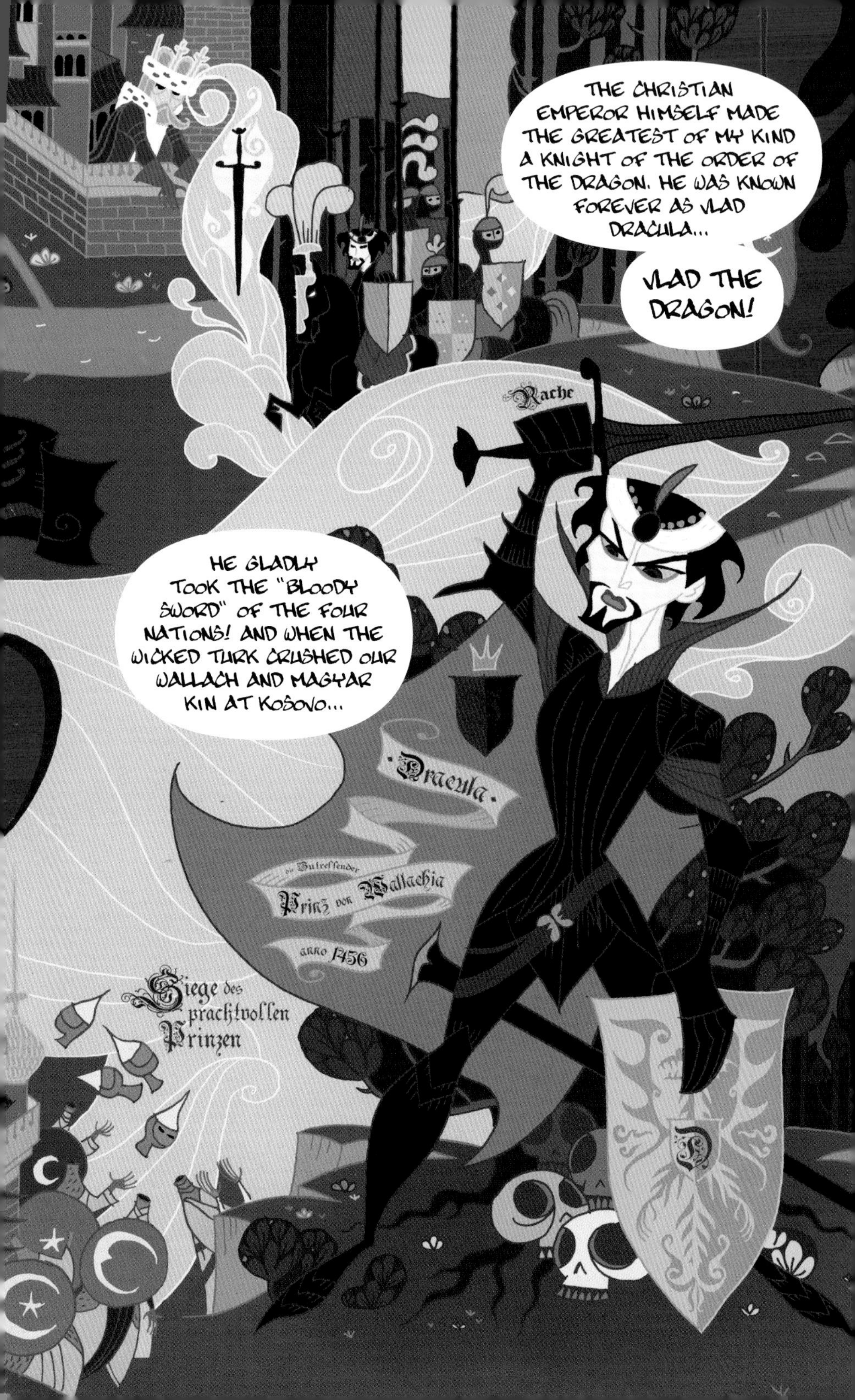
THE CHRISTIAN EMPEROR HIMSELF MADE THE GREATEST OF MY KIND A KNIGHT OF THE ORDER OF THE DRAGON. HE WAS KNOWN FOREVER AS VLAD DRACULA...
VLAD THE DRAGON!
Rache
HE GLADLY TOOK THE "BLOODY SWORD" OF THE FOUR NATIONS! AND WHEN THE WICKED TURK CRUSHED OUR WALLACH AND MAGYAR KIN AT KOSOVO...
Dracula
die Zutreffender
Prinz von Wallachia
anno 1456
Siege des prachtvollen Prinzen

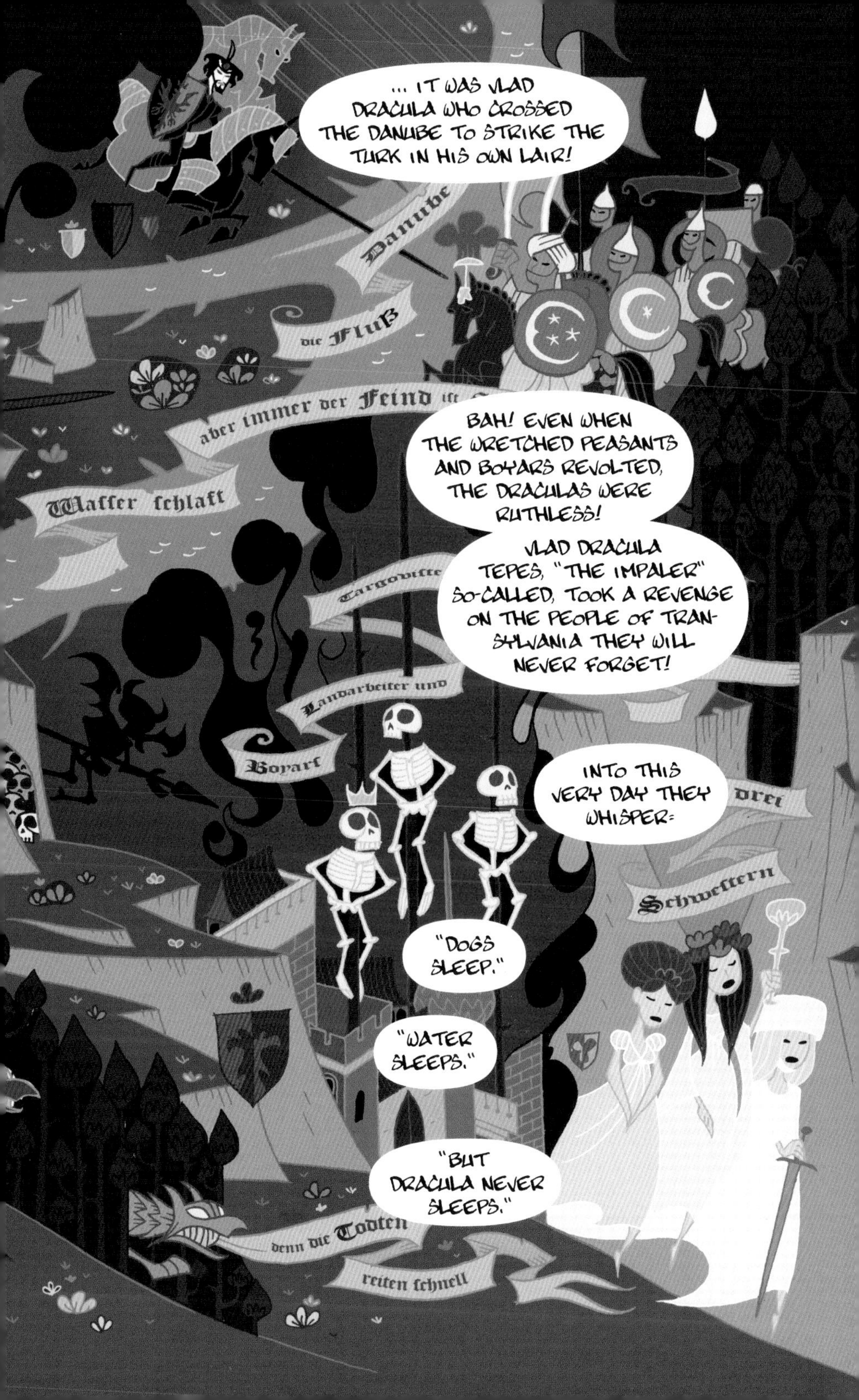
... IT WAS VLAD DRACULA WHO CROSSED THE DANUBE TO STRIKE THE TURK IN HIS OWN LAIR!
Danube
die Fluß
aber immer der Feind ist
Wasser schlaft
BAH! EVEN WHEN THE WRETCHED PEASANTS AND BOYARS REVOLTED, THE DRACULAS WERE RUTHLESS!
VLAD DRACULA TEPES, "THE IMPALER" SO-CALLED, TOOK A REVENGE ON THE PEOPLE OF TRANSYLVANIA THEY WILL NEVER FORGET!
Landarbeiter und
Boyars
INTO THIS VERY DAY THEY WHISPER:
drei
Schwestern
"DOGS SLEEP."
"WATER SLEEPS."
"BUT DRACULA NEVER SLEEPS."
denn die Todten
reiten schnell

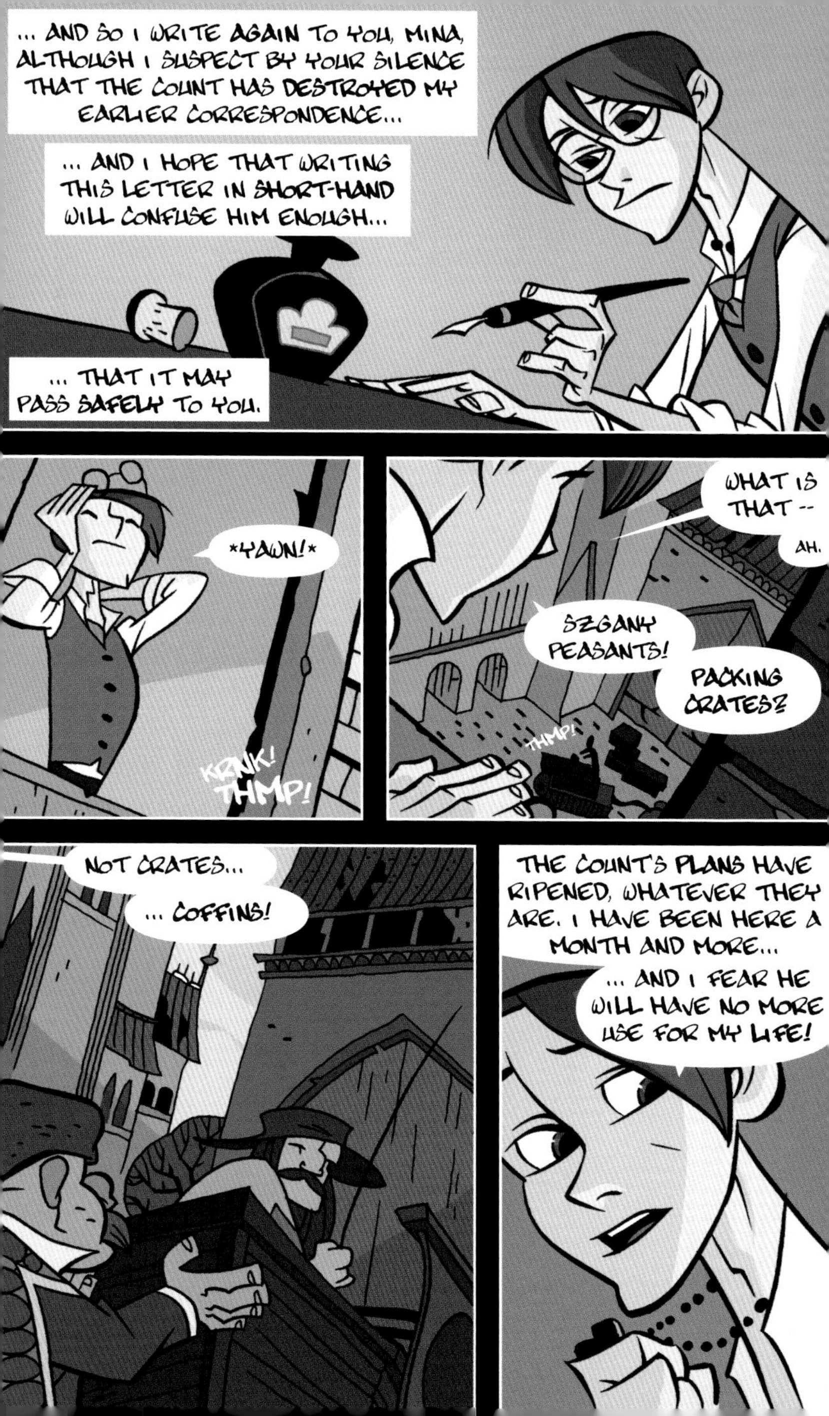
... AND SO I WRITE AGAIN TO YOU, MINA, ALTHOUGH I SUSPECT BY YOUR SILENCE THAT THE COUNT HAS DESTROYED MY EARLIER CORRESPONDENCE...
... AND I HOPE THAT WRITING THIS LETTER IN SHORT-HAND WILL CONFUSE HIM ENOUGH...
... THAT IT MAY PASS SAFELY TO YOU.
YAWN!
KRNK! THMP!
WHAT IS THAT --
AH.
SZGANY PEASANTS!
PACKING CRATES?
THMP!
NOT CRATES...
... COFFINS!
THE COUNT'S PLANS HAVE RIPENED, WHATEVER THEY ARE. I HAVE BEEN HERE A MONTH AND MORE...
... AND I FEAR HE WILL HAVE NO MORE USE FOR MY LIFE!

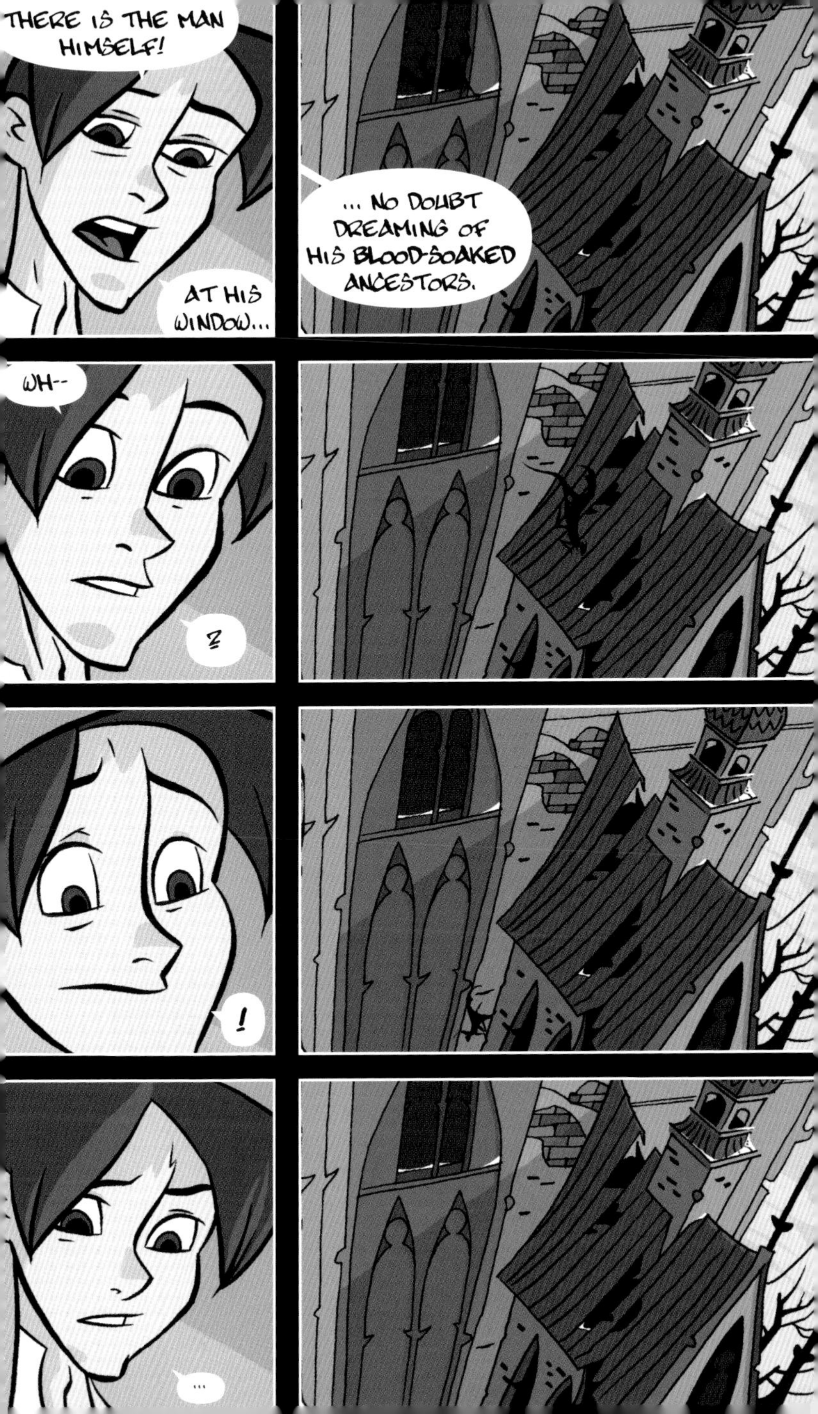
THERE IS THE MAN HIMSELF!
AT HIS WINDOW...
... NO DOUBT DREAMING OF HIS BLOOD-SOAKED ANCESTORS.
WH--
?
!
...

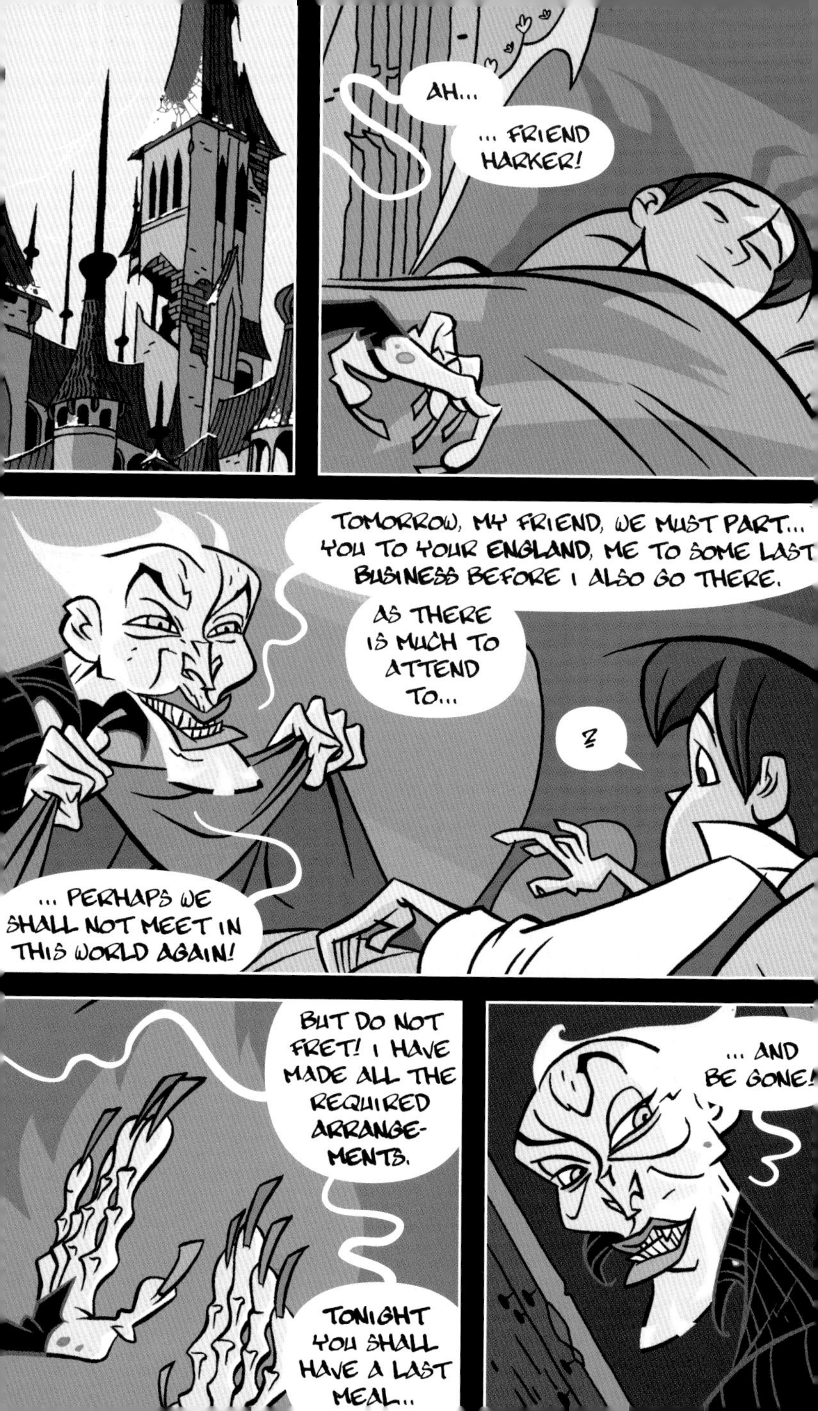
AH...
... FRIEND HARKER!
TOMORROW, MY FRIEND, WE MUST PART... YOU TO YOUR ENGLAND, ME TO SOME LAST BUSINESS BEFORE I ALSO GO THERE.
AS THERE IS MUCH TO ATTEND TO...
?
... PERHAPS WE SHALL NOT MEET IN THIS WORLD AGAIN!
BUT DO NOT FRET! I HAVE MADE ALL THE REQUIRED ARRANGE-MENTS.
TONIGHT YOU SHALL HAVE A LAST MEAL..
... AND BE GONE!

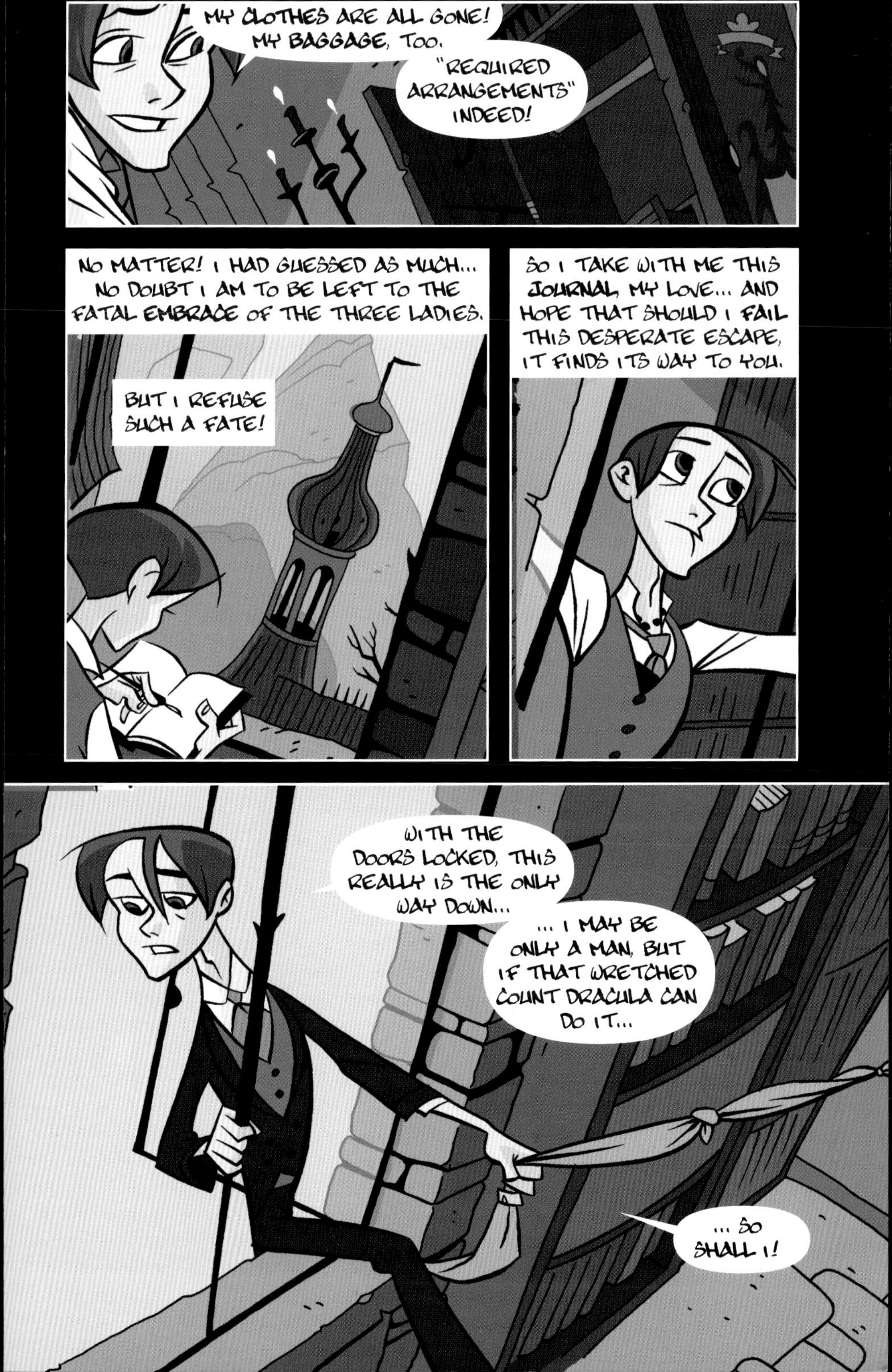
MY CLOTHES ARE ALL GONE! MY BAGGAGE, TOO.
"REQUIRED ARRANGEMENTS" INDEED!
NO MATTER! I HAD GUESSED AS MUCH... NO DOUBT I AM TO BE LEFT TO THE FATAL EMBRACE OF THE THREE LADIES.
BUT I REFUSE SUCH A FATE!
SO I TAKE WITH ME THIS JOURNAL, MY LOVE... AND HOPE THAT SHOULD I FAIL THIS DESPERATE ESCAPE, IT FINDS ITS WAY TO YOU.
WITH THE DOORS LOCKED, THIS REALLY IS THE ONLY WAY DOWN...
... I MAY BE ONLY A MAN, BUT IF THAT WRETCHED COUNT DRACULA CAN DO IT...
... SO SHALL I!

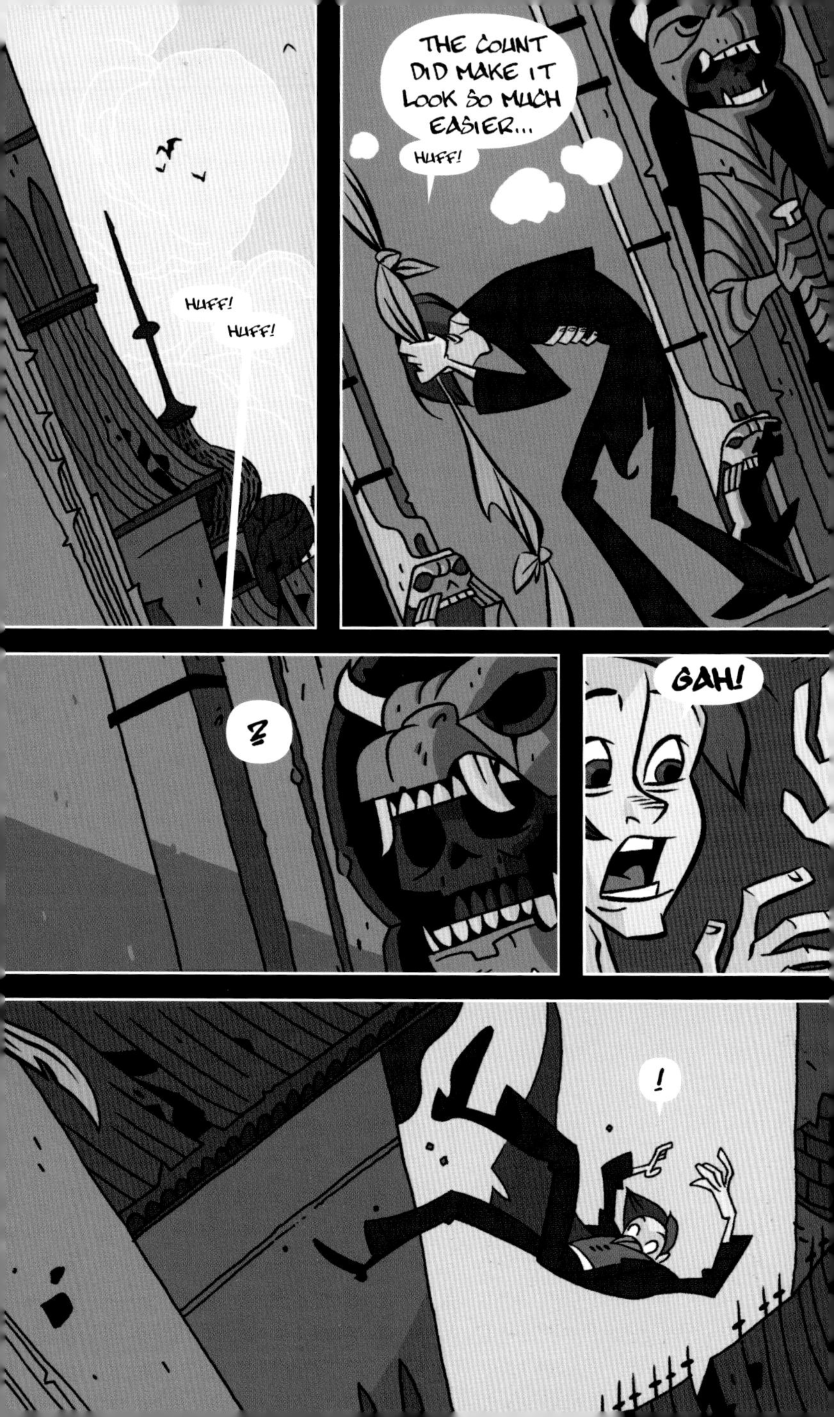
HUFF!
HUFF!
THE COUNT DID MAKE IT LOOK SO MUCH EASIER...
HUFF!
?
GAH!
!

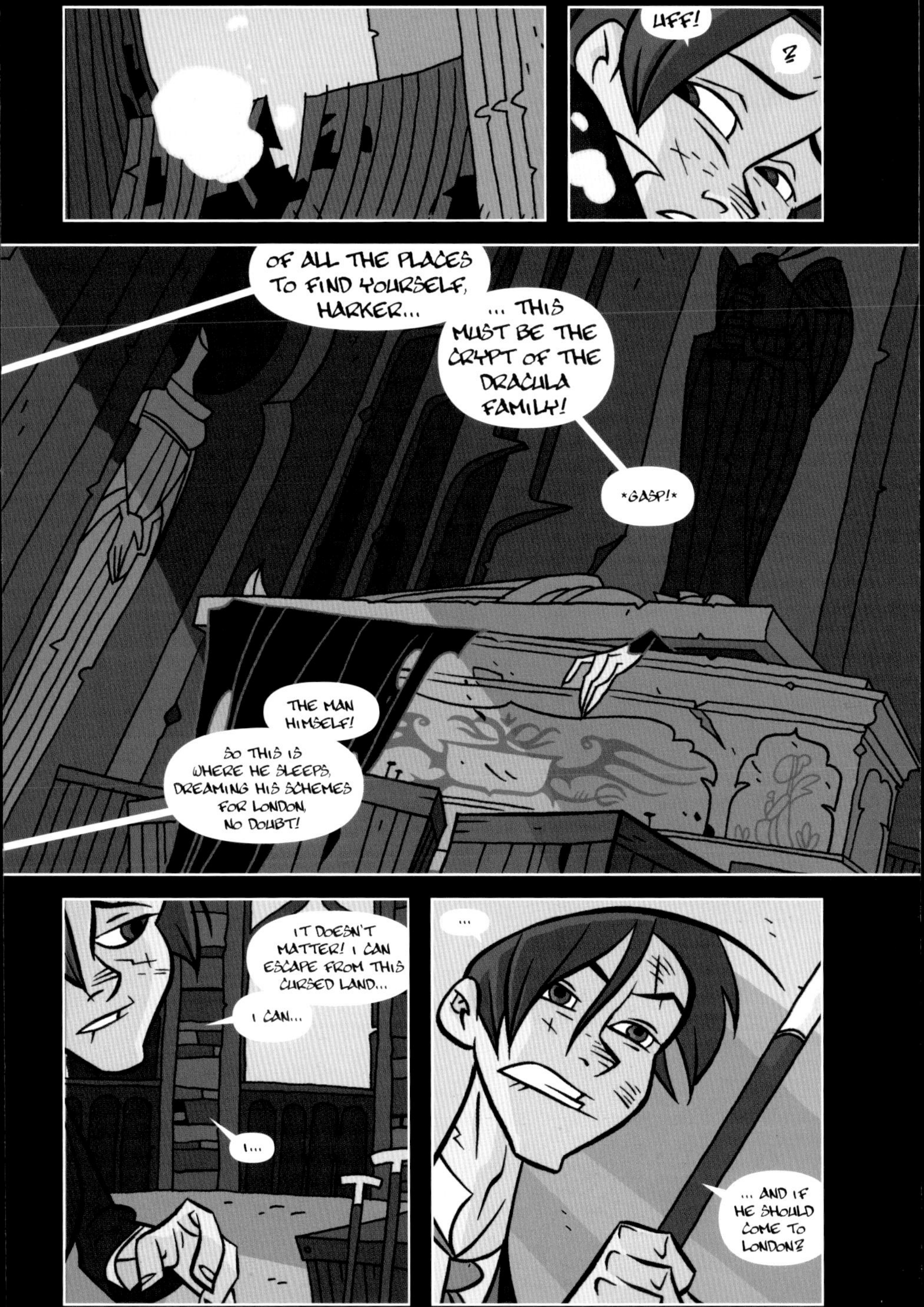
UFF!
?
OF ALL THE PLACES TO FIND YOURSELF, HARKER...
... THIS MUST BE THE CRYPT OF THE DRACULA FAMILY!
GASP!
THE MAN HIMSELF!
SO THIS IS WHERE HE SLEEPS, DREAMING HIS SCHEMES FOR LONDON, NO DOUBT!
IT DOESN'T MATTER! I CAN ESCAPE FROM THIS CURSED LAND...
I CAN...
I...
...
... AND IF HE SHOULD COME TO LONDON?

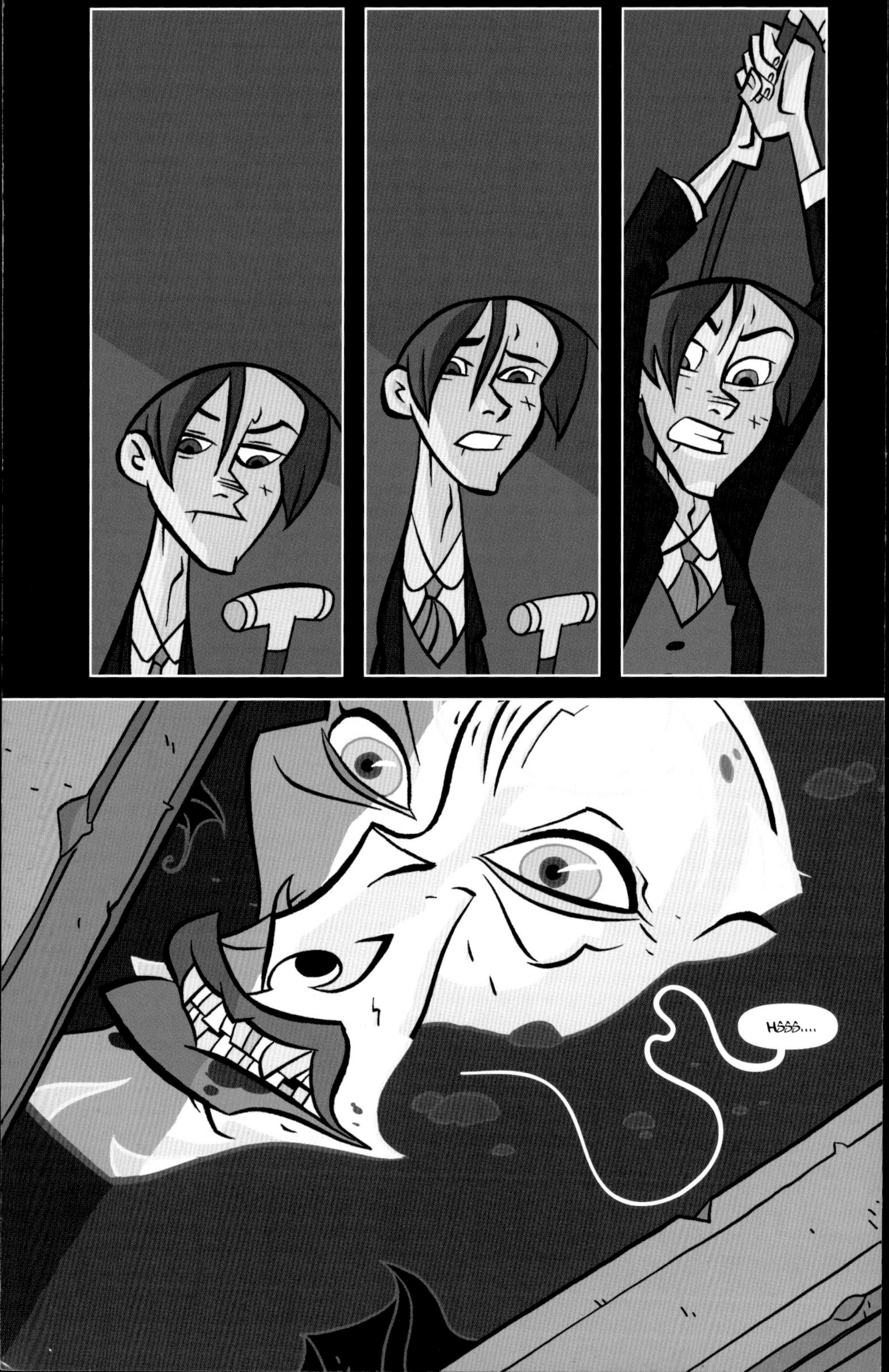
HSSS....

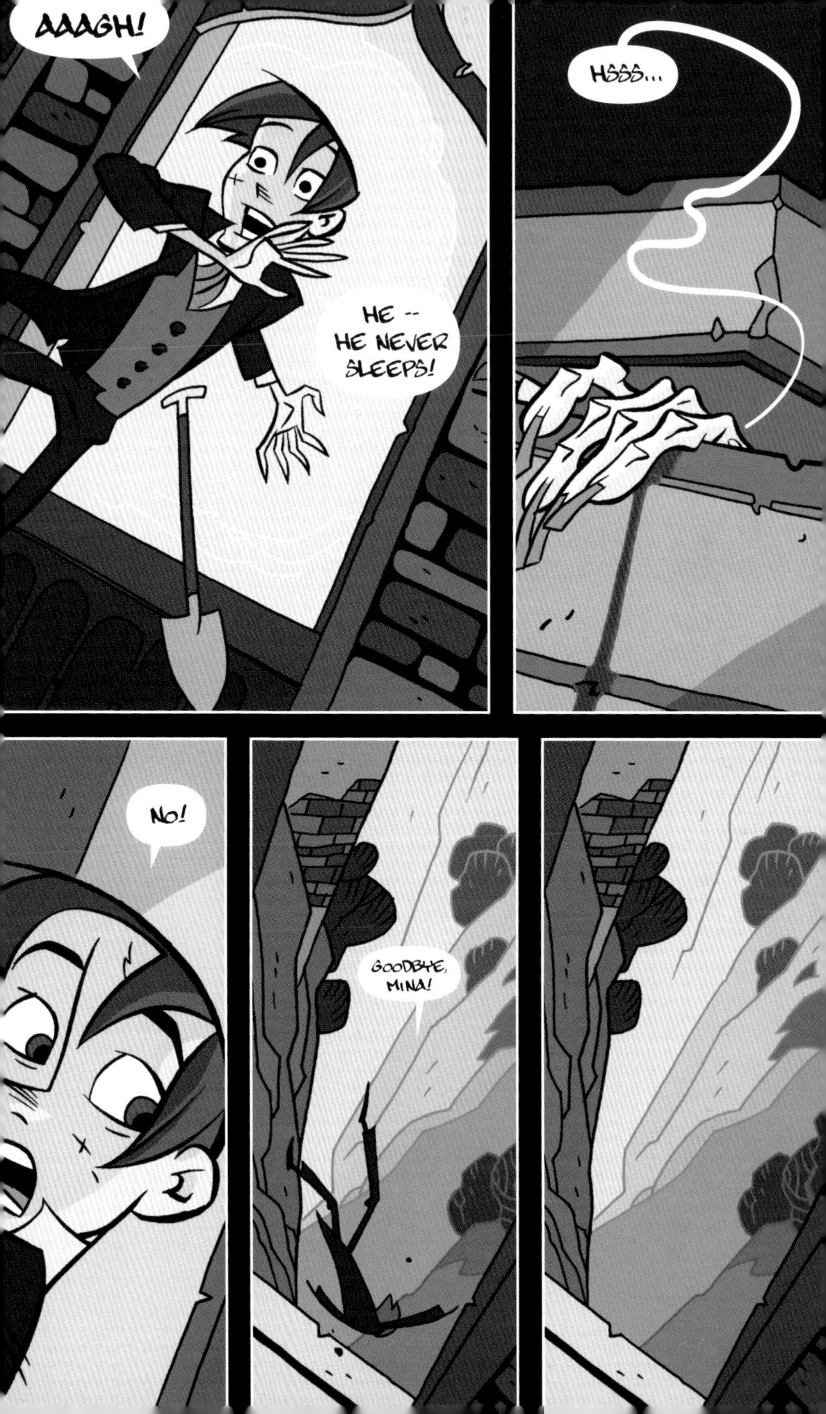
AAAGH!
HE -- HE NEVER SLEEPS!
HSSS...
NO!
GOODBYE, MINA!

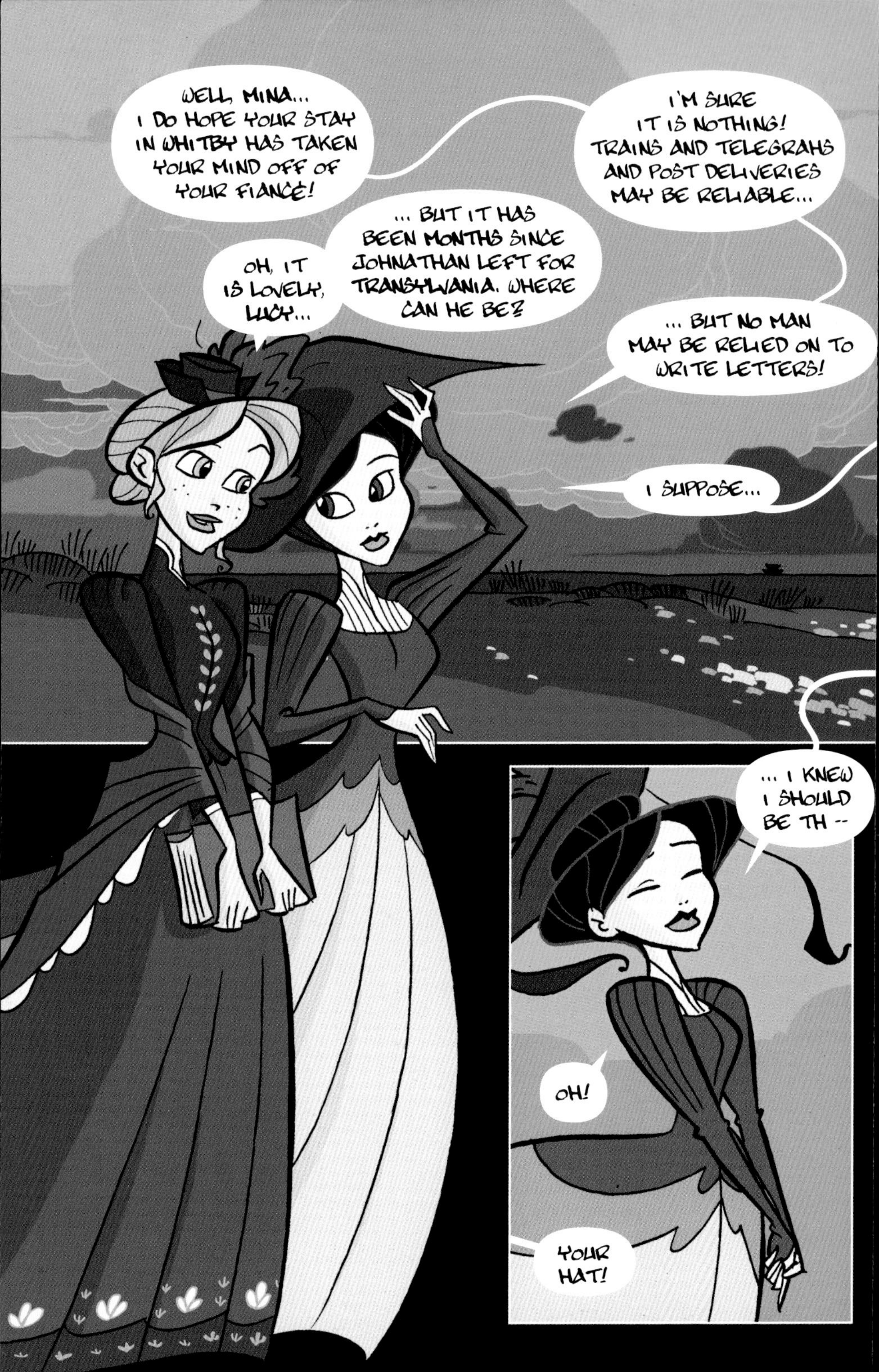
WELL, MINA... I DO HOPE YOUR STAY IN WHITBY HAS TAKEN YOUR MIND OFF OF YOUR FIANCÉ!
OH, IT IS LOVELY, LUCY...
... BUT IT HAS BEEN MONTHS SINCE JOHNATHAN LEFT FOR TRANSYLVANIA. WHERE CAN HE BE?
I'M SURE IT IS NOTHING! TRAINS AND TELEGRAHS AND POST DELIVERIES MAY BE RELIABLE...
... BUT NO MAN MAY BE RELIED ON TO WRITE LETTERS!
I SUPPOSE...
... I KNEW I SHOULD BE TH --
OH!
YOUR HAT!

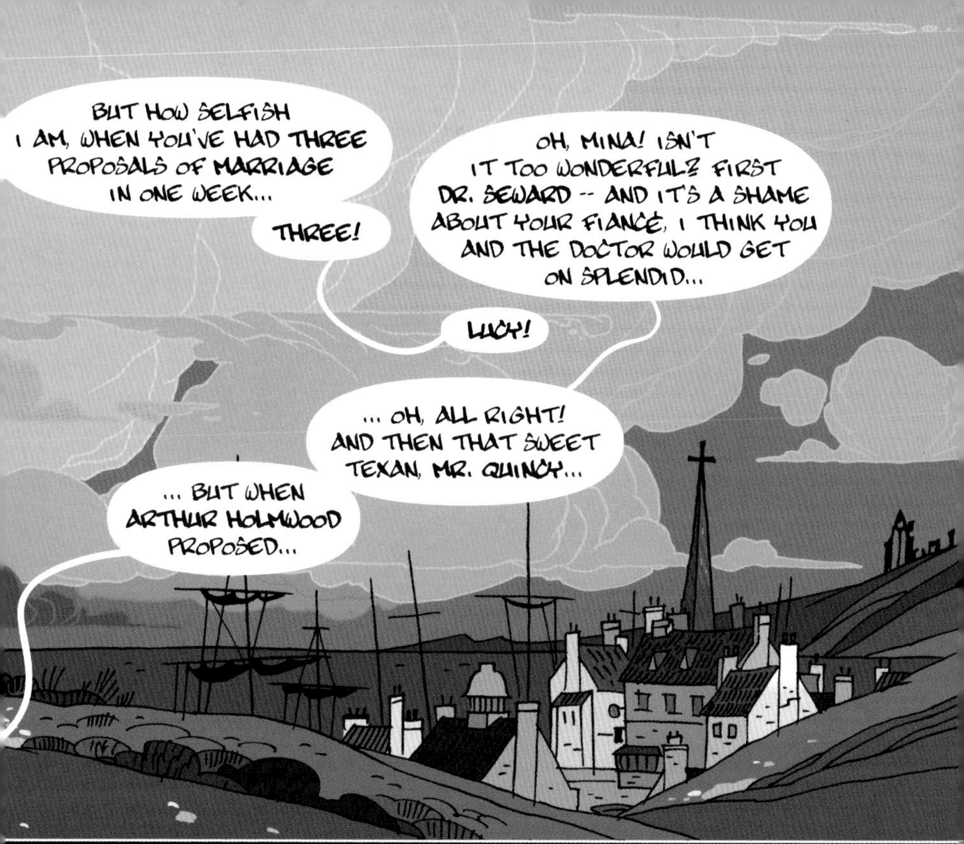
BUT HOW SELFISH I AM, WHEN YOU'VE HAD THREE PROPOSALS OF MARRIAGE IN ONE WEEK...
THREE!
OH, MINA! ISN'T IT TOO WONDERFUL? FIRST DR. SEWARD -- AND IT'S A SHAME ABOUT YOUR FIANCÉ, I THINK YOU AND THE DOCTOR WOULD GET ON SPLENDID...
LUCY!
... OH, ALL RIGHT! AND THEN THAT SWEET TEXAN, MR. QUINCY...
... BUT WHEN ARTHUR HOLMWOOD PROPOSED...

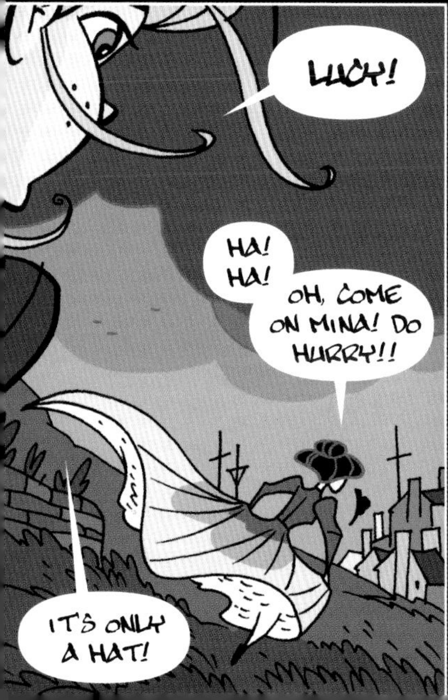
LUCY!
HA! HA!
OH, COME ON MINA! DO HURRY!!
IT'S ONLY A HAT!

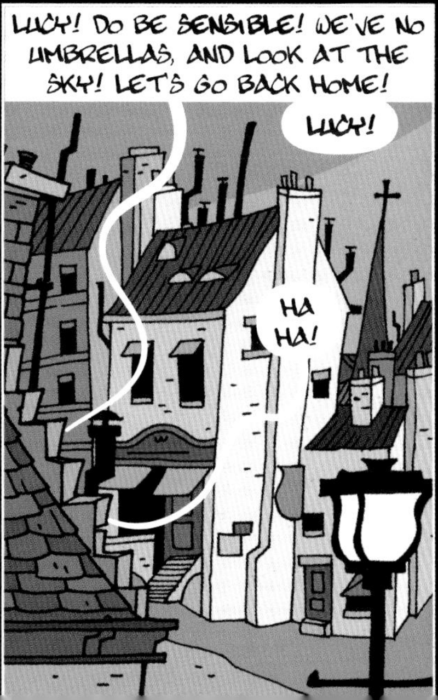
LUCY! DO BE SENSIBLE! WE'VE NO UMBRELLAS, AND LOOK AT THE SKY! LET'S GO BACK HOME!
LUCY!
HA HA!

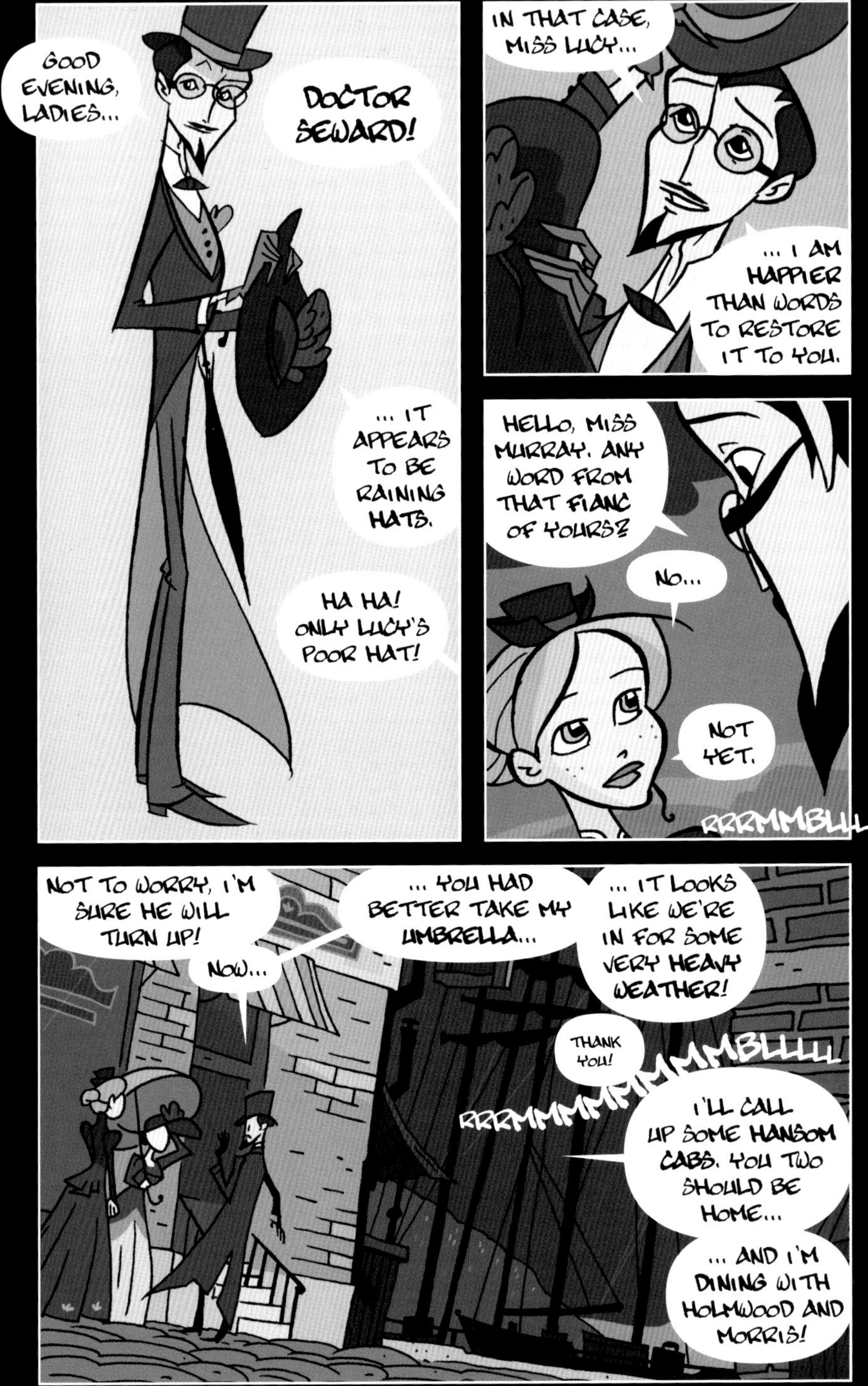
GOOD EVENING, LADIES...
DOCTOR SEWARD!
... IT APPEARS TO BE RAINING HATS.
HA HA! ONLY LUCY'S POOR HAT!
IN THAT CASE, MISS LUCY...
... I AM HAPPIER THAN WORDS TO RESTORE IT TO YOU.
HELLO, MISS MURRAY. ANY WORD FROM THAT FIANC OF YOURS?
NO...
NOT YET.
RRRMMBLLL
NOT TO WORRY, I'M SURE HE WILL TURN UP!
NOW...
... YOU HAD BETTER TAKE MY UMBRELLA...
... IT LOOKS LIKE WE'RE IN FOR SOME VERY HEAVY WEATHER!
THANK YOU!
RRRMMMMMMMMMBLLLLL
I'LL CALL UP SOME HANSOM CABS. YOU TWO SHOULD BE HOME...
... AND I'M DINING WITH HOLMWOOD AND MORRIS!

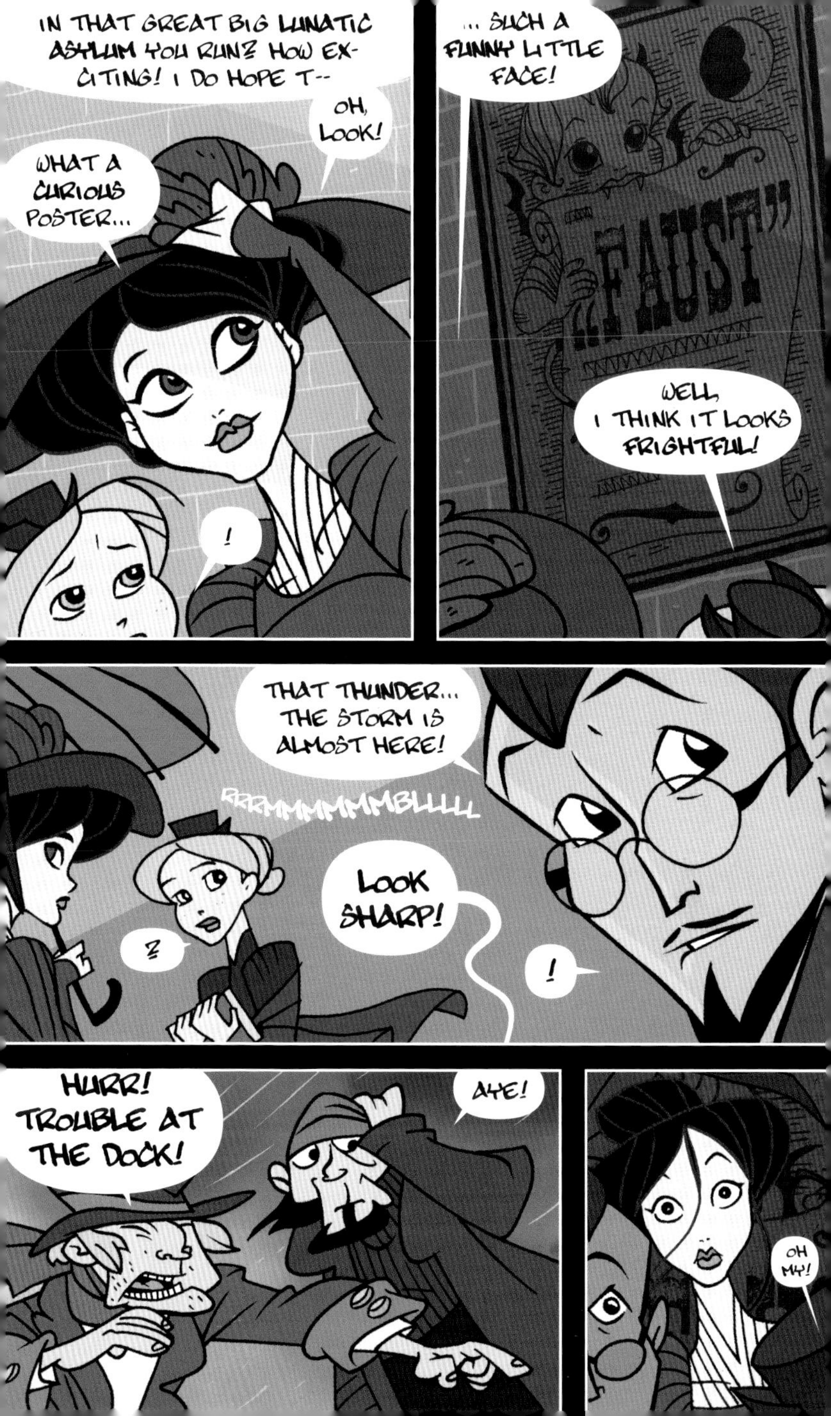
IN THAT GREAT BIG LUNATIC ASYLUM YOU RUN? HOW EXCITING! I DO HOPE T--
OH, LOOK!
WHAT A CURIOUS POSTER...
!
... SUCH A FUNNY LITTLE FACE!
"FAUST"
WELL, I THINK IT LOOKS FRIGHTFUL!
THAT THUNDER... THE STORM IS ALMOST HERE!
RRRMMMMMMBLLLLL
LOOK SHARP!
?
!
HURR! TROUBLE AT THE DOCK!
AYE!
OH MY!

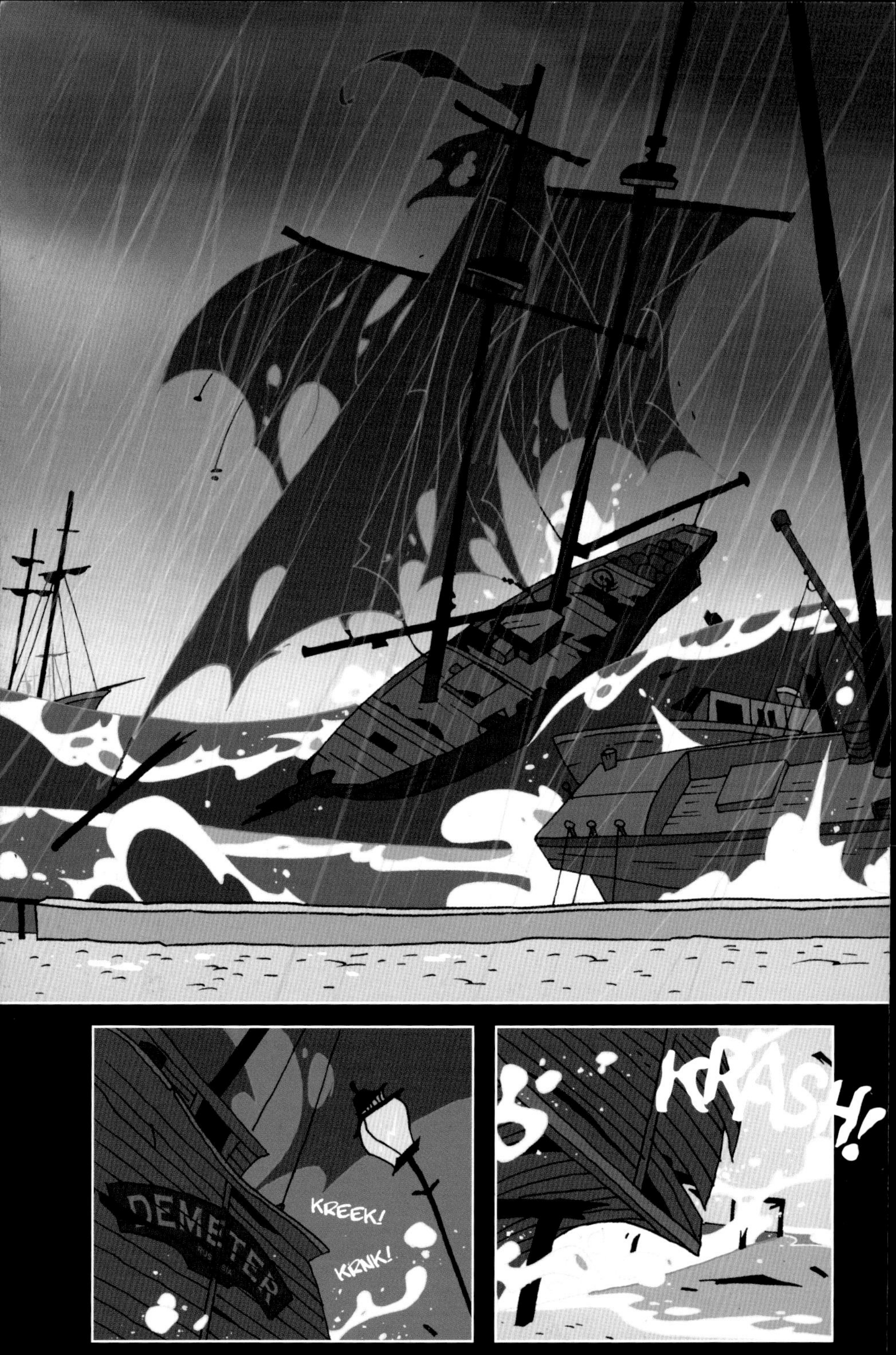
DEMETER
KREEK!
KRNK!
KRASH!!

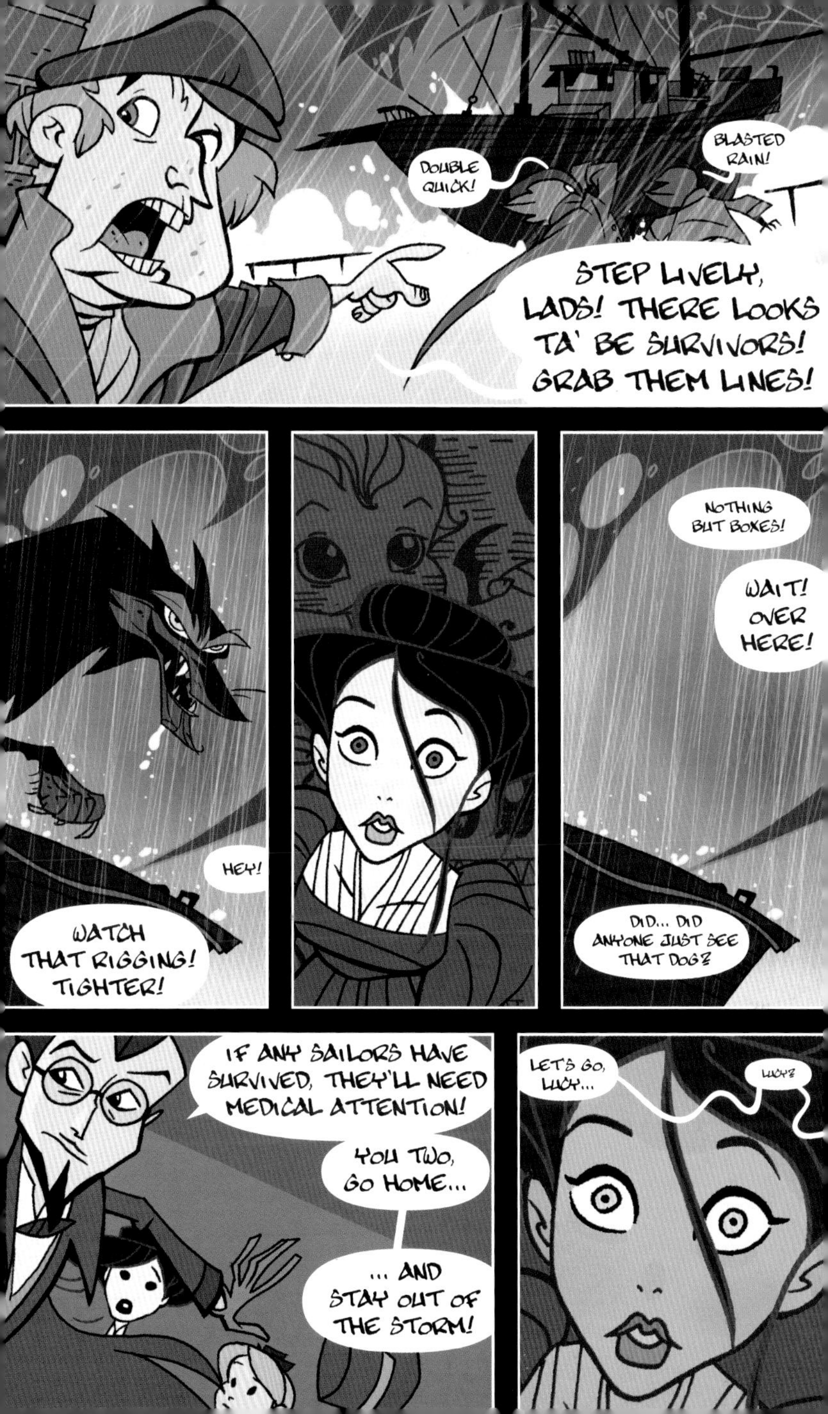
DOUBLE QUICK!
BLASTED RAIN!
STEP LIVELY, LADS! THERE LOOKS TA' BE SURVIVORS! GRAB THEM LINES!
HEY!
WATCH THAT RIGGING! TIGHTER!
NOTHING BUT BOXES!
WAIT! OVER HERE!
DID... DID ANYONE JUST SEE THAT DOG?
IF ANY SAILORS HAVE SURVIVED, THEY'LL NEED MEDICAL ATTENTION!
YOU TWO, GO HOME...
... AND STAY OUT OF THE STORM!
LET'S GO, LUCY...
LUCY?

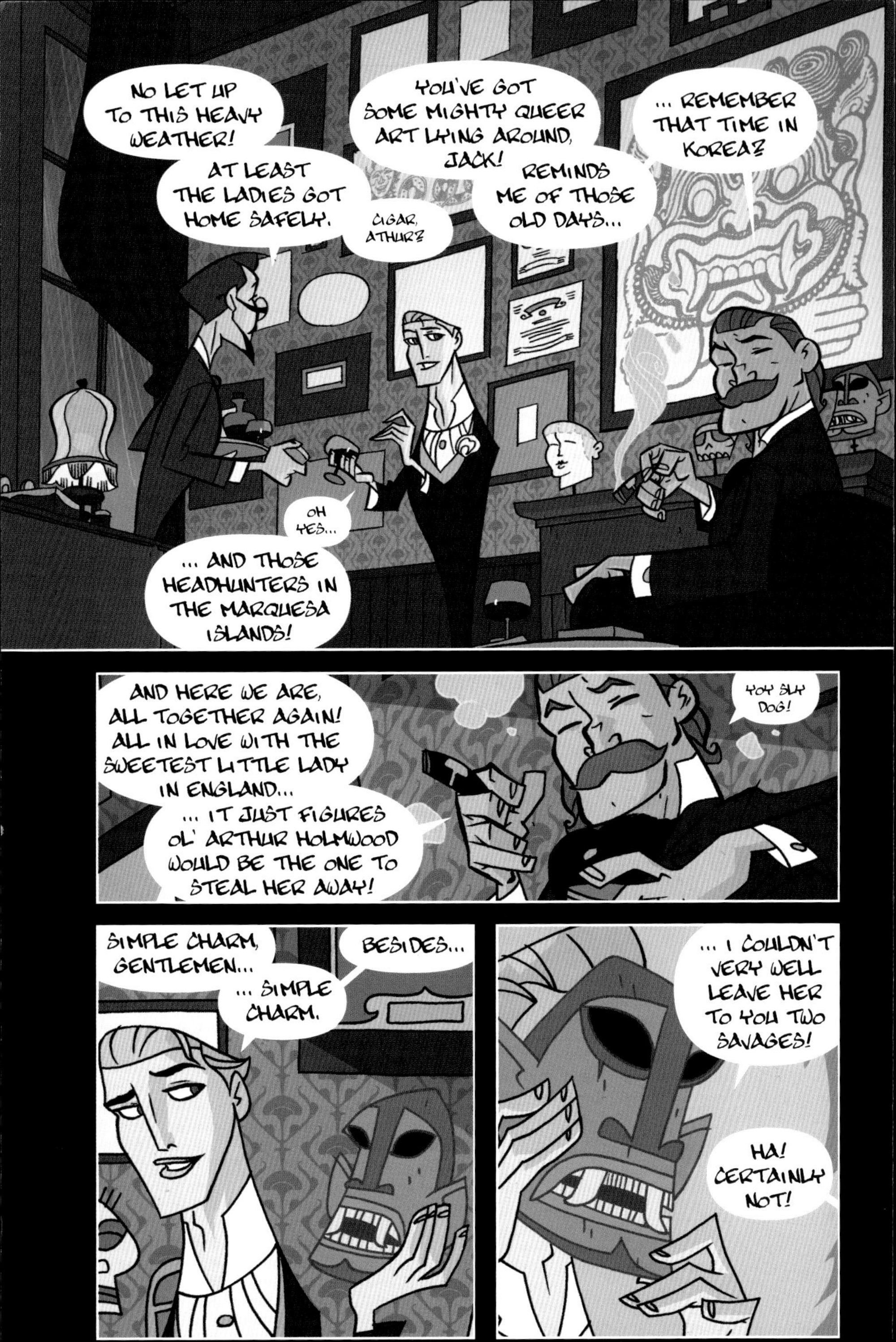
NO LET UP TO THIS HEAVY WEATHER!
AT LEAST THE LADIES GOT HOME SAFELY.
YOU'VE GOT SOME MIGHTY QUEER ART LYING AROUND, JACK!
CIGAR, ATHUR?
REMINDS ME OF THOSE OLD DAYS...
... REMEMBER THAT TIME IN KOREA?
OH YES...
... AND THOSE HEADHUNTERS IN THE MARQUESA ISLANDS!
AND HERE WE ARE, ALL TOGETHER AGAIN! ALL IN LOVE WITH THE SWEETEST LITTLE LADY IN ENGLAND...
... IT JUST FIGURES OL' ARTHUR HOLMWOOD WOULD BE THE ONE TO STEAL HER AWAY!
YOU SLY DOG!
SIMPLE CHARM, GENTLEMEN...
... SIMPLE CHARM.
BESIDES...
... I COULDN'T VERY WELL LEAVE HER TO YOU TWO SAVAGES!
HA! CERTAINLY NOT!

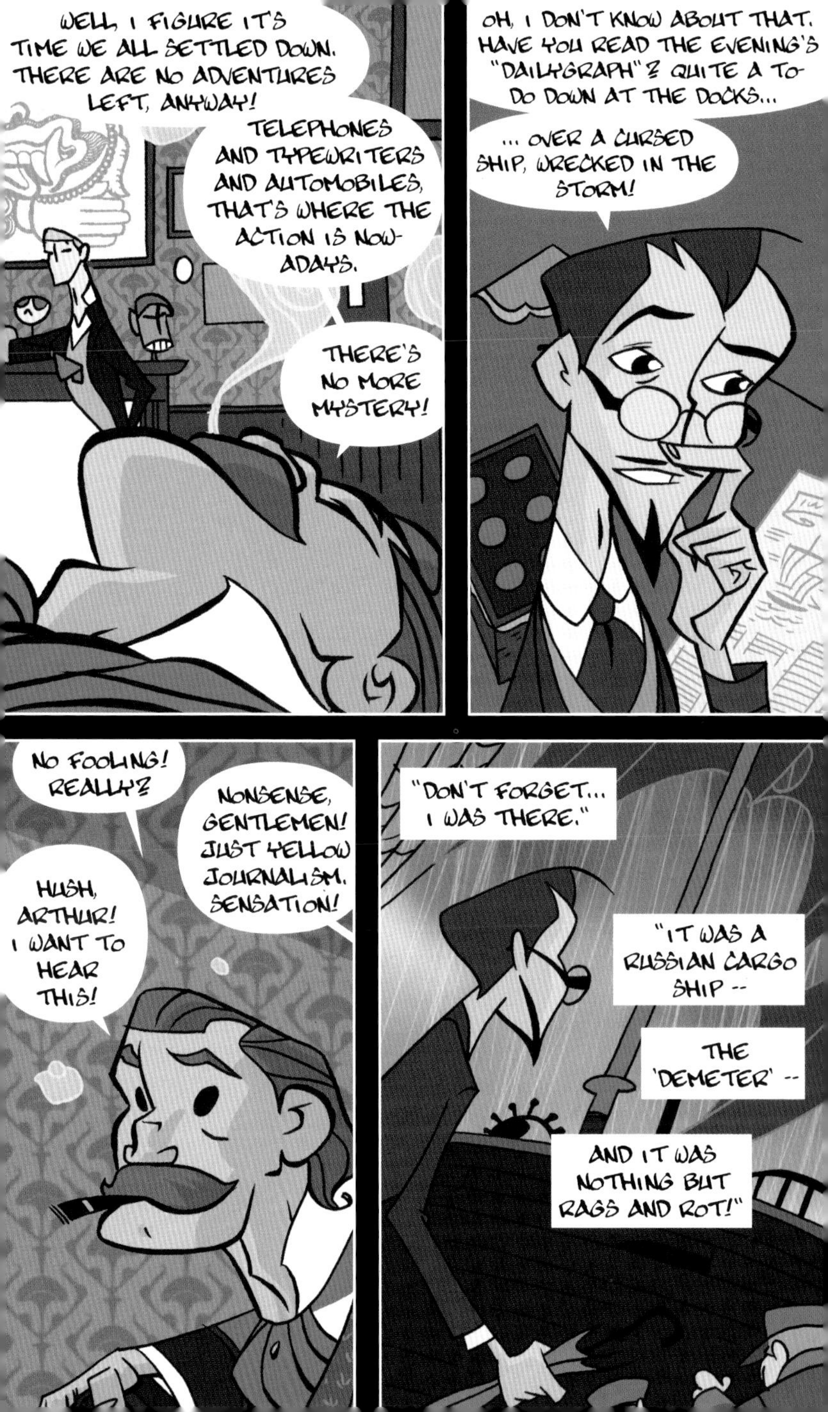
WELL, I FIGURE IT'S TIME WE ALL SETTLED DOWN. THERE ARE NO ADVENTURES LEFT, ANYWAY!
TELEPHONES AND TYPEWRITERS AND AUTOMOBILES, THAT'S WHERE THE ACTION IS NOWADAYS.
THERE'S NO MORE MYSTERY!
OH, I DON'T KNOW ABOUT THAT. HAVE YOU READ THE EVENING'S "DAILYGRAPH"? QUITE A TO-DO DOWN AT THE DOCKS...
... OVER A CURSED SHIP, WRECKED IN THE STORM!
NO FOOLING! REALLY?
NONSENSE, GENTLEMEN! JUST YELLOW JOURNALISM. SENSATION!
HUSH, ARTHUR! I WANT TO HEAR THIS!
"DON'T FORGET... I WAS THERE."
"IT WAS A RUSSIAN CARGO SHIP --
THE 'DEMETER' --
AND IT WAS NOTHING BUT RAGS AND ROT!"

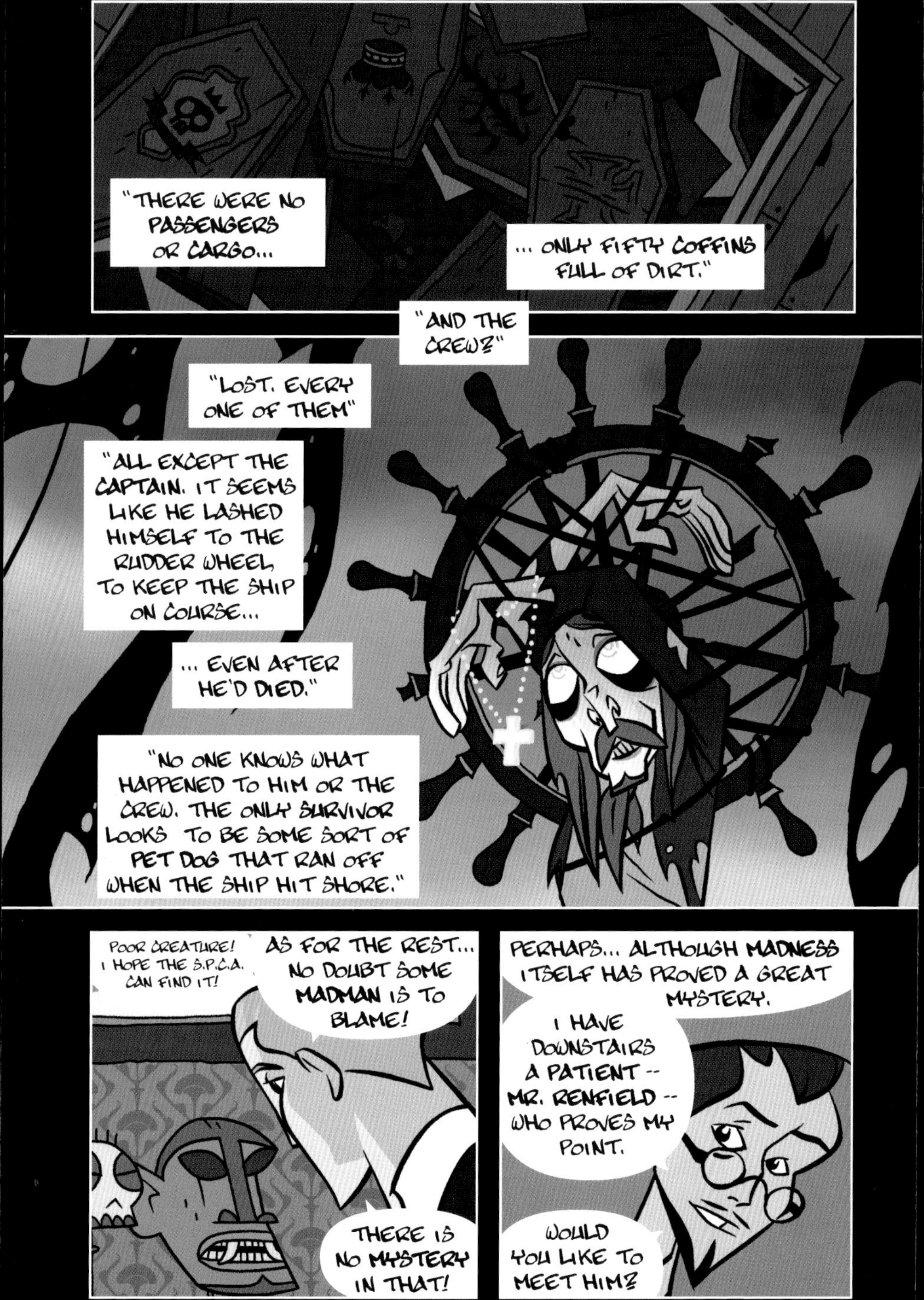
"THERE WERE NO PASSENGERS OR CARGO...
... ONLY FIFTY COFFINS FULL OF DIRT."
"AND THE CREW?"
"LOST. EVERY ONE OF THEM"
"ALL EXCEPT THE CAPTAIN. IT SEEMS LIKE HE LASHED HIMSELF TO THE RUDDER WHEEL, TO KEEP THE SHIP ON COURSE...
... EVEN AFTER HE'D DIED."
"NO ONE KNOWS WHAT HAPPENED TO HIM OR THE CREW. THE ONLY SURVIVOR LOOKS TO BE SOME SORT OF PET DOG THAT RAN OFF WHEN THE SHIP HIT SHORE."
POOR CREATURE! I HOPE THE S.P.C.A. CAN FIND IT!
AS FOR THE REST... NO DOUBT SOME MADMAN IS TO BLAME!
THERE IS NO MYSTERY IN THAT!
PERHAPS... ALTHOUGH MADNESS ITSELF HAS PROVED A GREAT MYSTERY.
I HAVE DOWNSTAIRS A PATIENT -- MR. RENFIELD -- WHO PROVES MY POINT.
WOULD YOU LIKE TO MEET HIM?

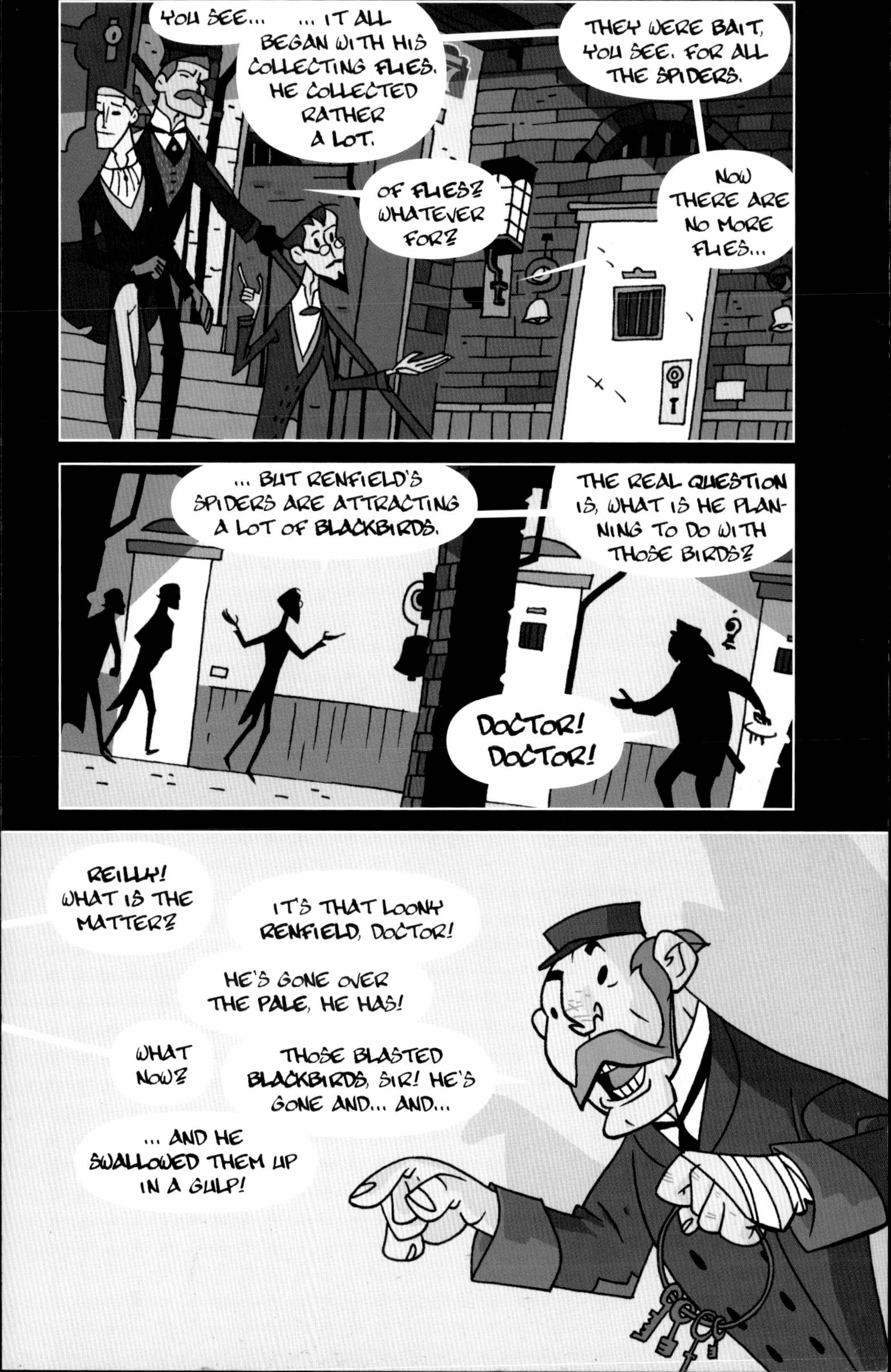
YOU SEE...
... IT ALL BEGAN WITH HIS COLLECTING FLIES. HE COLLECTED RATHER A LOT.
OF FLIES? WHATEVER FOR?
THEY WERE BAIT, YOU SEE. FOR ALL THE SPIDERS.
NOW THERE ARE NO MORE FLIES...
... BUT RENFIELD'S SPIDERS ARE ATTRACTING A LOT OF BLACKBIRDS.
THE REAL QUESTION IS, WHAT IS HE PLANNING TO DO WITH THOSE BIRDS?
DOCTOR! DOCTOR!
REILLY! WHAT IS THE MATTER?
IT'S THAT LOONY RENFIELD, DOCTOR!
HE'S GONE OVER THE PALE, HE HAS!
WHAT NOW?
THOSE BLASTED BLACKBIRDS, SIR! HE'S GONE AND... AND...
... AND HE SWALLOWED THEM UP IN A GULP!

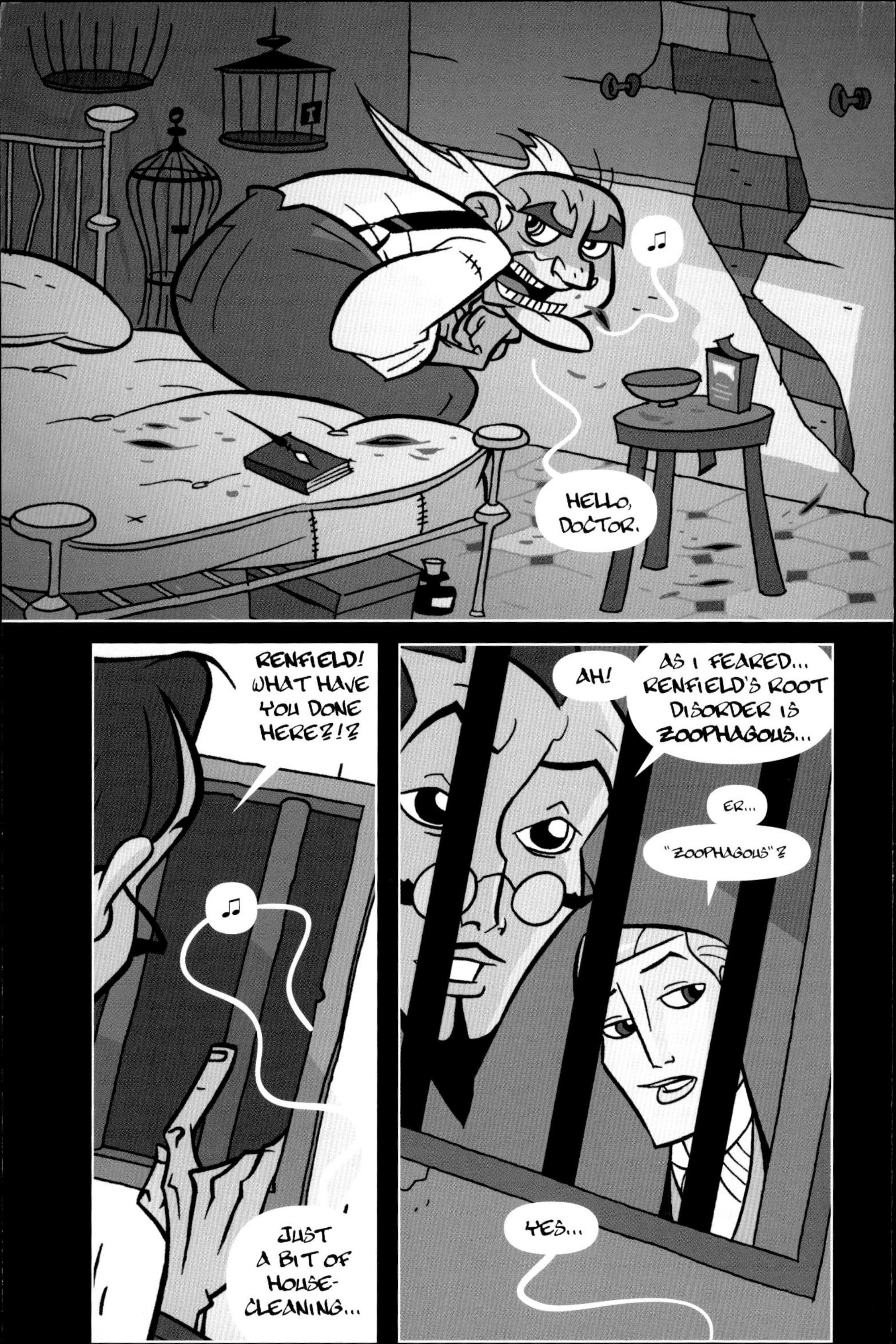

HELLO, DOCTOR.
RENFIELD! WHAT HAVE YOU DONE HERE?!?
JUST A BIT OF HOUSE-CLEANING...
AH!
AS I FEARED... RENFIELD'S ROOT DISORDER IS ZOOPHAGOUS...
ER...
"ZOOPHAGOUS"?
YES...

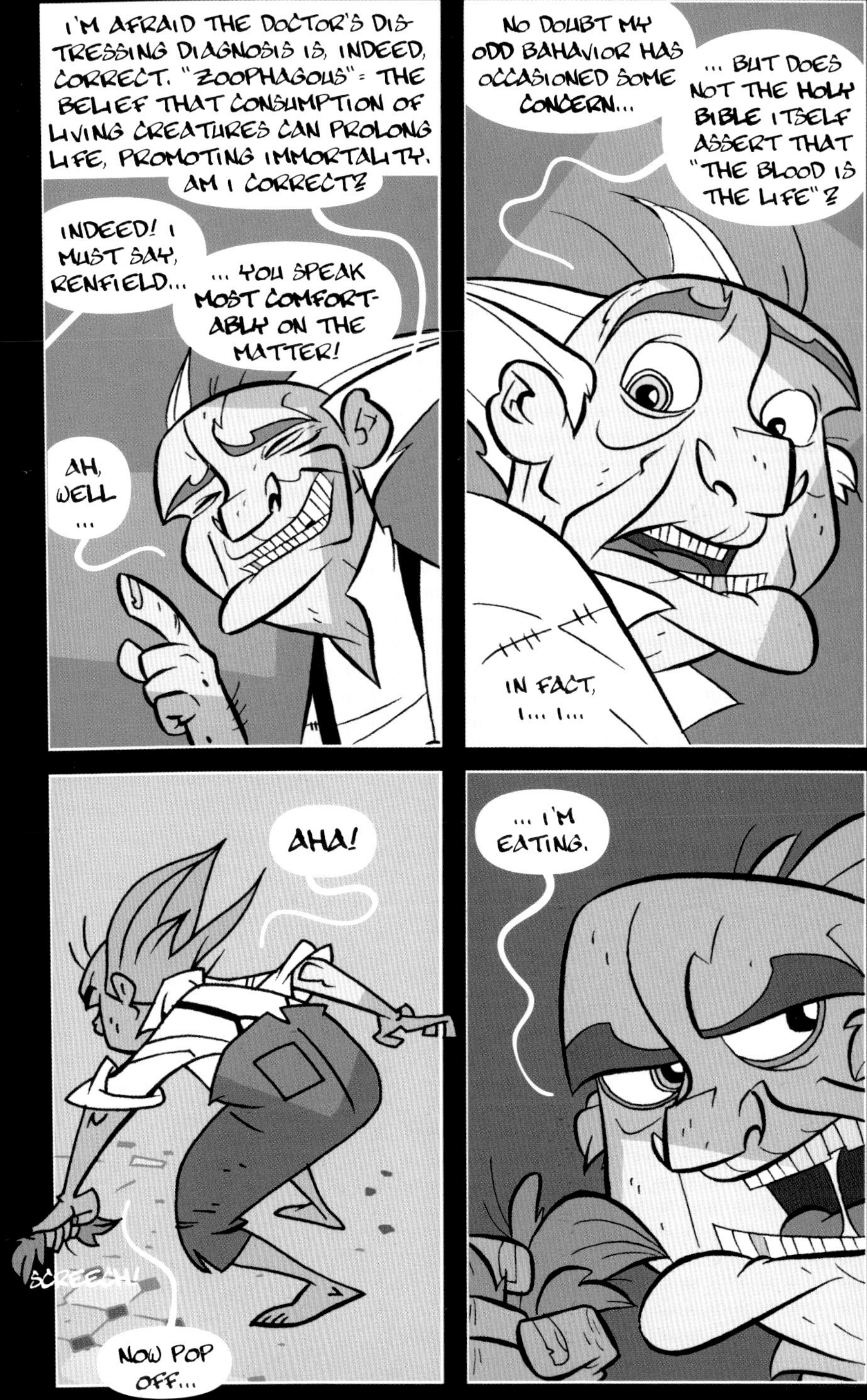
I'M AFRAID THE DOCTOR'S DISTRESSING DIAGNOSIS IS, INDEED, CORRECT. "ZOOPHAGOUS" = THE BELIEF THAT CONSUMPTION OF LIVING CREATURES CAN PROLONG LIFE, PROMOTING IMMORTALITY. AM I CORRECT?
INDEED! I MUST SAY, RENFIELD...
... YOU SPEAK MOST COMFORTABLY ON THE MATTER!
AH, WELL ...
NO DOUBT MY ODD BAHAVIOR HAS OCCASIONED SOME CONCERN...
... BUT DOES NOT THE HOLY BIBLE ITSELF ASSERT THAT "THE BLOOD IS THE LIFE"?
IN FACT, I... I...
AHA!
SCREECH!
NOW POP OFF...
... I'M EATING.

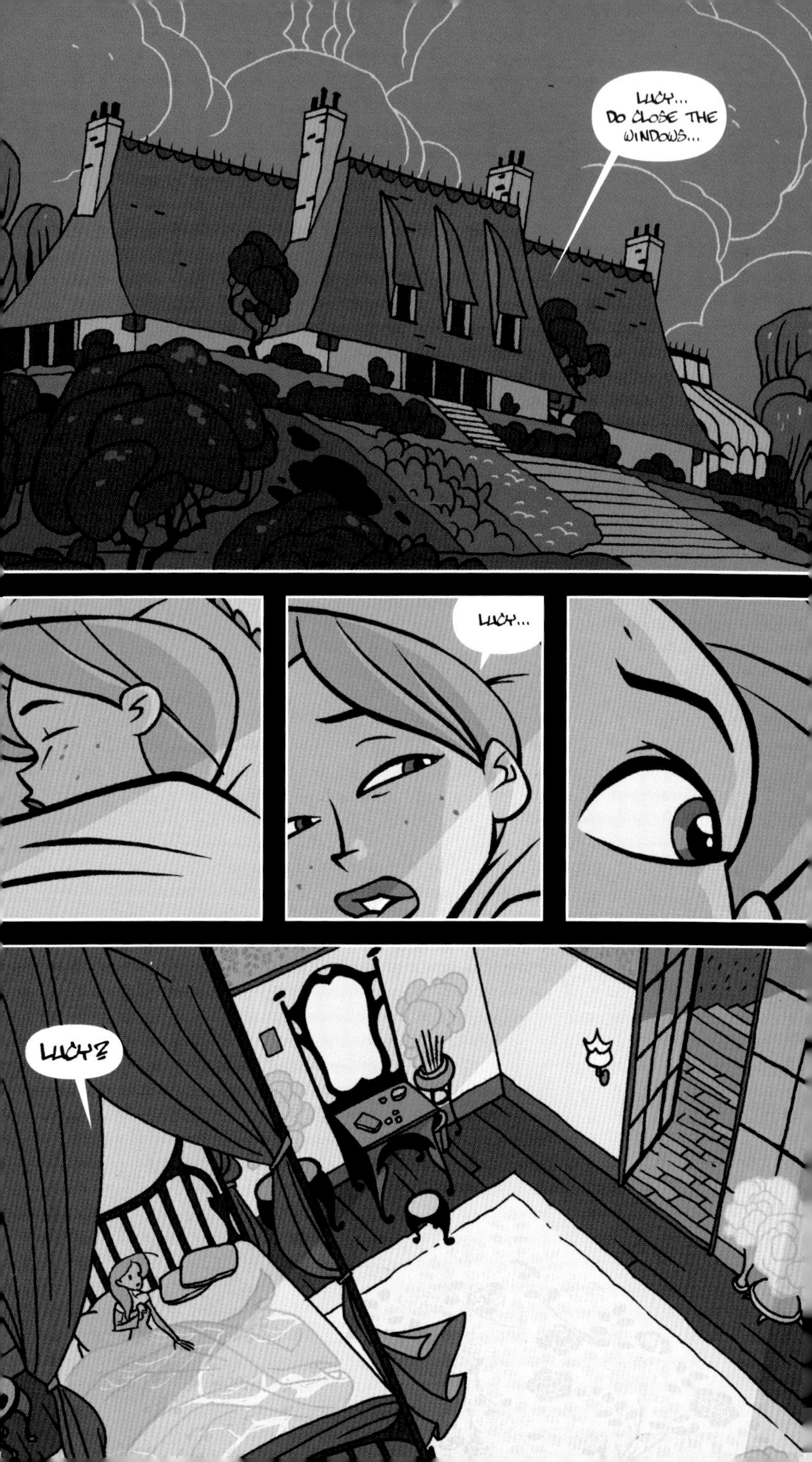
LUCY...
DO CLOSE THE WINDOWS...
LUCY...
LUCY?

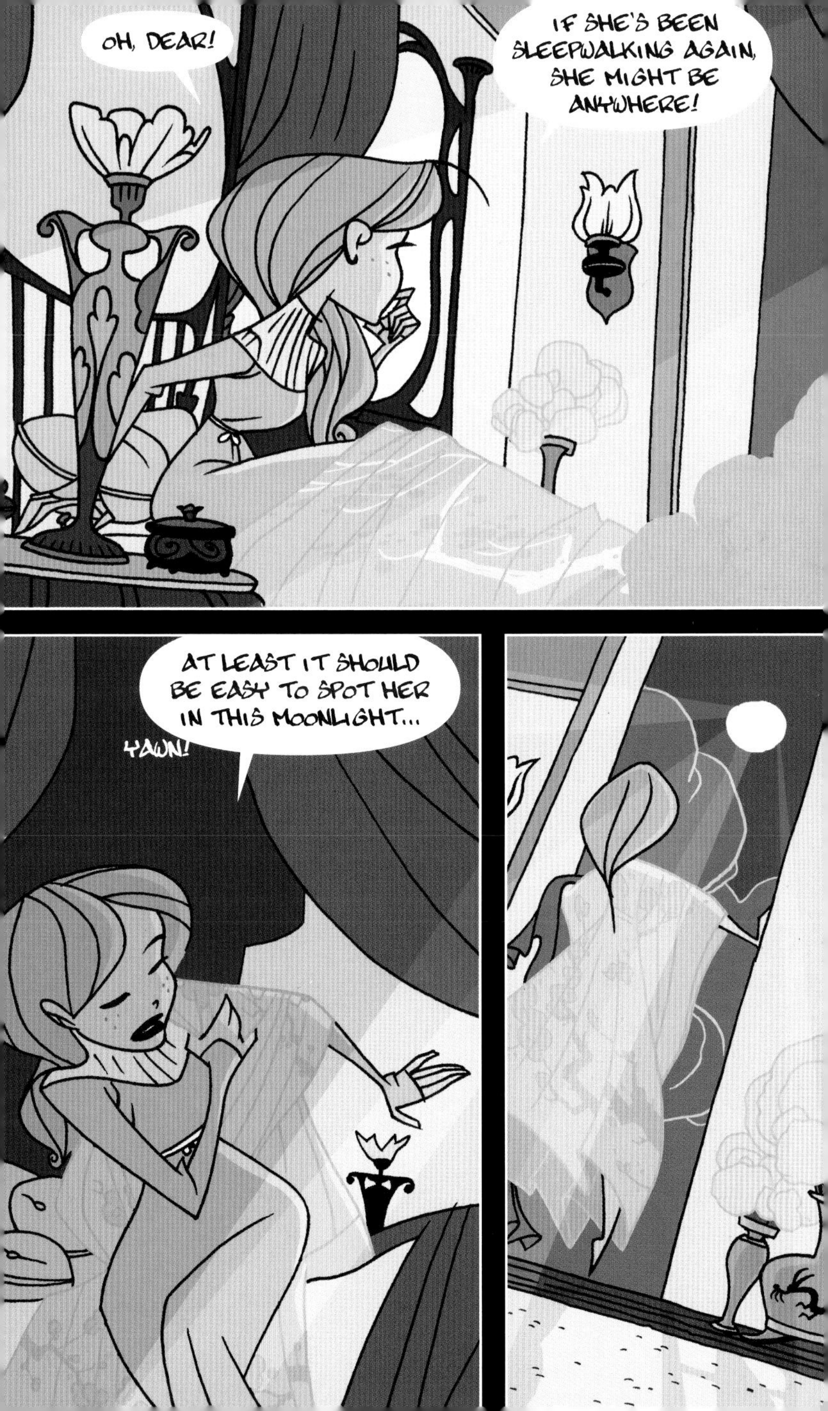
OH, DEAR!
IF SHE'S BEEN SLEEPWALKING AGAIN, SHE MIGHT BE ANYWHERE!
YAWN!
AT LEAST IT SHOULD BE EASY TO SPOT HER IN THIS MOONLIGHT...

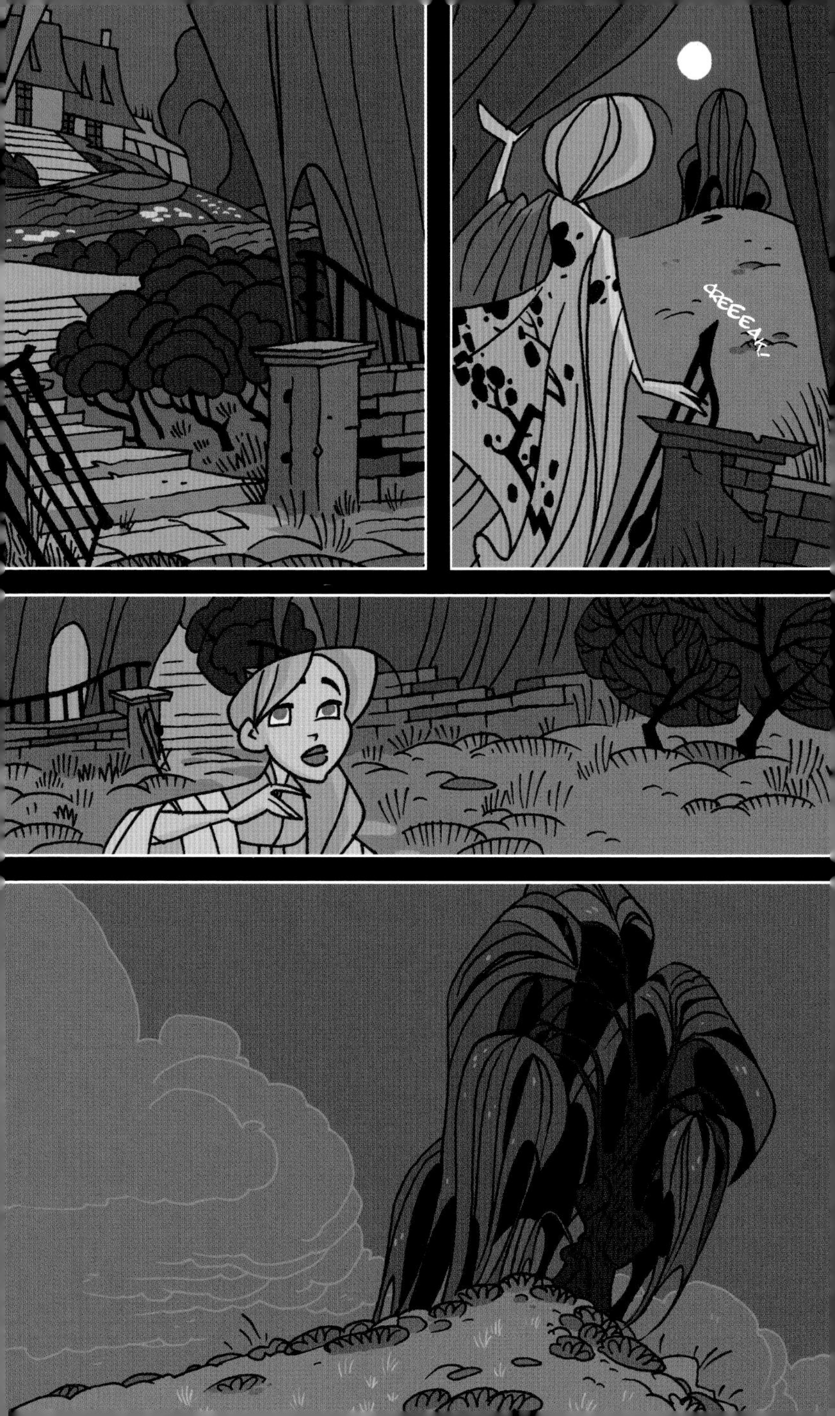
CREEEAK!

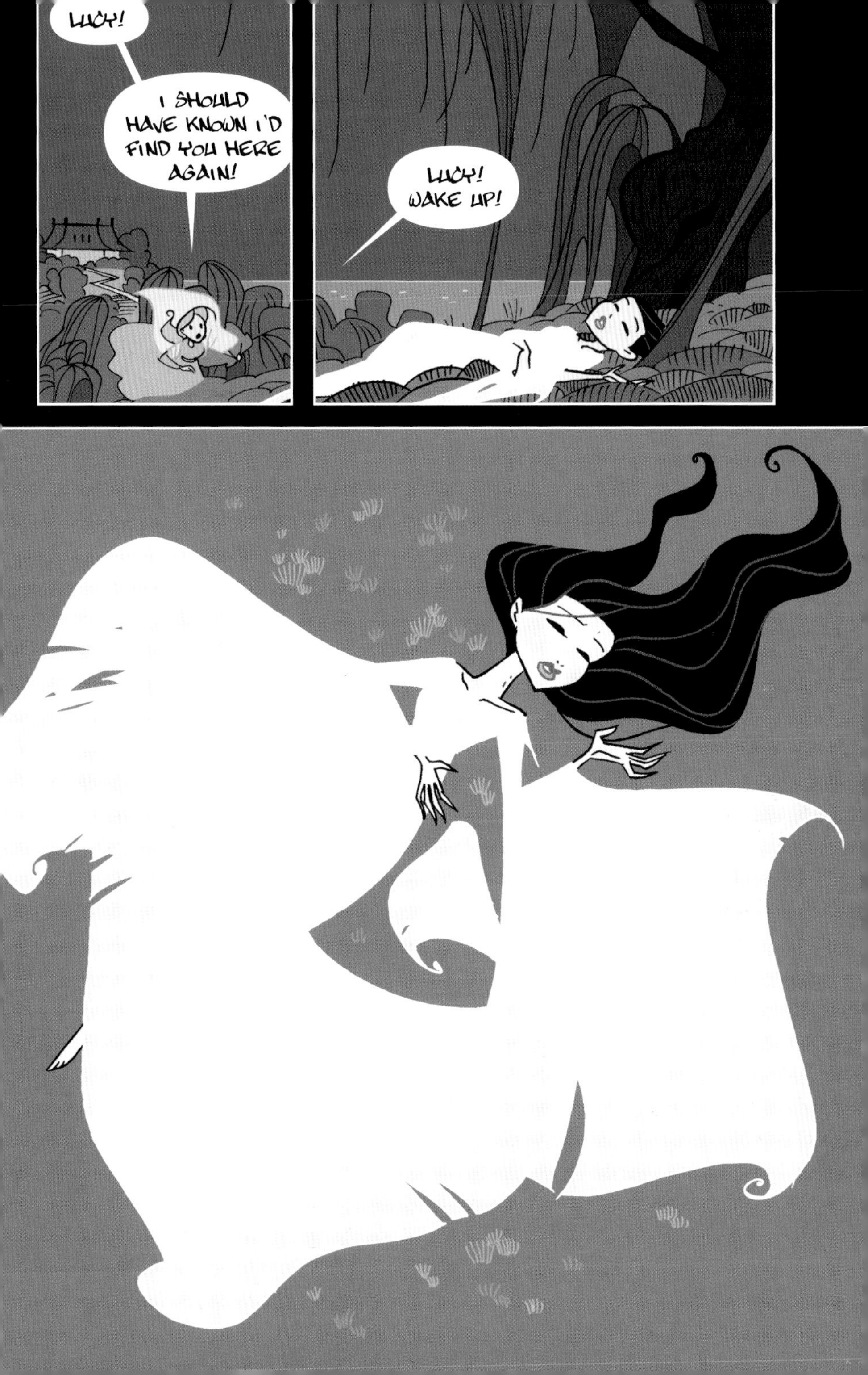
LUCY!
I SHOULD HAVE KNOWN I'D FIND YOU HERE AGAIN!
LUCY! WAKE UP!

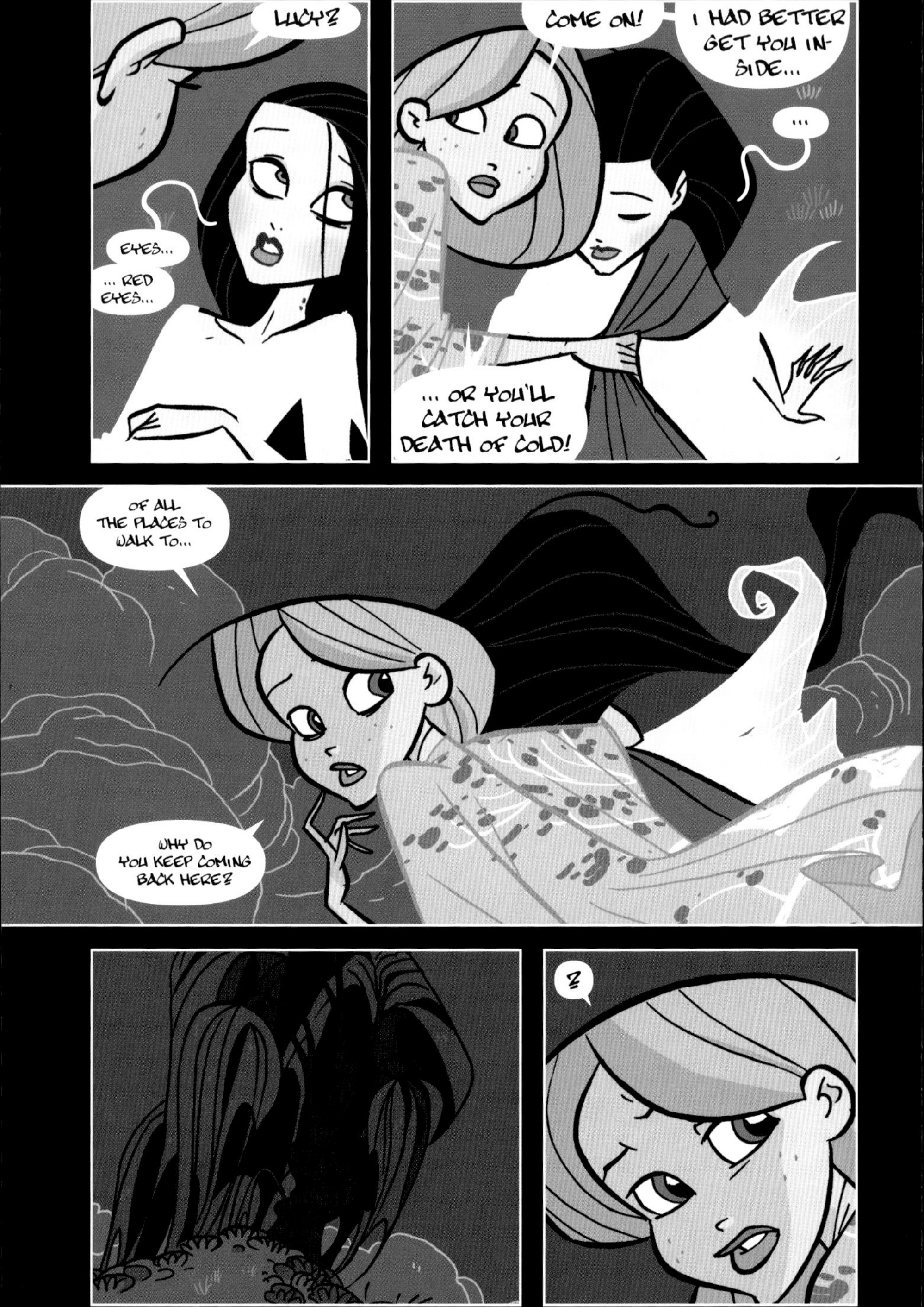
LUCY?
EYES...
... RED EYES...
COME ON!
I HAD BETTER GET YOU IN-SIDE...
...
... OR YOU'LL CATCH YOUR DEATH OF COLD!
OF ALL THE PLACES TO WALK TO...
WHY DO YOU KEEP COMING BACK HERE?
?

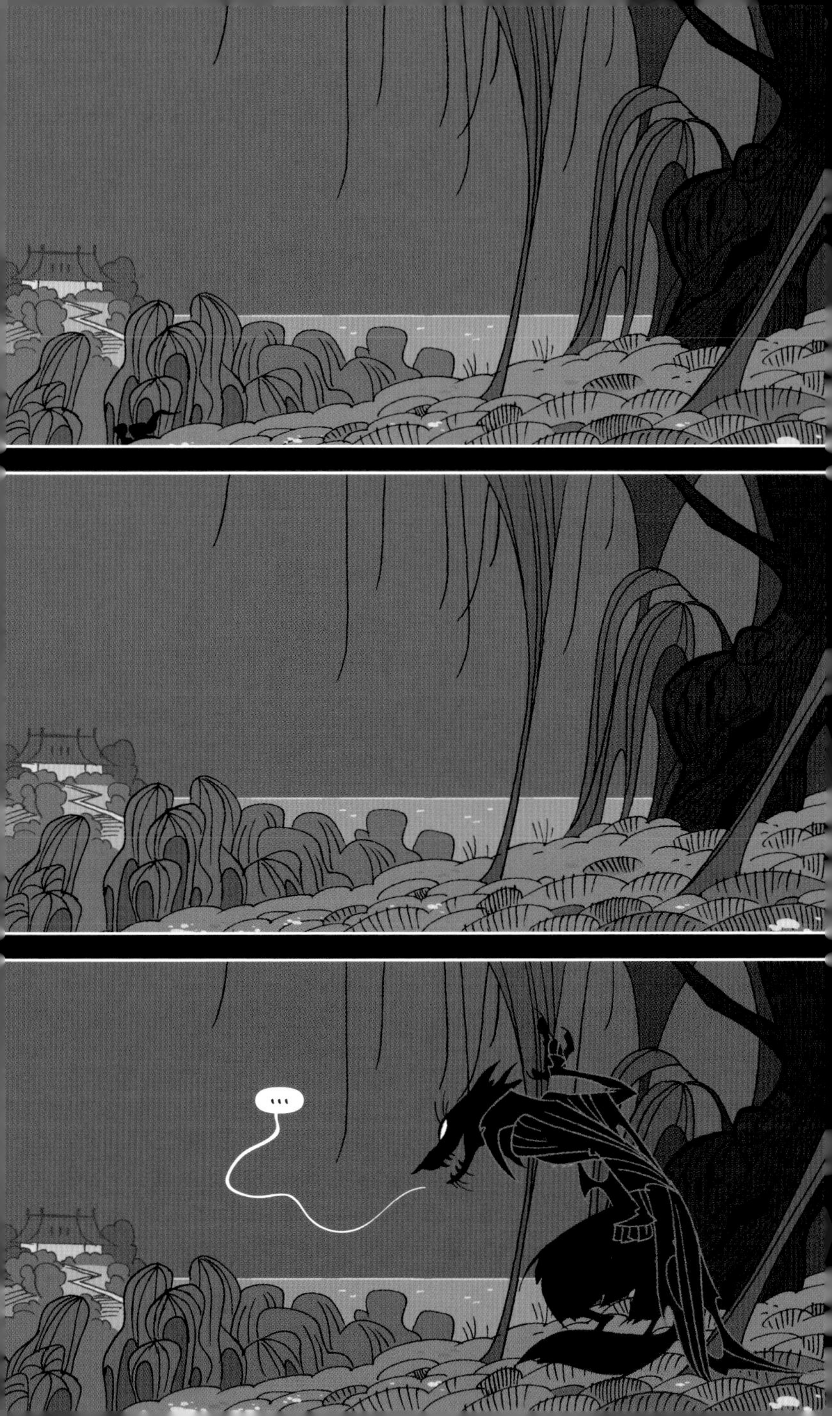
...

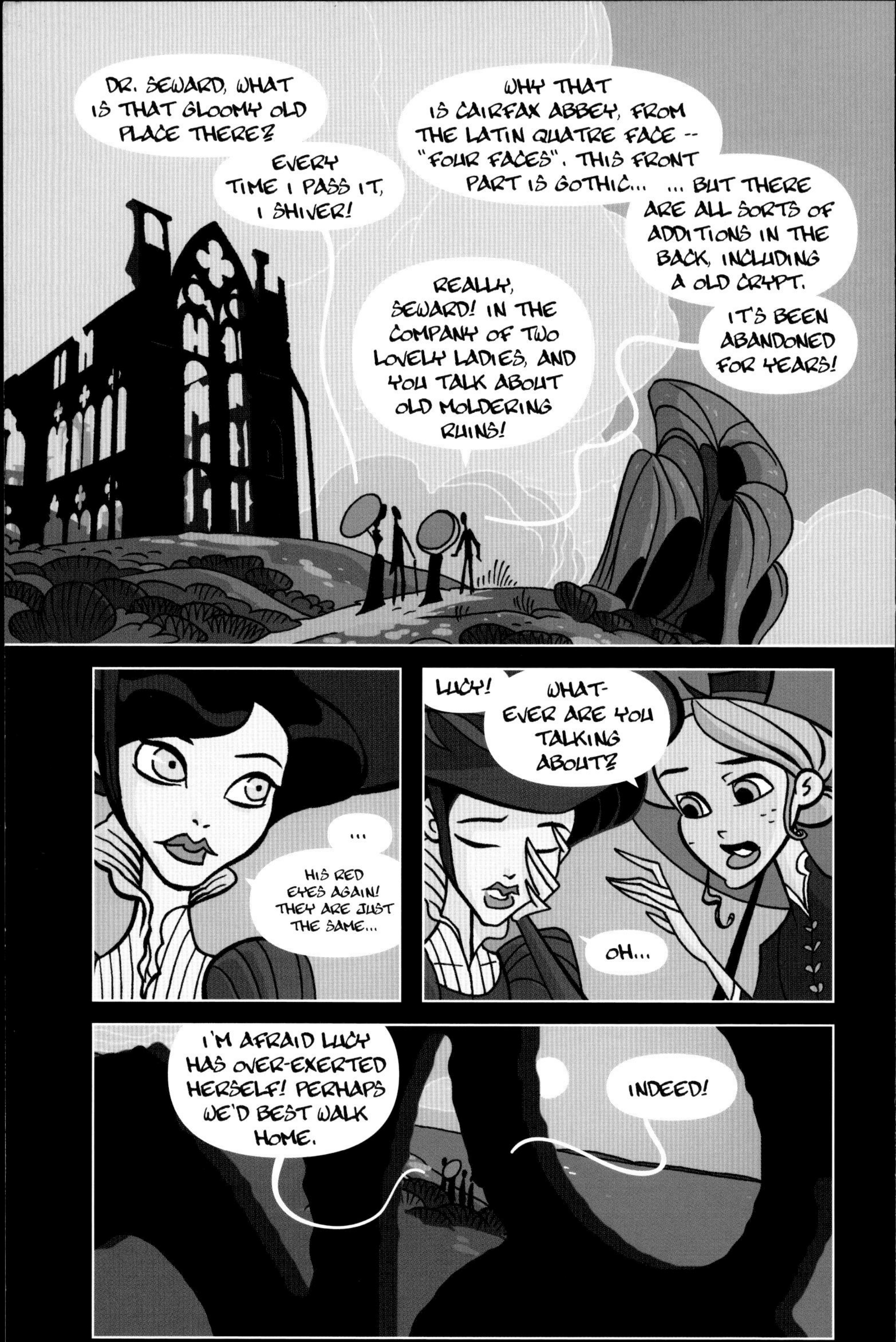
DR. SEWARD, WHAT IS THAT GLOOMY OLD PLACE THERE?
EVERY TIME I PASS IT, I SHIVER!
WHY THAT IS CAIRFAX ABBEY, FROM THE LATIN QUATRE FACE -- "FOUR FACES". THIS FRONT PART IS GOTHIC...
... BUT THERE ARE ALL SORTS OF ADDITIONS IN THE BACK, INCLUDING A OLD CRYPT.
IT'S BEEN ABANDONED FOR YEARS!
REALLY, SEWARD! IN THE COMPANY OF TWO LOVELY LADIES, AND YOU TALK ABOUT OLD MOLDERING RUINS!
...
HIS RED EYES AGAIN! THEY ARE JUST THE SAME...
LUCY!
WHATEVER ARE YOU TALKING ABOUT?
OH...
I'M AFRAID LUCY HAS OVER-EXERTED HERSELF! PERHAPS WE'D BEST WALK HOME.
INDEED!

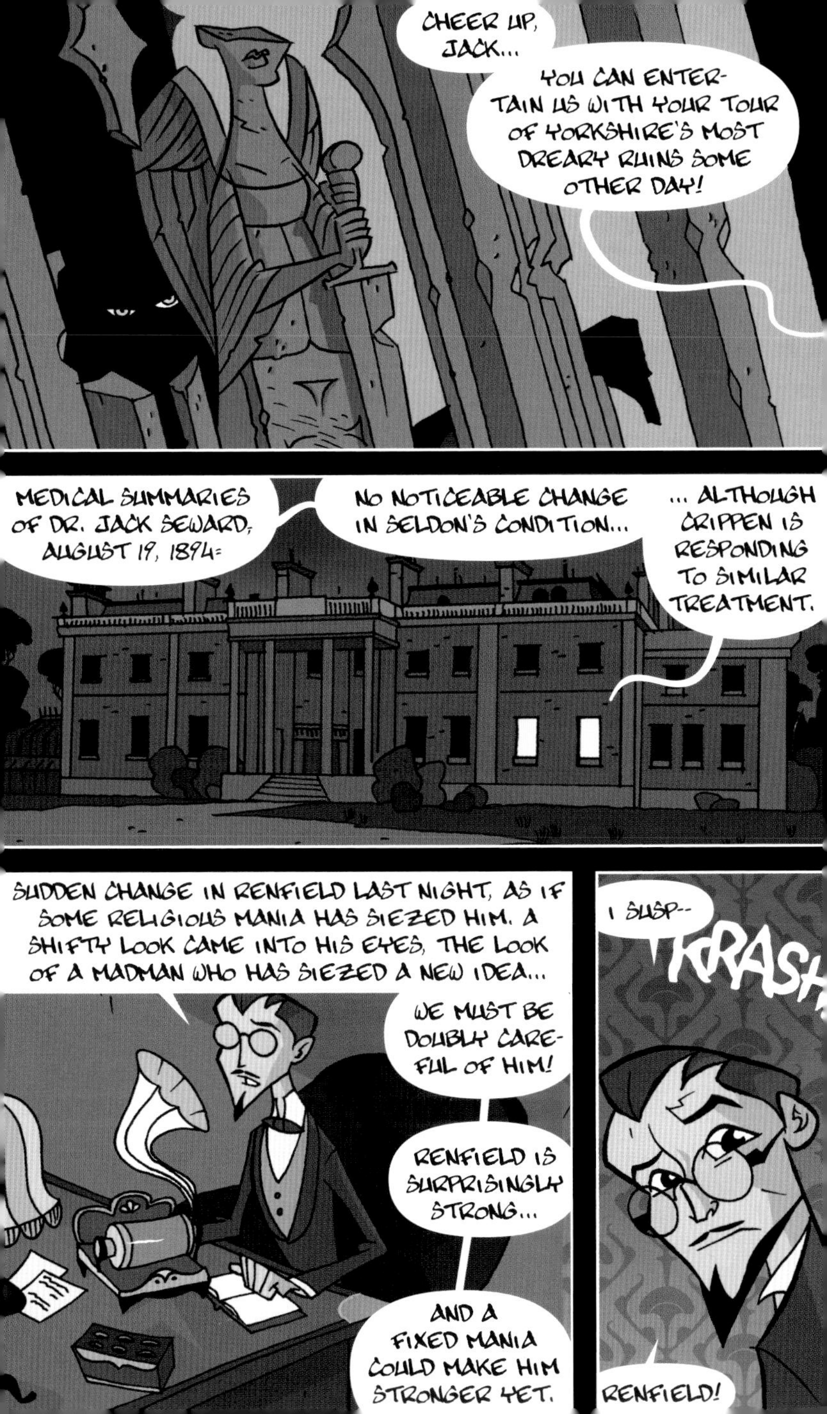
CHEER UP, JACK...
YOU CAN ENTERTAIN US WITH YOUR TOUR OF YORKSHIRE'S MOST DREARY RUINS SOME OTHER DAY!
MEDICAL SUMMARIES OF DR. JACK SEWARD, AUGUST 19, 1894:
NO NOTICEABLE CHANGE IN SELDON'S CONDITION...
... ALTHOUGH CRIPPEN IS RESPONDING TO SIMILAR TREATMENT.
SUDDEN CHANGE IN RENFIELD LAST NIGHT, AS IF SOME RELIGIOUS MANIA HAS SIEZED HIM. A SHIFTY LOOK CAME INTO HIS EYES, THE LOOK OF A MADMAN WHO HAS SIEZED A NEW IDEA...
WE MUST BE DOUBLY CAREFUL OF HIM!
RENFIELD IS SURPRISINGLY STRONG...
AND A FIXED MANIA COULD MAKE HIM STRONGER YET.
I SUSP--
KRASH!
RENFIELD!

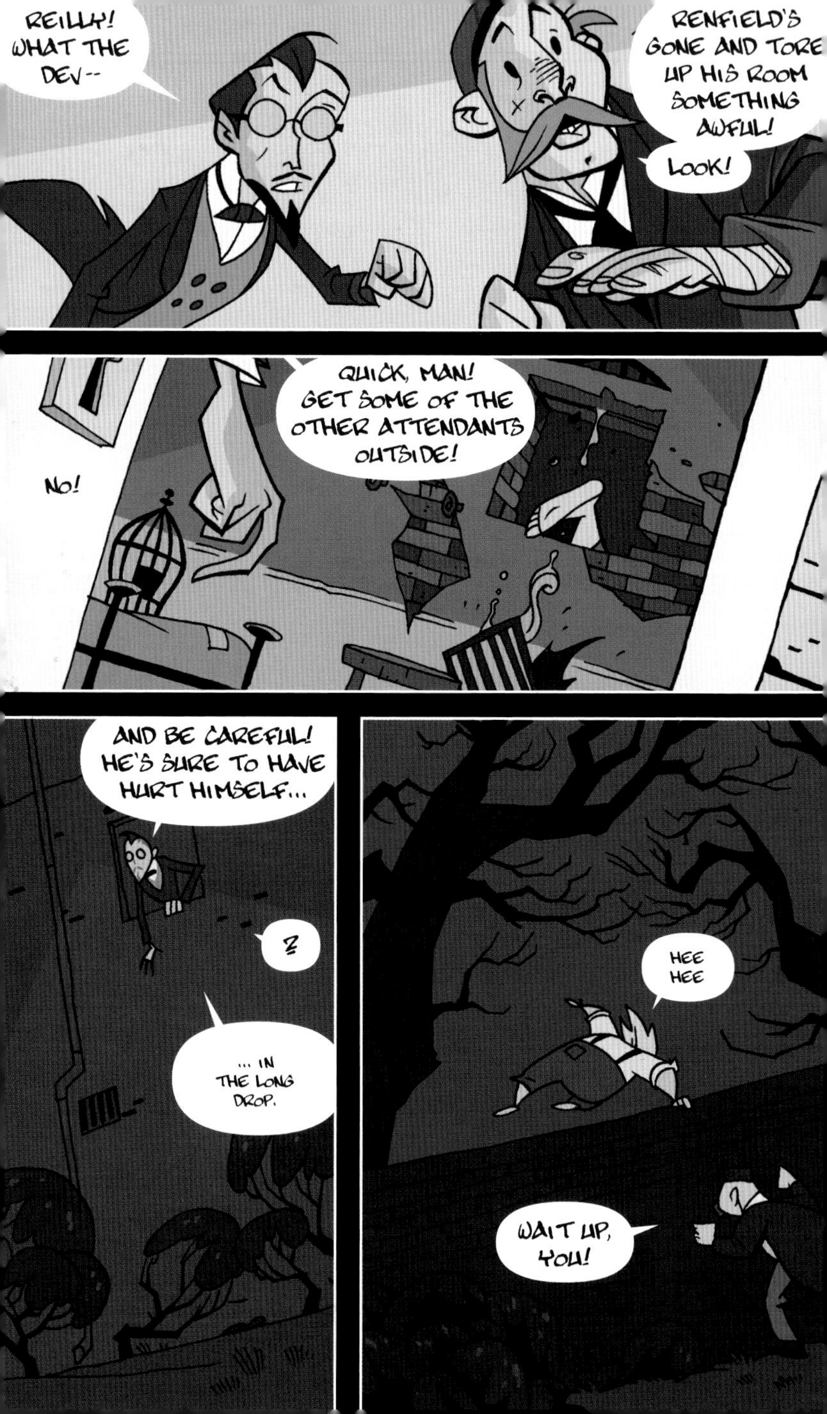
REILLY! WHAT THE DEV--
RENFIELD'S GONE AND TORE UP HIS ROOM SOMETHING AWFUL!
LOOK!
QUICK, MAN! GET SOME OF THE OTHER ATTENDANTS OUTSIDE!
NO!
AND BE CAREFUL! HE'S SURE TO HAVE HURT HIMSELF...
?
... IN THE LONG DROP.
HEE HEE
WAIT UP, YOU!

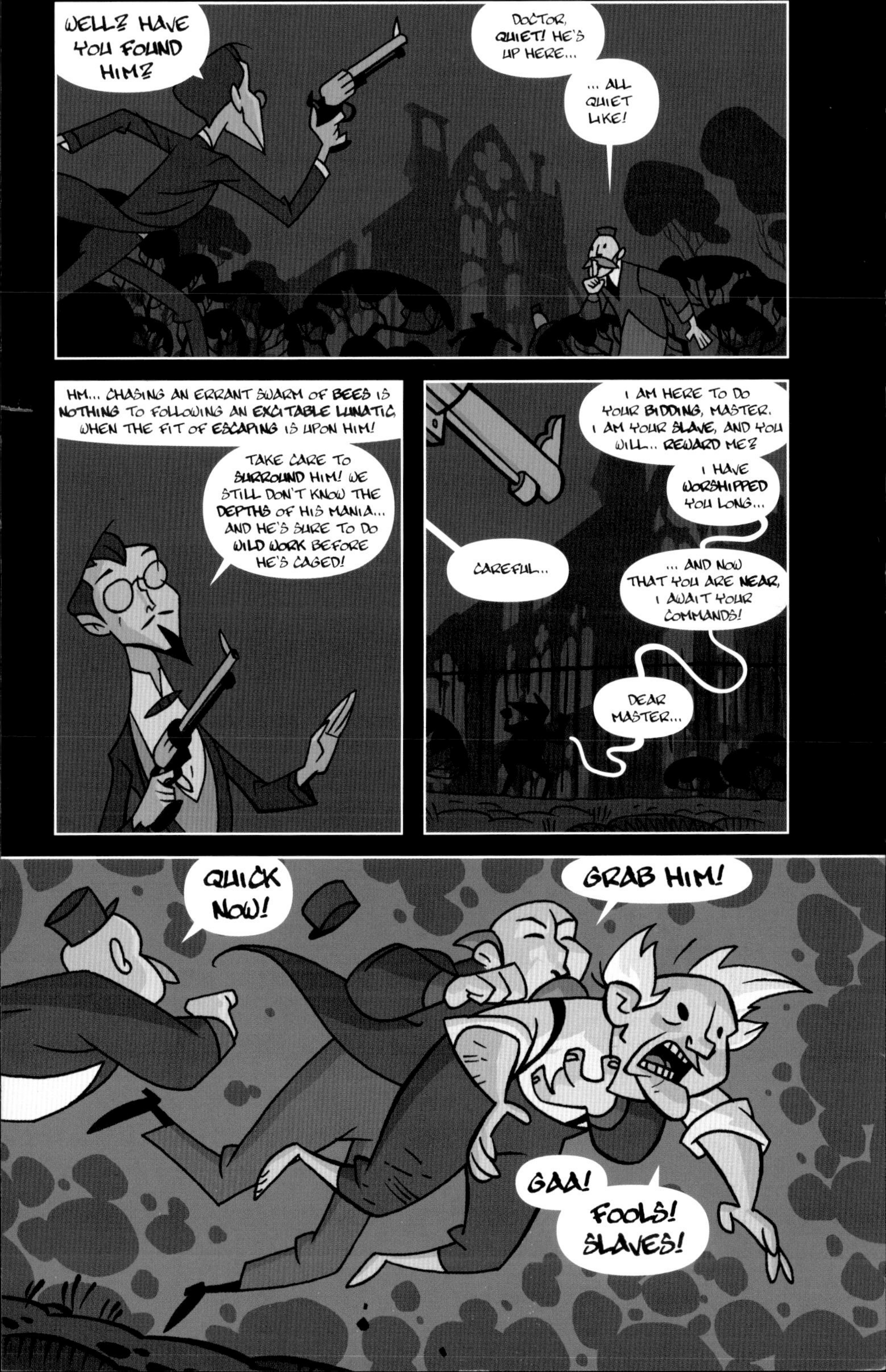
WELL? HAVE YOU FOUND HIM?
DOCTOR, QUIET! HE'S UP HERE...
... ALL QUIET LIKE!
HM... CHASING AN ERRANT SWARM OF BEES IS NOTHING TO FOLLOWING AN EXCITABLE LUNATIC WHEN THE FIT OF ESCAPING IS UPON HIM!
TAKE CARE TO SURROUND HIM! WE STILL DON'T KNOW THE DEPTHS OF HIS MANIA... AND HE'S SURE TO DO WILD WORK BEFORE HE'S CAGED!
I AM HERE TO DO YOUR BIDDING, MASTER. I AM YOUR SLAVE, AND YOU WILL... REWARD ME?
I HAVE WORSHIPPED YOU LONG...
CAREFUL...
... AND NOW THAT YOU ARE NEAR, I AWAIT YOUR COMMANDS!
DEAR MASTER...
QUICK NOW!
GRAB HIM!
GAA!
FOOLS! SLAVES!

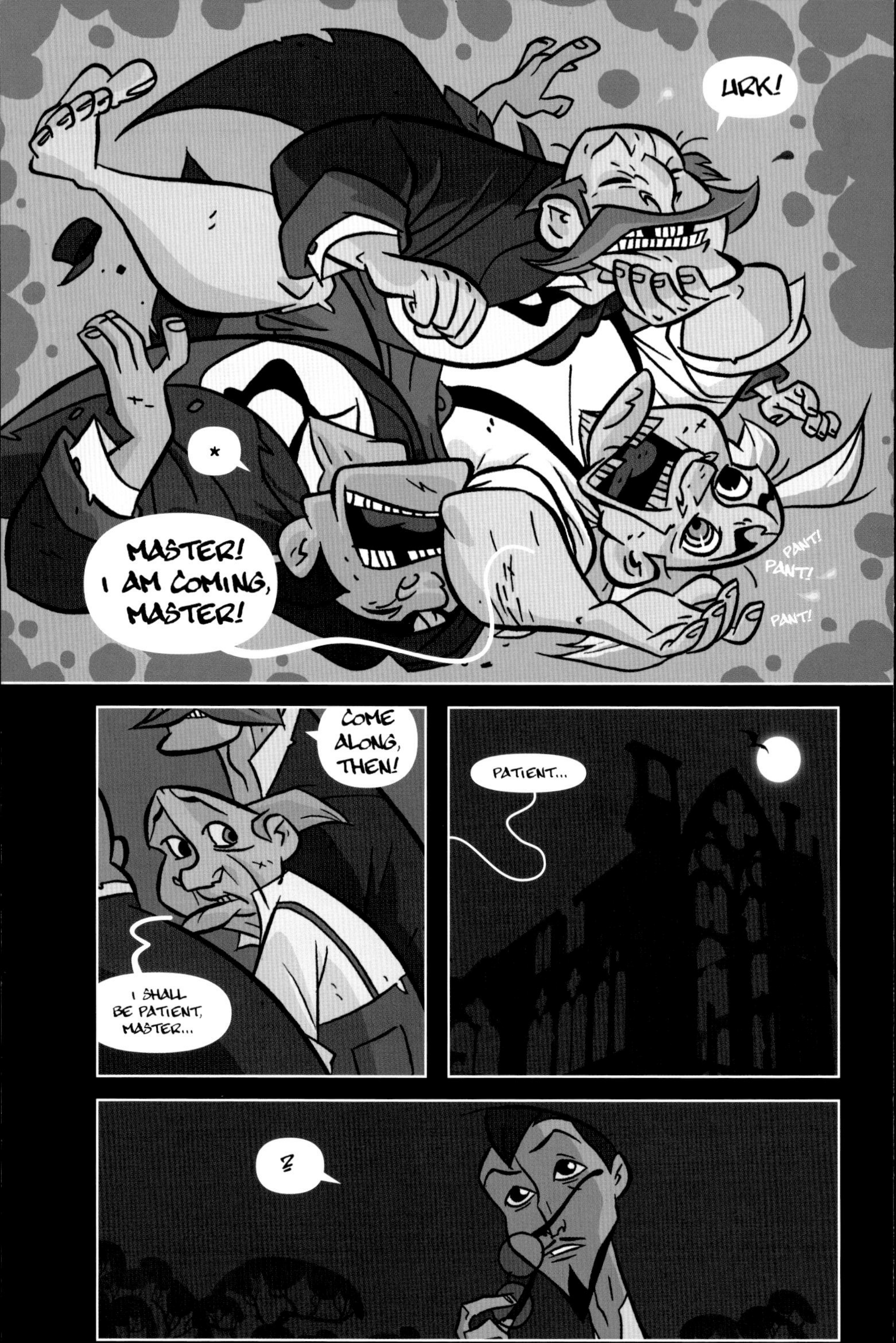
URK!
*
MASTER! I AM COMING, MASTER!
PANT! PANT! PANT!
COME ALONG, THEN!
I SHALL BE PATIENT, MASTER...
PATIENT...
?

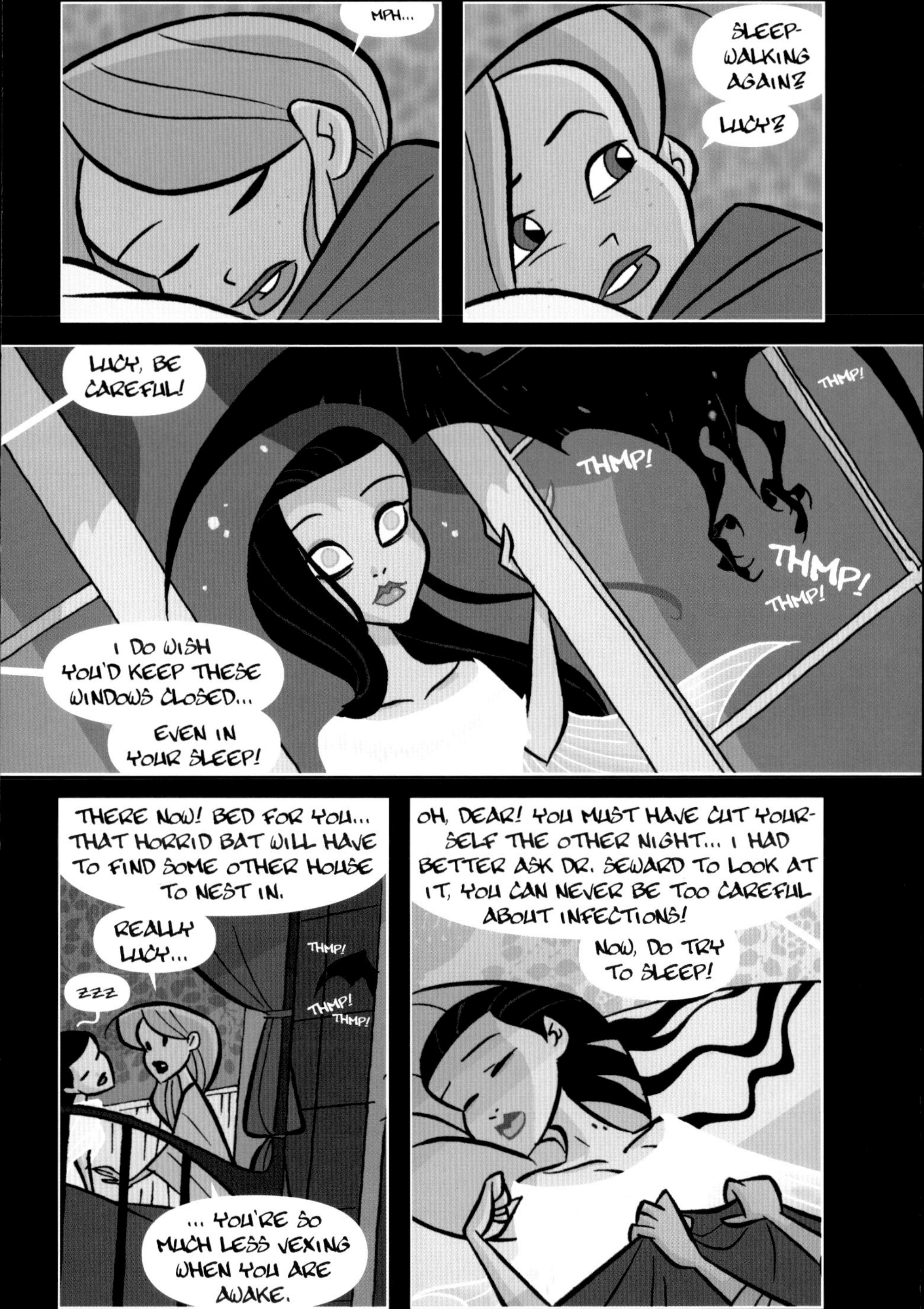
MPH...
SLEEP-WALKING AGAIN?
LUCY?
LUCY, BE CAREFUL!
THMP!
THMP!
THMP!
THMP!
I DO WISH YOU'D KEEP THESE WINDOWS CLOSED...
EVEN IN YOUR SLEEP!
THERE NOW! BED FOR YOU... THAT HORRID BAT WILL HAVE TO FIND SOME OTHER HOUSE TO NEST IN.
REALLY LUCY...
ZZZ
THMP!
THMP!
THMP!
... YOU'RE SO MUCH LESS VEXING WHEN YOU ARE AWAKE.
OH, DEAR! YOU MUST HAVE CUT YOURSELF THE OTHER NIGHT... I HAD BETTER ASK DR. SEWARD TO LOOK AT IT, YOU CAN NEVER BE TOO CAREFUL ABOUT INFECTIONS!
NOW, DO TRY TO SLEEP!

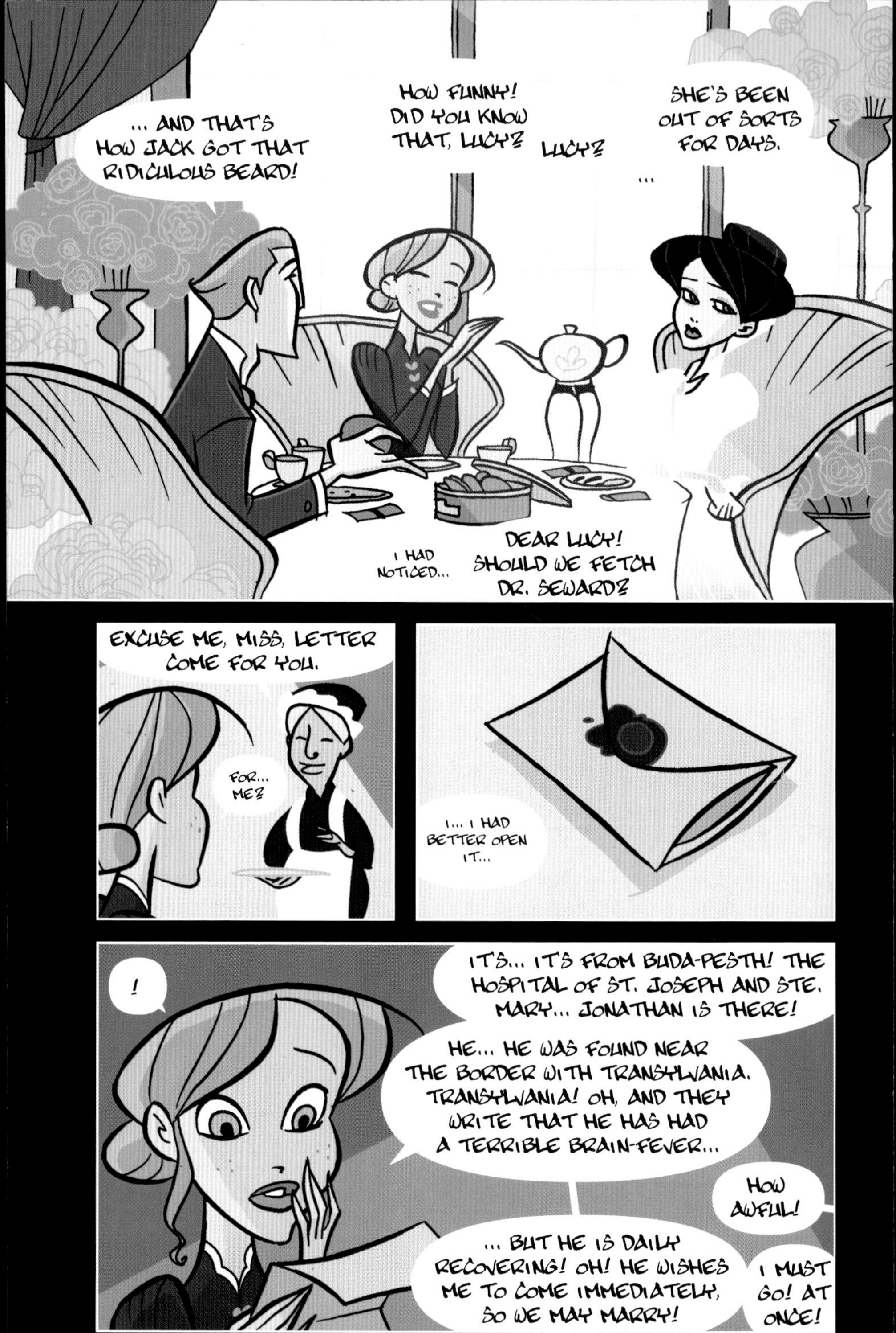
... AND THAT'S HOW JACK GOT THAT RIDICULOUS BEARD!
HOW FUNNY! DID YOU KNOW THAT, LUCY?
LUCY?
SHE'S BEEN OUT OF SORTS FOR DAYS.
...
I HAD NOTICED...
DEAR LUCY! SHOULD WE FETCH DR. SEWARD?
EXCUSE ME, MISS, LETTER COME FOR YOU.
FOR... ME?
I... I HAD BETTER OPEN IT...
!
IT'S... IT'S FROM BUDA-PESTH! THE HOSPITAL OF ST. JOSEPH AND STE. MARY... JONATHAN IS THERE!
HE... HE WAS FOUND NEAR THE BORDER WITH TRANSYLVANIA. TRANSYLVANIA! OH, AND THEY WRITE THAT HE HAS HAD A TERRIBLE BRAIN-FEVER...
HOW AWFUL!
... BUT HE IS DAILY RECOVERING! OH! HE WISHES ME TO COME IMMEDIATELY, SO WE MAY MARRY!
I MUST GO! AT ONCE!

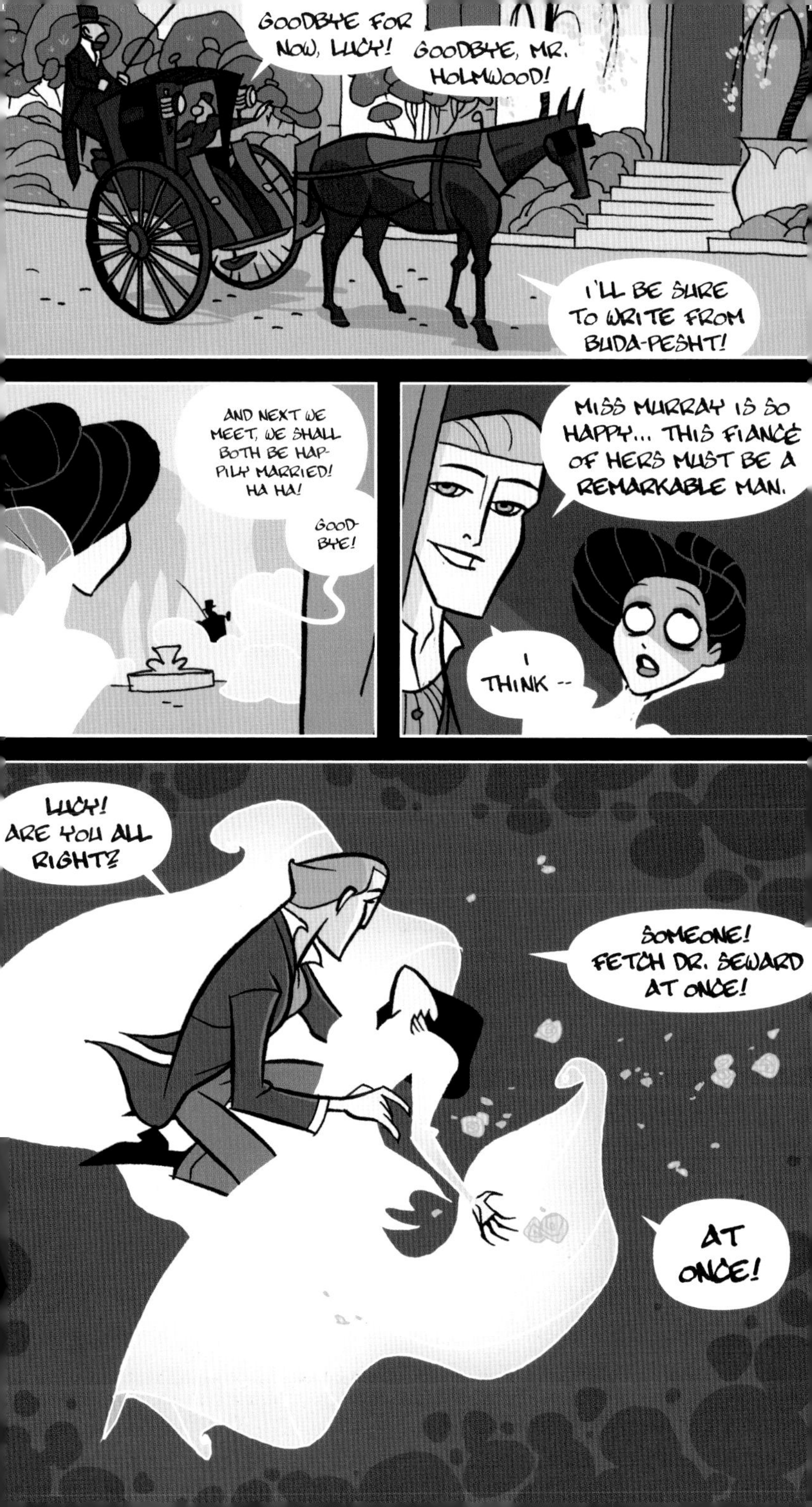

GOODBYE FOR NOW, LUCY!
GOODBYE, MR. HOLMWOOD!
I'LL BE SURE TO WRITE FROM BUDA-PESHT!
AND NEXT WE MEET, WE SHALL BOTH BE HAPPILY MARRIED! HA HA!
GOOD-BYE!
MISS MURRAY IS SO HAPPY... THIS FIANCÉ OF HERS MUST BE A REMARKABLE MAN.
I THINK --
LUCY! ARE YOU ALL RIGHT?
SOMEONE! FETCH DR. SEWARD AT ONCE!
AT ONCE!

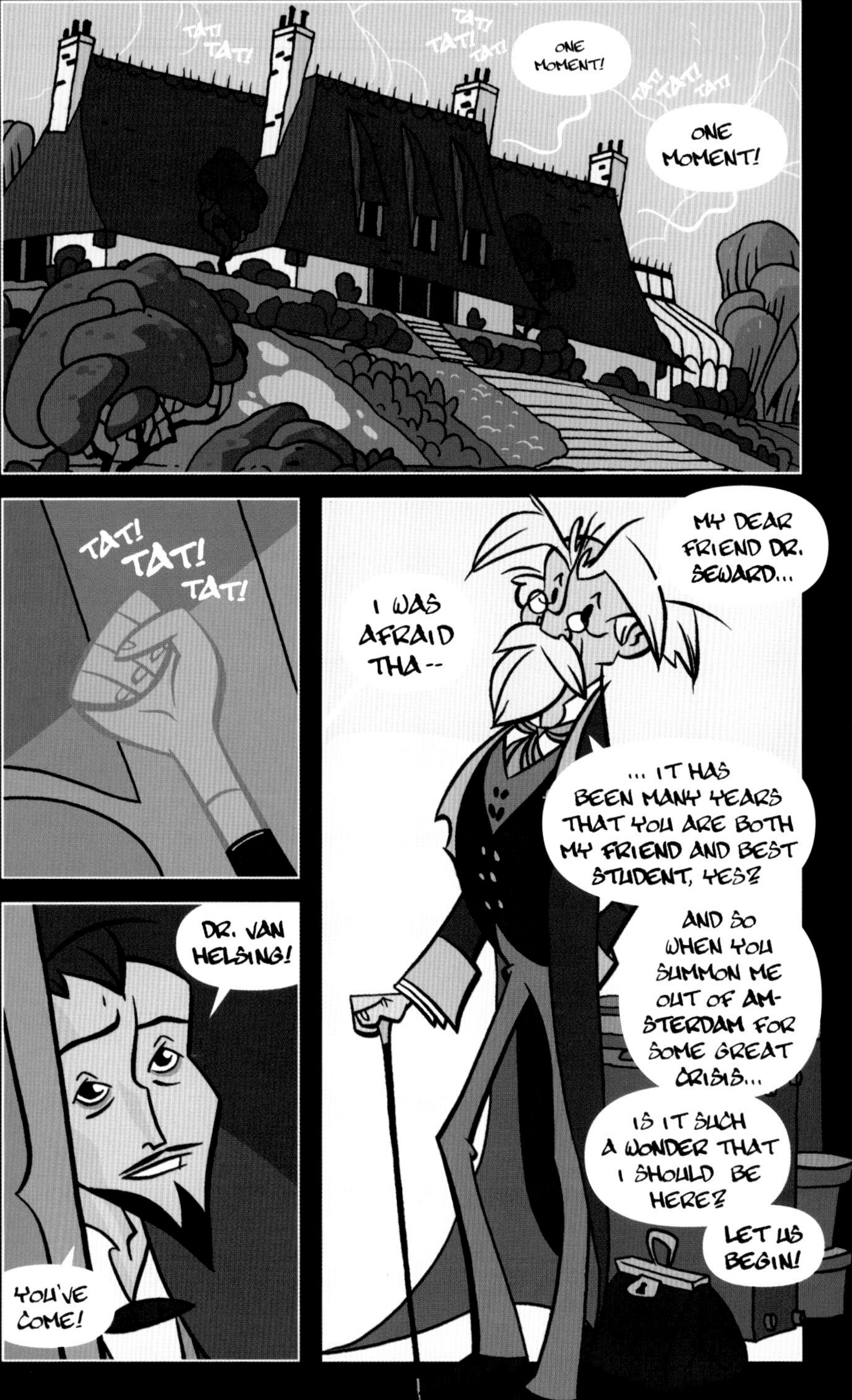
TAT! TAT!
TAT! TAT! TAT!
ONE MOMENT!
TAT! TAT! TAT!
ONE MOMENT!
TAT! TAT! TAT!
DR. VAN HELSING!
YOU'VE COME!
I WAS AFRAID THA--
MY DEAR FRIEND DR. SEWARD...
... IT HAS BEEN MANY YEARS THAT YOU ARE BOTH MY FRIEND AND BEST STUDENT, YES?
AND SO WHEN YOU SUMMON ME OUT OF AMSTERDAM FOR SOME GREAT CRISIS...
IS IT SUCH A WONDER THAT I SHOULD BE HERE?
LET US BEGIN!

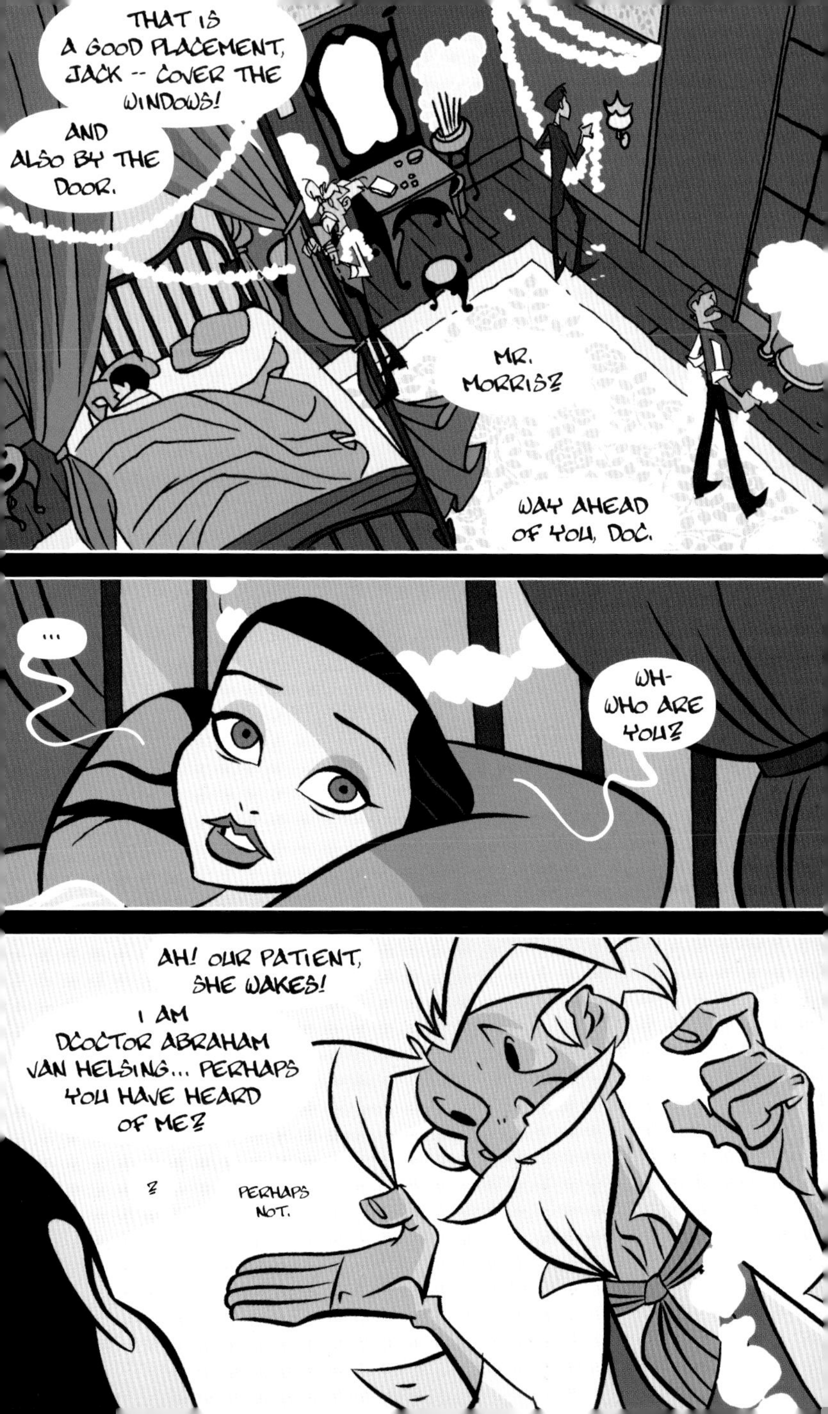
THAT IS A GOOD PLACEMENT, JACK -- COVER THE WINDOWS!
AND ALSO BY THE DOOR.
MR. MORRIS?
WAY AHEAD OF YOU, DOC.
...
WH- WHO ARE YOU?
AH! OUR PATIENT, SHE WAKES!
I AM DCOCTOR ABRAHAM VAN HELSING... PERHAPS YOU HAVE HEARD OF ME?
?
PERHAPS NOT.

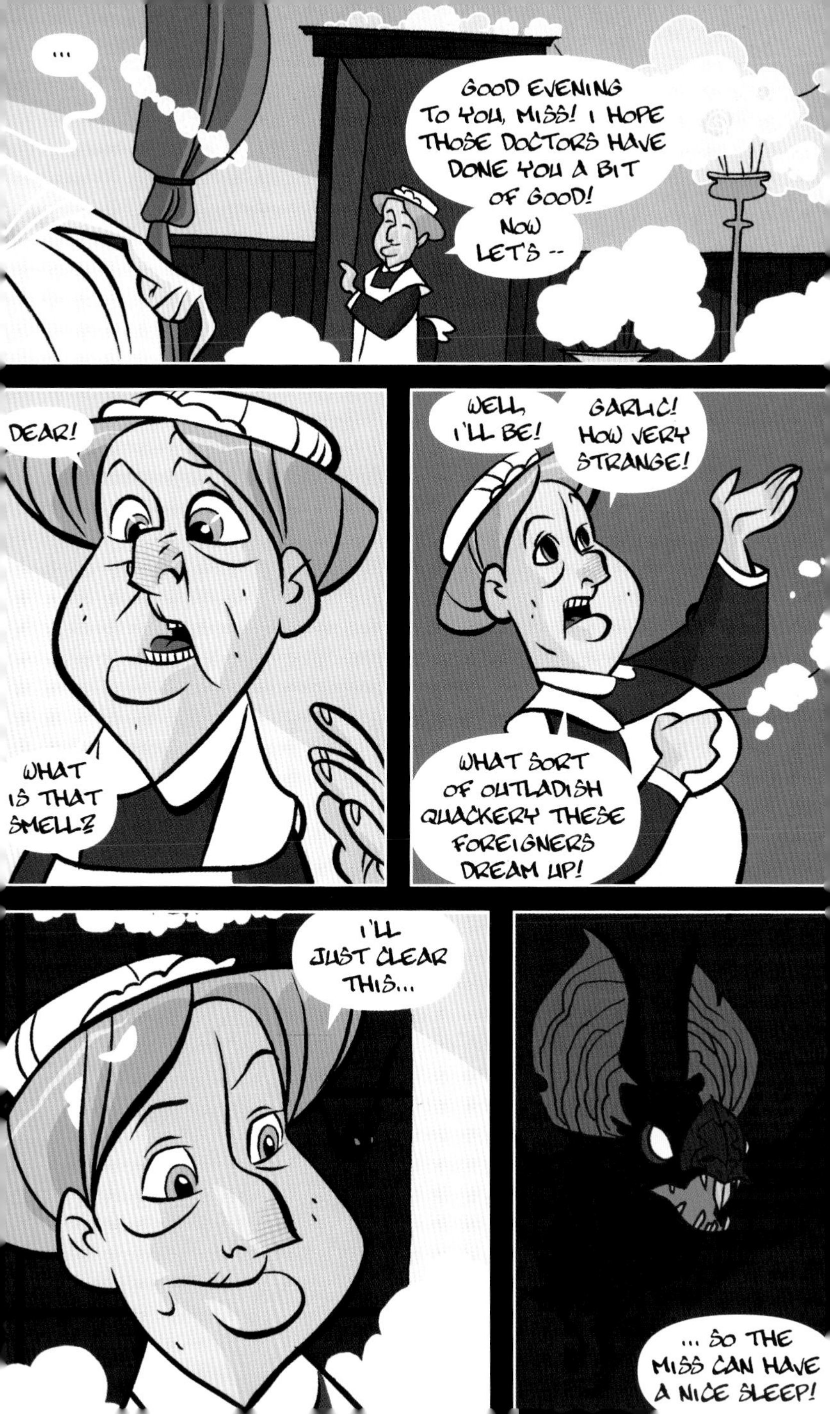
...
GOOD EVENING TO YOU, MISS! I HOPE THOSE DOCTORS HAVE DONE YOU A BIT OF GOOD!
NOW LET'S --
DEAR!
WHAT IS THAT SMELL?
WELL, I'LL BE!
GARLIC! HOW VERY STRANGE!
WHAT SORT OF OUTLADISH QUACKERY THESE FOREIGNERS DREAM UP!
I'LL JUST CLEAR THIS...
... SO THE MISS CAN HAVE A NICE SLEEP!

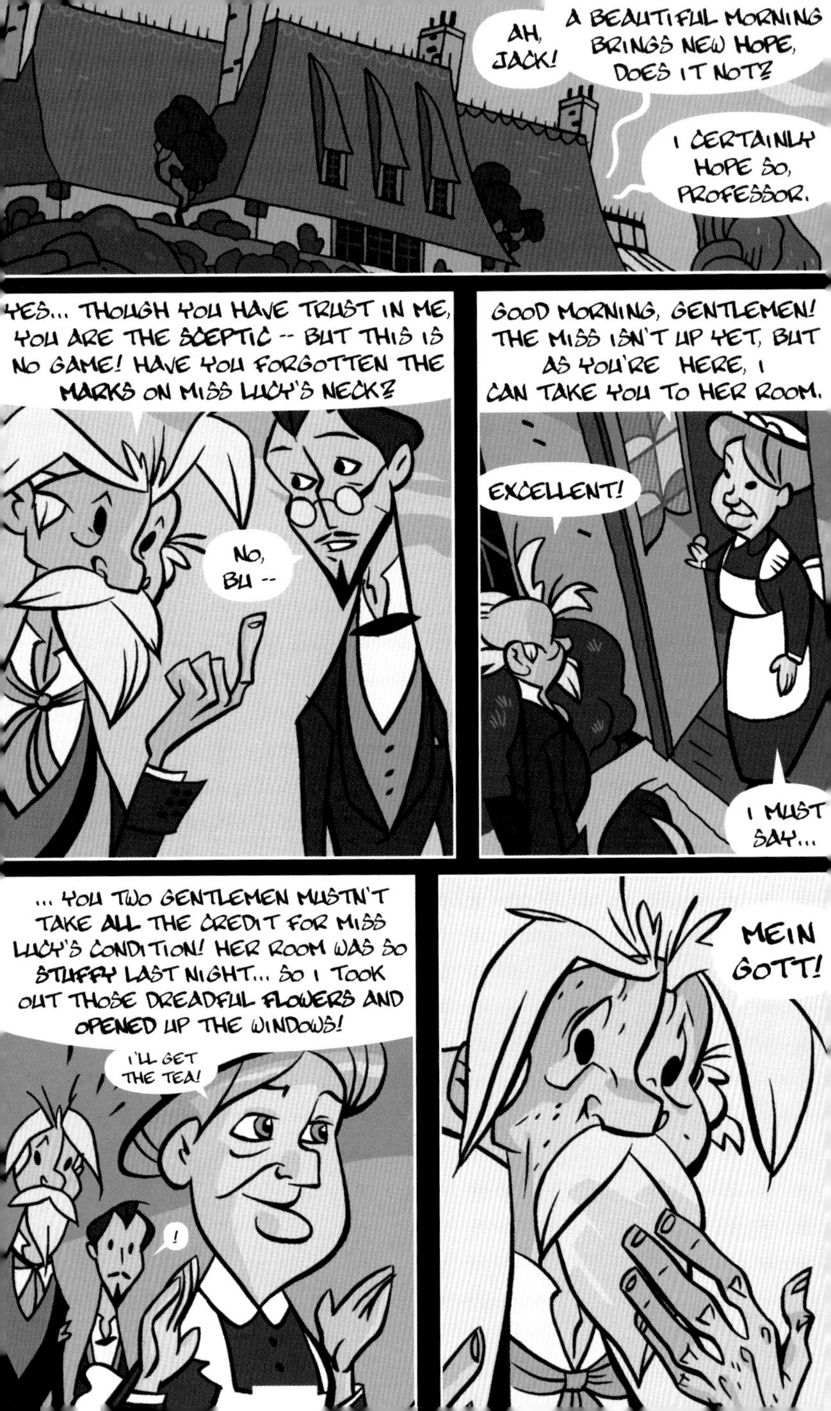
AH, JACK!
A BEAUTIFUL MORNING BRINGS NEW HOPE, DOES IT NOT?
I CERTAINLY HOPE SO, PROFESSOR.
YES... THOUGH YOU HAVE TRUST IN ME, YOU ARE THE SCEPTIC -- BUT THIS IS NO GAME! HAVE YOU FORGOTTEN THE MARKS ON MISS LUCY'S NECK?
NO, BU --
GOOD MORNING, GENTLEMEN! THE MISS ISN'T UP YET, BUT AS YOU'RE HERE, I CAN TAKE YOU TO HER ROOM.
EXCELLENT!
I MUST SAY...
... YOU TWO GENTLEMEN MUSTN'T TAKE ALL THE CREDIT FOR MISS LUCY'S CONDITION! HER ROOM WAS SO STUFFY LAST NIGHT... SO I TOOK OUT THOSE DREADFUL FLOWERS AND OPENED UP THE WINDOWS!
I'LL GET THE TEA!
!
MEIN GOTT!

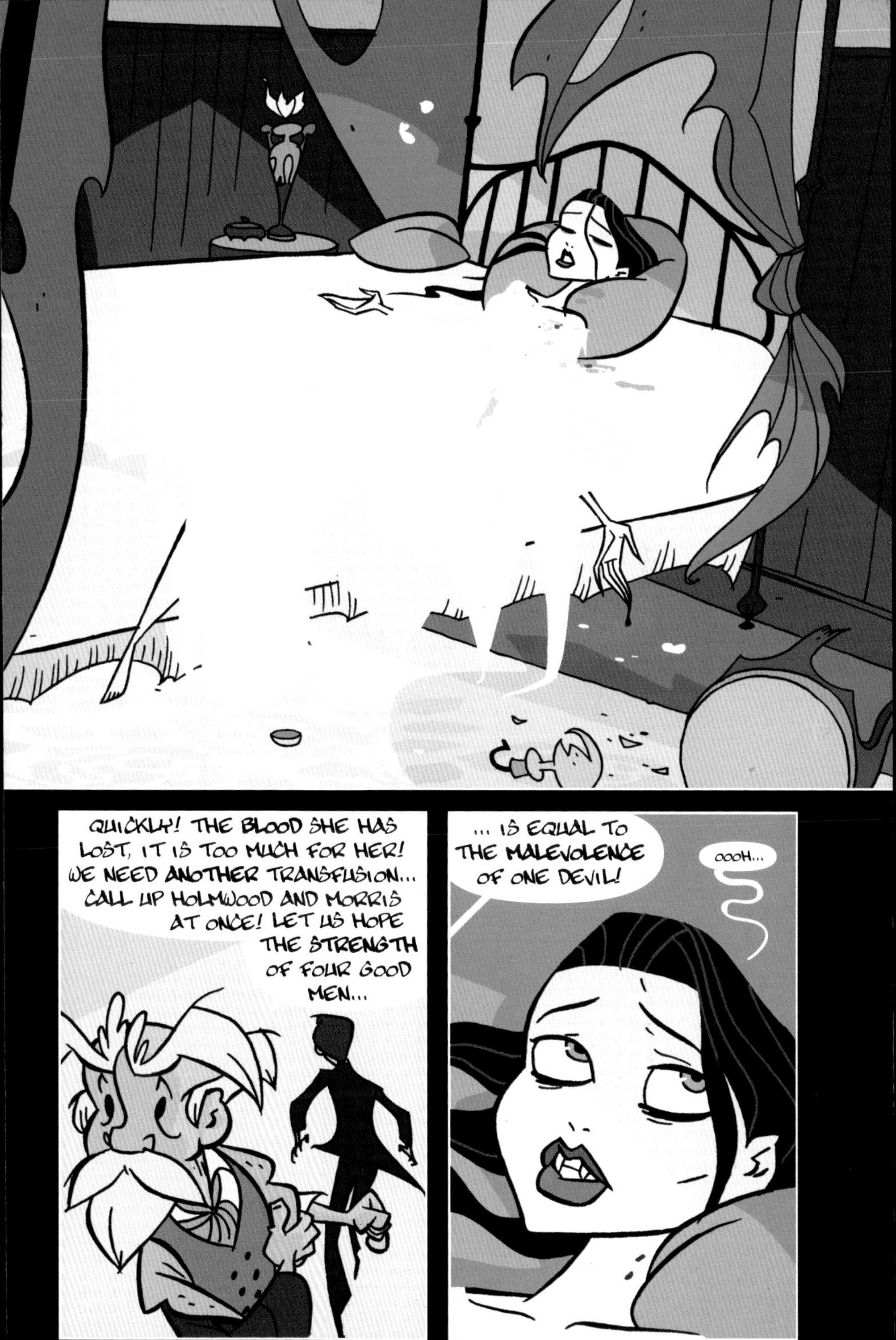
QUICKLY! THE BLOOD SHE HAS LOST, IT IS TOO MUCH FOR HER! WE NEED ANOTHER TRANSFUSION... CALL UP HOLMWOOD AND MORRIS AT ONCE! LET US HOPE THE STRENGTH OF FOUR GOOD MEN...
... IS EQUAL TO THE MALEVOLENCE OF ONE DEVIL!
OOOH...

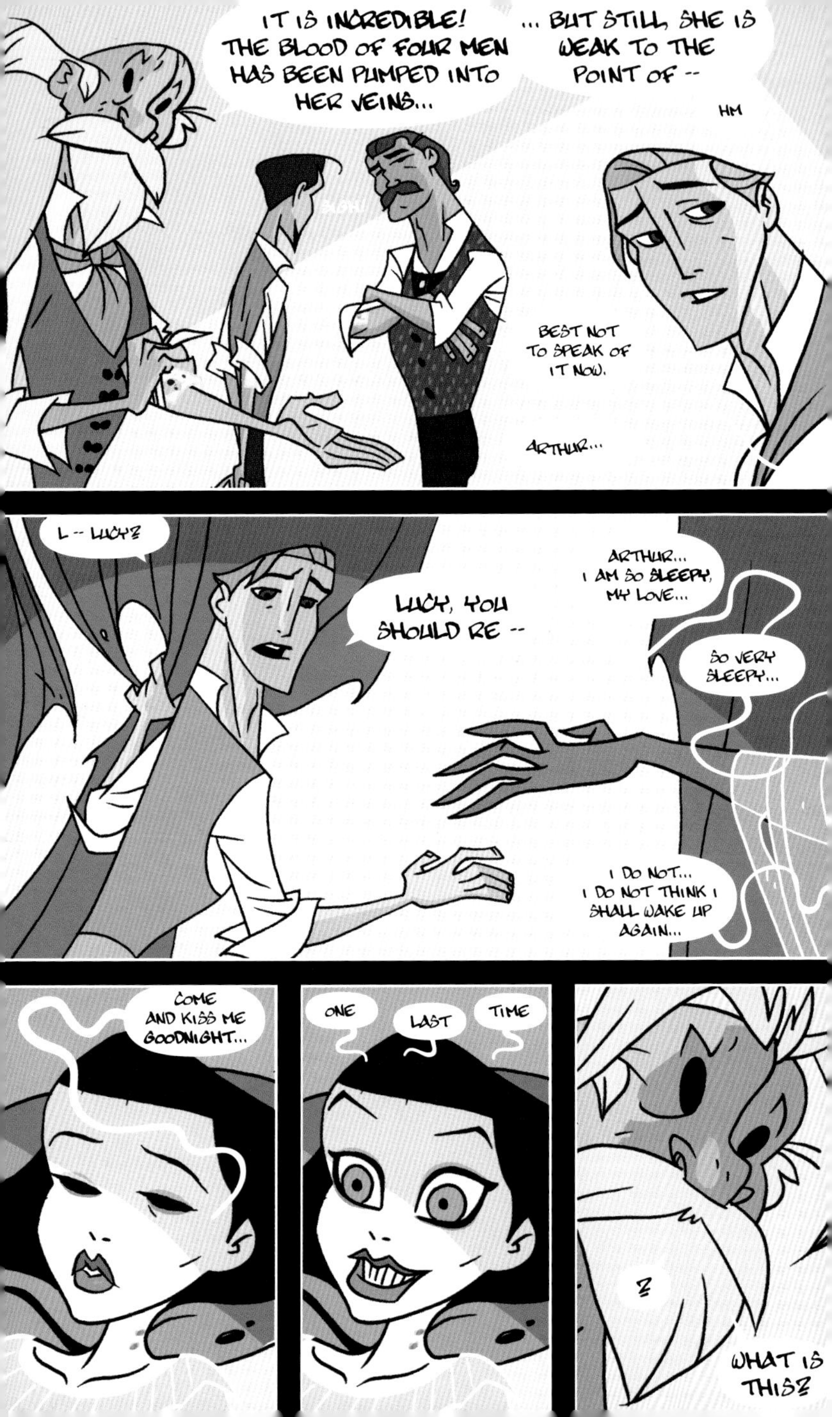
IT IS INCREDIBLE! THE BLOOD OF FOUR MEN HAS BEEN PUMPED INTO HER VEINS...
... BUT STILL, SHE IS WEAK TO THE POINT OF --
HM
BEST NOT TO SPEAK OF IT NOW.
ARTHUR...
L -- LUCY?
LUCY, YOU SHOULD RE --
ARTHUR... I AM SO SLEEPY, MY LOVE...
SO VERY SLEEPY...
I DO NOT... I DO NOT THINK I SHALL WAKE UP AGAIN...
COME AND KISS ME GOODNIGHT...
ONE
LAST
TIME
?
WHAT IS THIS?

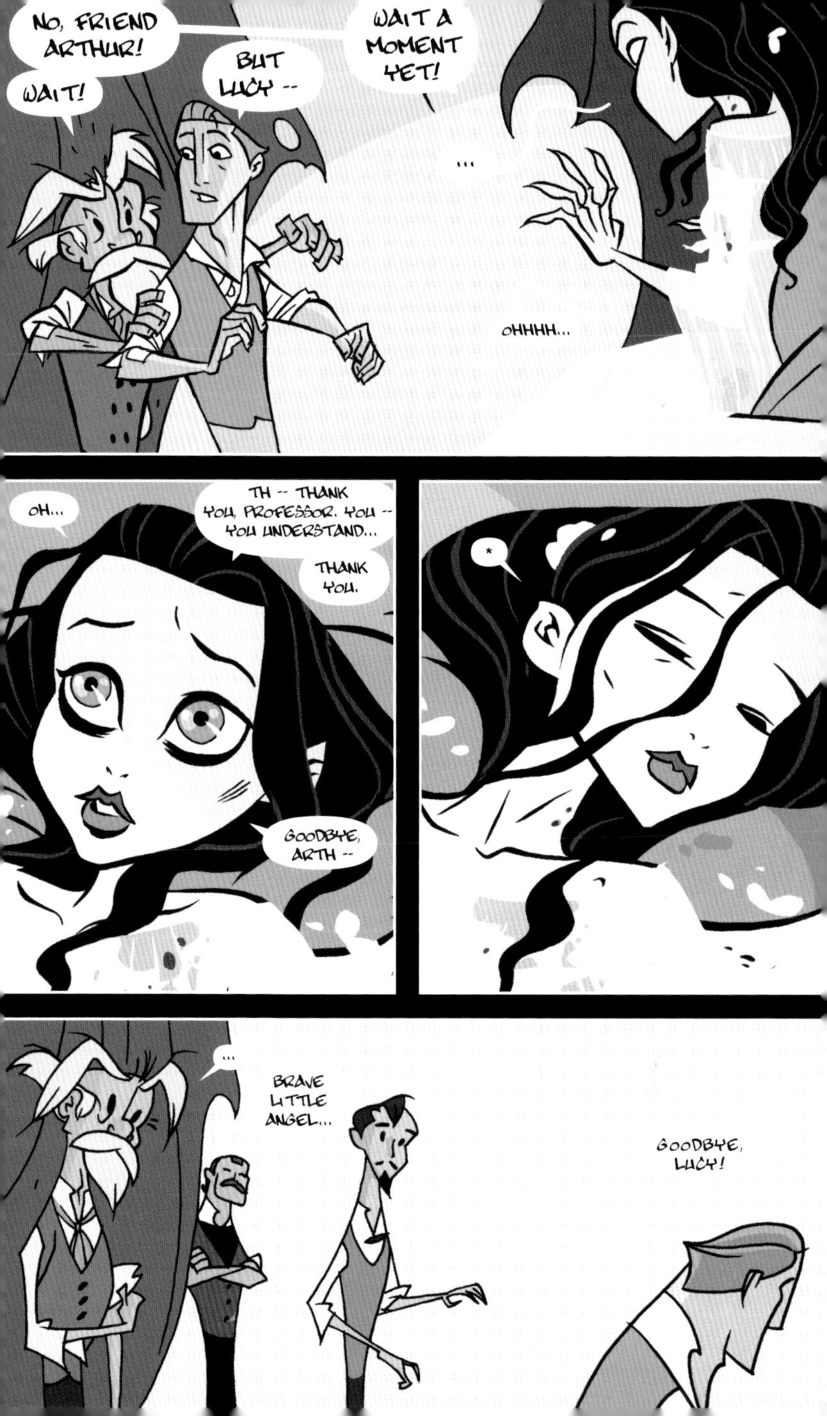
NO, FRIEND ARTHUR!
WAIT!
BUT LUCY --
WAIT A MOMENT YET!
...
OHHHH...
OH...
TH -- THANK YOU, PROFESSOR. YOU -- YOU UNDERSTAND...
THANK YOU.
GOODBYE, ARTH --
*
...
BRAVE LITTLE ANGEL...
GOODBYE, LUCY!

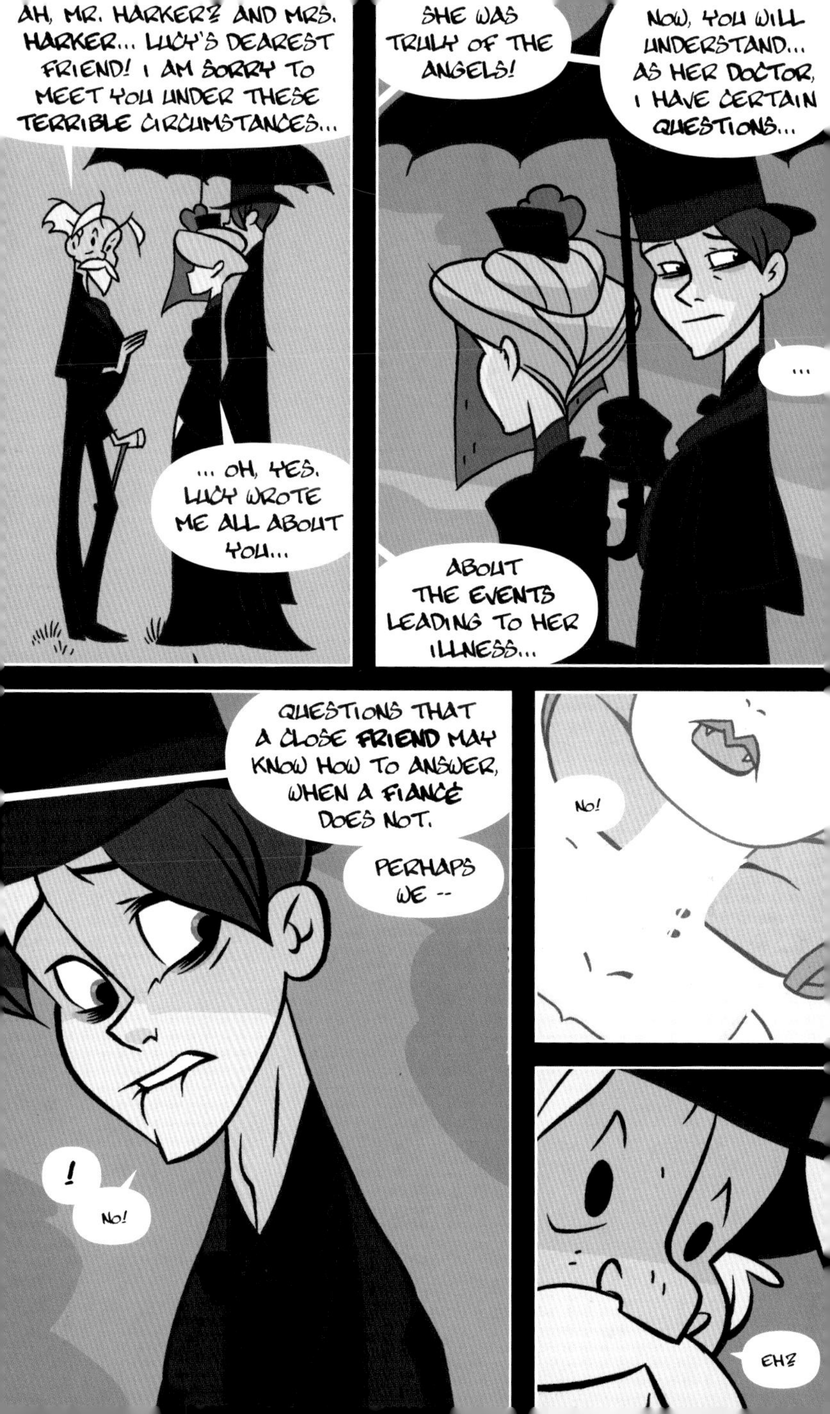
AH, MR. HARKER? AND MRS. HARKER... LUCY'S DEAREST FRIEND! I AM SORRY TO MEET YOU UNDER THESE TERRIBLE CIRCUMSTANCES...
... OH, YES. LUCY WROTE ME ALL ABOUT YOU...
SHE WAS TRULY OF THE ANGELS!
NOW, YOU WILL UNDERSTAND... AS HER DOCTOR, I HAVE CERTAIN QUESTIONS...
...
ABOUT THE EVENTS LEADING TO HER ILLNESS...
QUESTIONS THAT A CLOSE FRIEND MAY KNOW HOW TO ANSWER, WHEN A FIANCÉ DOES NOT.
PERHAPS WE --
!
NO!
NO!
EH?

I SHOULD KNOW... I MADE THE ARRANGEMENTS FOR EVERY ESTATE PURCHASE, CUSTOMS FEE, AND SHIPPING RECIEPT THE COUNT REQUIRED! FIFTY COFFINS, BILLED AS PERSONAL ITEMS...

... SHIPPED BY THE SCHOONER DEMETER...

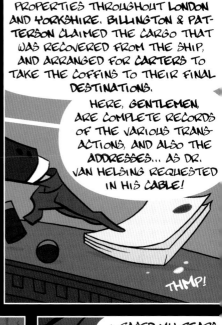

... THEN CRATED TO TWENTY THREE PROPERTIES THROUGHOUT LONDON AND YORKSHIRE. BILLINGTON & PATTERSON CLAIMED THE CARGO THAT WAS RECOVERED FROM THE SHIP, AND ARRANGED FOR CARTERS TO TAKE THE COFFINS TO THEIR FINAL DESTINATIONS.

HERE, GENTLEMEN, ARE COMPLETE RECORDS OF THE VARIOUS TRANSACTIONS, AND ALSO THE ADDRESSES... AS DR. VAN HELSING REQUESTED IN HIS CABLE!

THMP!

IMPRESSIVE, MR. HARKER.

NO DOUBT YOU MAKE A FIRST-RATE ESTATE AGENT...

... BUT DO YOU HAVE THE NERVES TO WORK AGAINST THIS...

... THIS COUNT DRACULA?

I FACED MY FEARS IN TRANSYLVANIA...

KNOWING IT WAS NOT ALL SOME... NIGHTMARE HAS RESTORED ME! AND WHEN THE TIME --

BLAM! BLAM!

AAI!!!

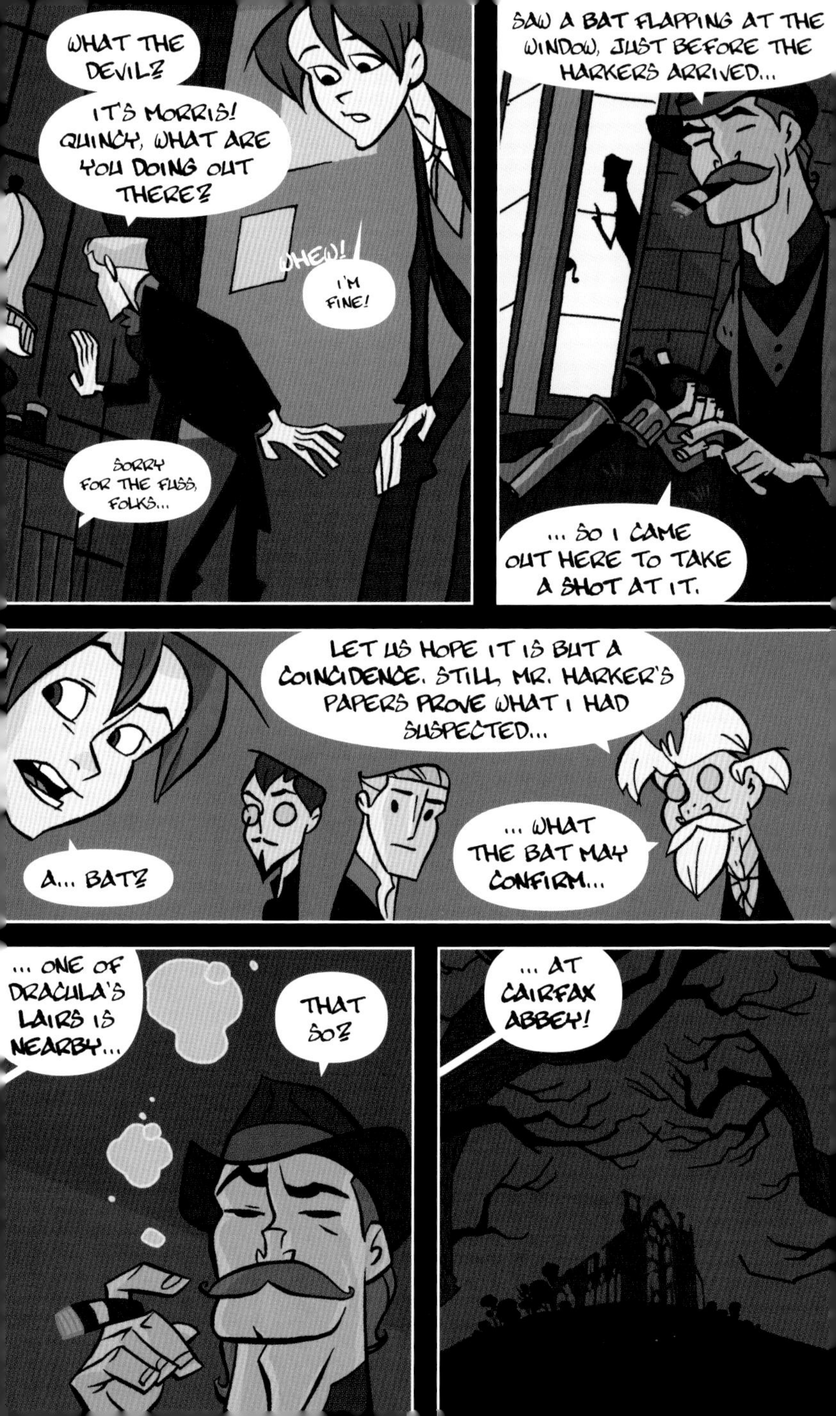
WHAT THE DEVIL?
IT'S MORRIS! QUINCY, WHAT ARE YOU DOING OUT THERE?
WHEW!
I'M FINE!
SORRY FOR THE FUSS, FOLKS...
SAW A BAT FLAPPING AT THE WINDOW, JUST BEFORE THE HARKERS ARRIVED...
... SO I CAME OUT HERE TO TAKE A SHOT AT IT.
A... BAT?
LET US HOPE IT IS BUT A COINCIDENCE. STILL, MR. HARKER'S PAPERS PROVE WHAT I HAD SUSPECTED...
... WHAT THE BAT MAY CONFIRM...
... ONE OF DRACULA'S LAIRS IS NEARBY...
THAT SO?
... AT CAIRFAX ABBEY!

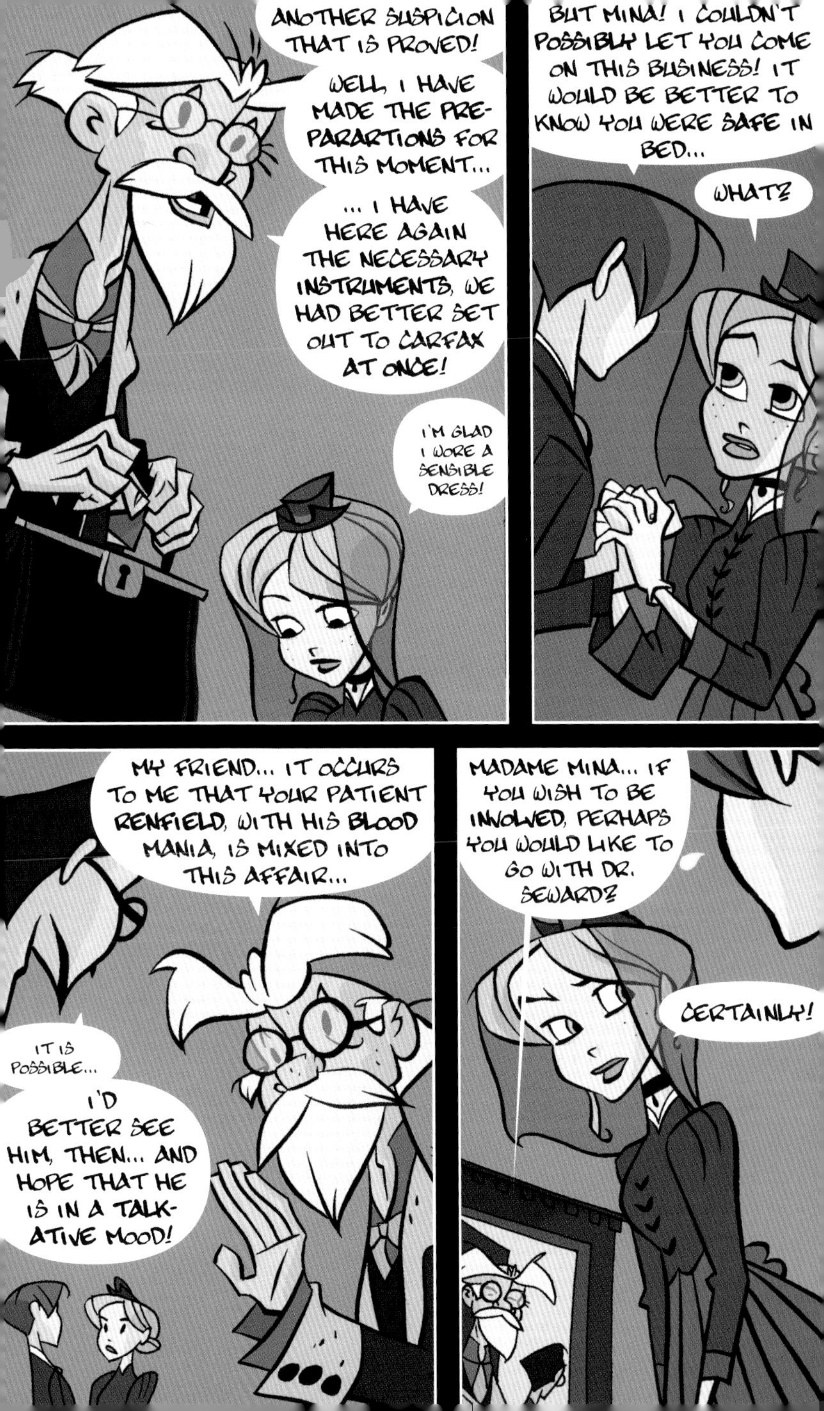
ANOTHER SUSPICION THAT IS PROVED!
WELL, I HAVE MADE THE PRE-PARARTIONS FOR THIS MOMENT...
... I HAVE HERE AGAIN THE NECESSARY INSTRUMENTS, WE HAD BETTER SET OUT TO CARFAX AT ONCE!
I'M GLAD I WORE A SENSIBLE DRESS!
BUT MINA! I COULDN'T POSSIBLY LET YOU COME ON THIS BUSINESS! IT WOULD BE BETTER TO KNOW YOU WERE SAFE IN BED...
WHAT?
MY FRIEND... IT OCCURS TO ME THAT YOUR PATIENT RENFIELD, WITH HIS BLOOD MANIA, IS MIXED INTO THIS AFFAIR...
IT IS POSSIBLE...
I'D BETTER SEE HIM, THEN... AND HOPE THAT HE IS IN A TALK-ATIVE MOOD!
MADAME MINA... IF YOU WISH TO BE INVOLVED, PERHAPS YOU WOULD LIKE TO GO WITH DR. SEWARD?
CERTAINLY!

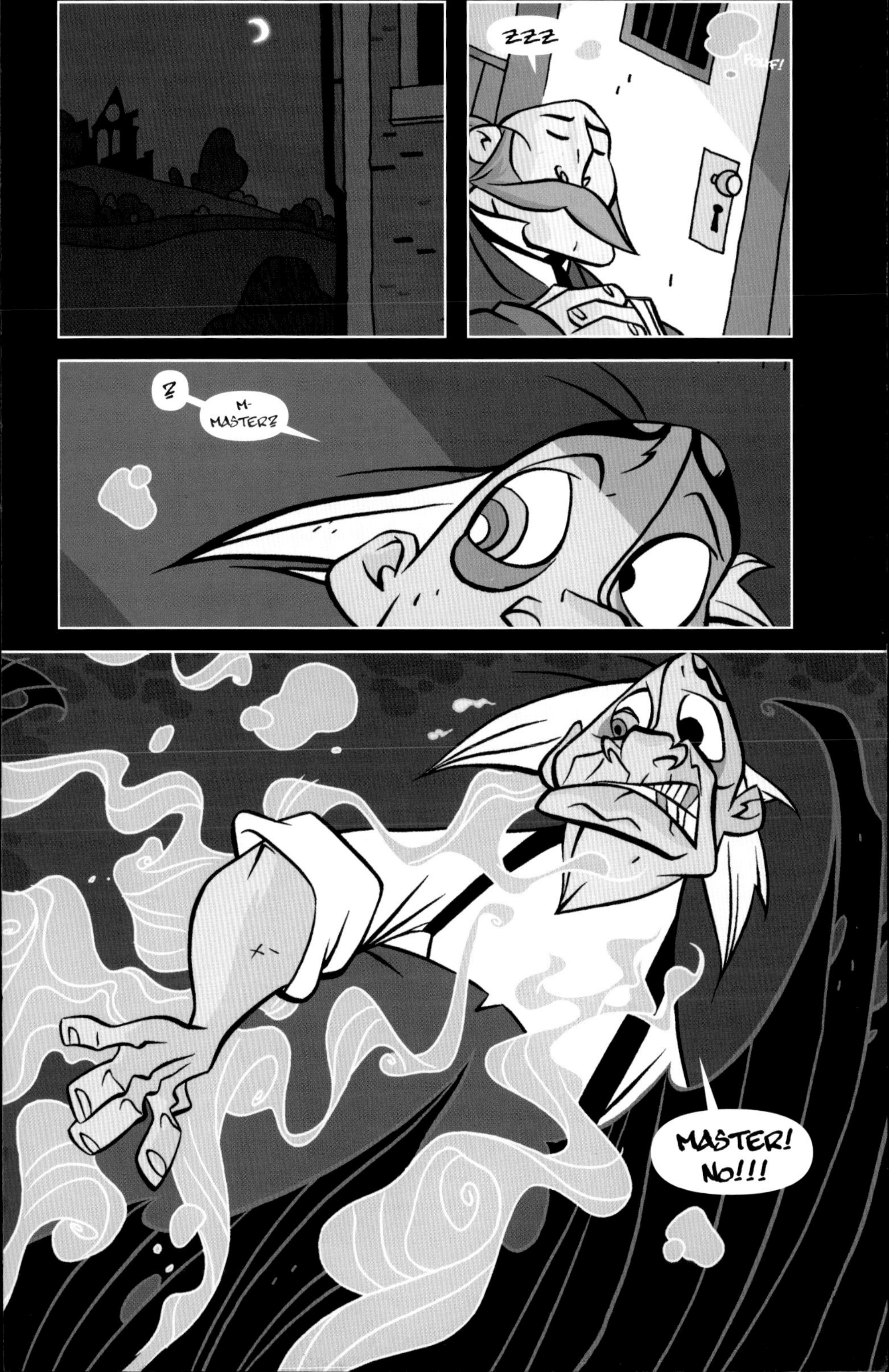
ZZZ
POUF!
?
M-
MASTER?
MASTER!
NO!!!

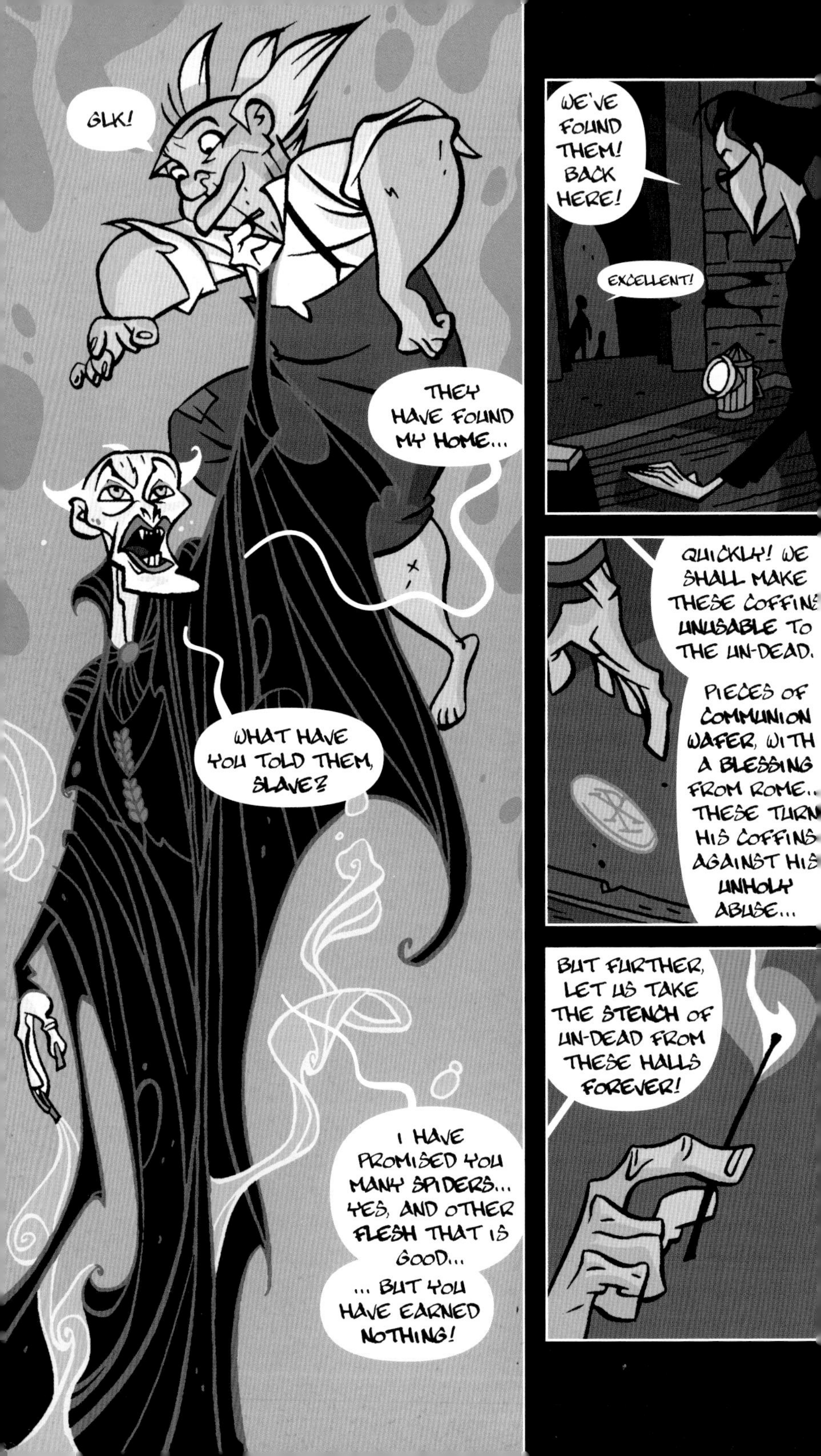
GLK!
THEY HAVE FOUND MY HOME...
WHAT HAVE YOU TOLD THEM, SLAVE?
I HAVE PROMISED YOU MANY SPIDERS... YES, AND OTHER FLESH THAT IS GOOD...
... BUT YOU HAVE EARNED NOTHING!
WE'VE FOUND THEM! BACK HERE!
EXCELLENT!
QUICKLY! WE SHALL MAKE THESE COFFINS UNUSABLE TO THE UN-DEAD.
PIECES OF COMMUNION WAFER, WITH A BLESSING FROM ROME... THESE TURN HIS COFFINS AGAINST HIS UNHOLY ABUSE...
BUT FURTHER, LET US TAKE THE STENCH OF UN-DEAD FROM THESE HALLS FOREVER!

SO! DRACULA HAS COME AGAIN INTO THIS COUNTRY, HE IS BEING CARRIED THROUGH THE MOUNTAINS BY SLEIGH OR HORSE-CART...
... ANOTHER DAY, AT MOST, AND HE WILL BE HERE!
MR. MORRIS HAS MADE OUR PLANS.
EXCELLENT! IT WILL BE YOUR WORK TO STOP THE COUNT ON THE HIGH ROAD. MADAME MINA AND I SHALL STAY BEHIND, TO TAKE OTHER PRECAUTIONS...
BUT MINA --
DO NOT FEAR, FRIEND JONATHAN! I PLACE THIS WAFER OF THE SACRED HOST AGAINST HER FOREHEAD...
TO PROTECT HER FROM THE DAR --
PUF!
AH!
GASP!
QUICKLY! THE POWER OF DRACULA GROWS OVER MISS MINA! BY TOMORROW'S SUNSET, IT WILL BE TOO LATE! YOU MUST GO NOW!
NO!
STAY WITH VAN HELSING, DARLING! AND STAY STRONG...
JACK! MR. HOLMWOOD! MR. MORRIS!
WE WILL DESTROY THE MONSTER BEFORE ANOTHER DAY IS OUT!

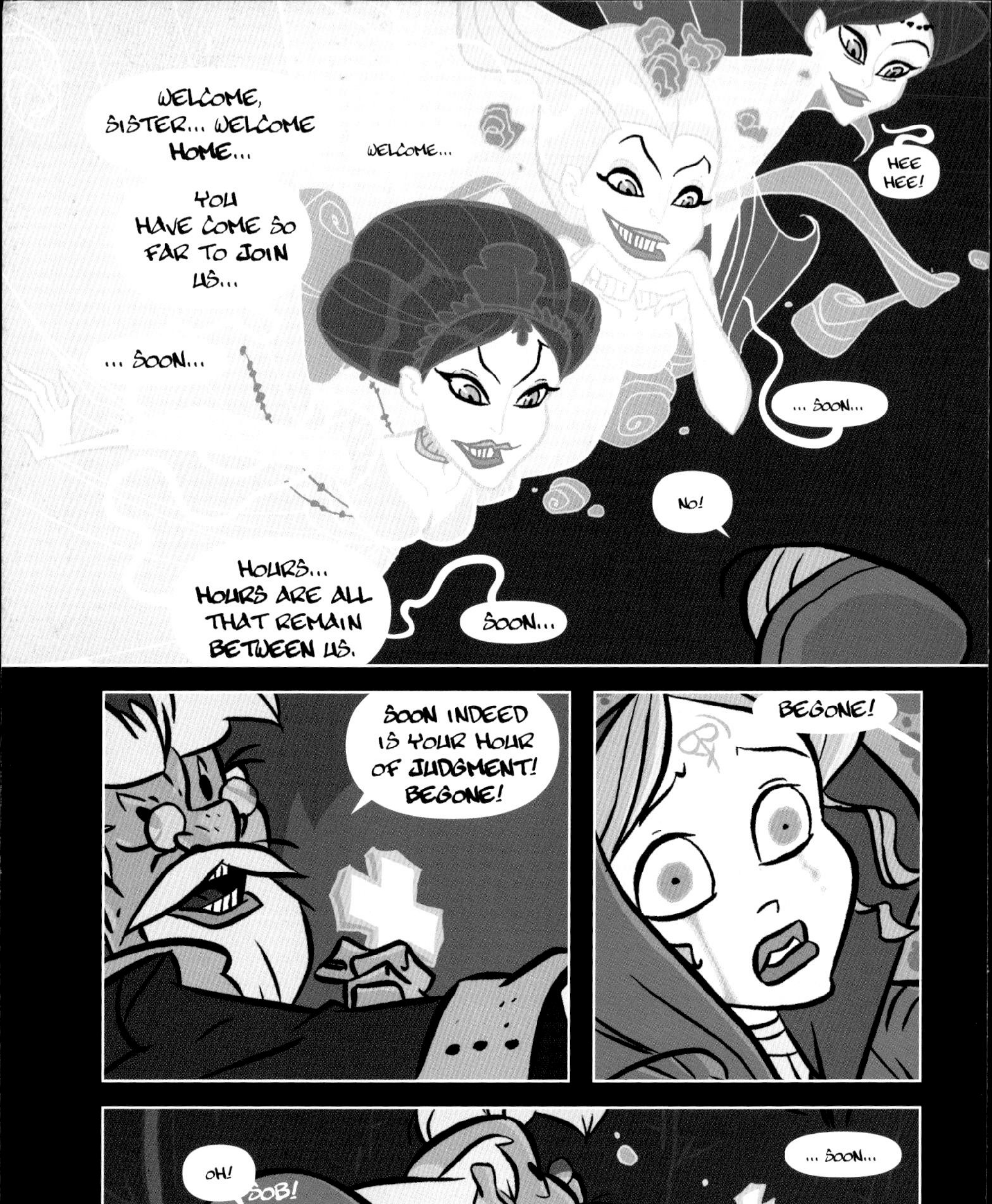
WELCOME, SISTER... WELCOME HOME...
WELCOME...
HEE HEE!
YOU HAVE COME SO FAR TO JOIN US...
... SOON...
... SOON...
NO!
HOURS... HOURS ARE ALL THAT REMAIN BETWEEN US.
SOON...
SOON INDEED IS YOUR HOUR OF JUDGMENT! BEGONE!
BEGONE!
OH!
SOB!
... SOON...

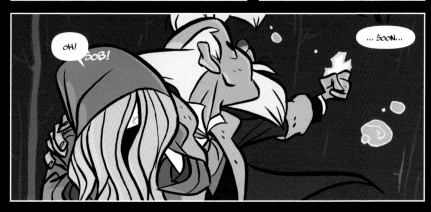

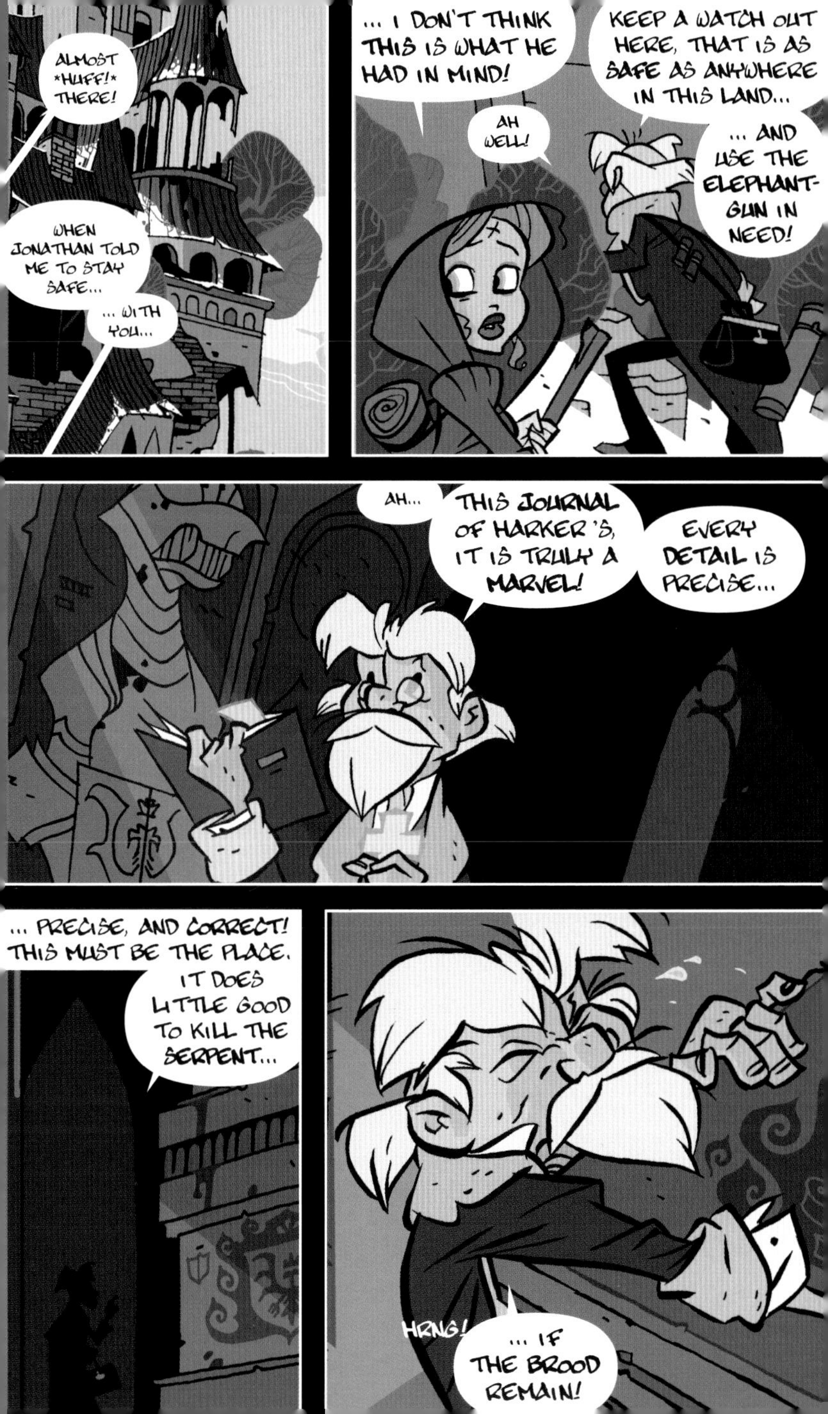
ALMOST *HUFF!* THERE!
WHEN JONATHAN TOLD ME TO STAY SAFE...
... WITH YOU...
... I DON'T THINK THIS IS WHAT HE HAD IN MIND!
AH WELL!
KEEP A WATCH OUT HERE, THAT IS AS SAFE AS ANYWHERE IN THIS LAND...
... AND USE THE ELEPHANT-GUN IN NEED!
AH...
THIS JOURNAL OF HARKER'S, IT IS TRULY A MARVEL!
EVERY DETAIL IS PRECISE...
... PRECISE, AND CORRECT! THIS MUST BE THE PLACE.
IT DOES LITTLE GOOD TO KILL THE SERPENT...
HRNG!
... IF THE BROOD REMAIN!

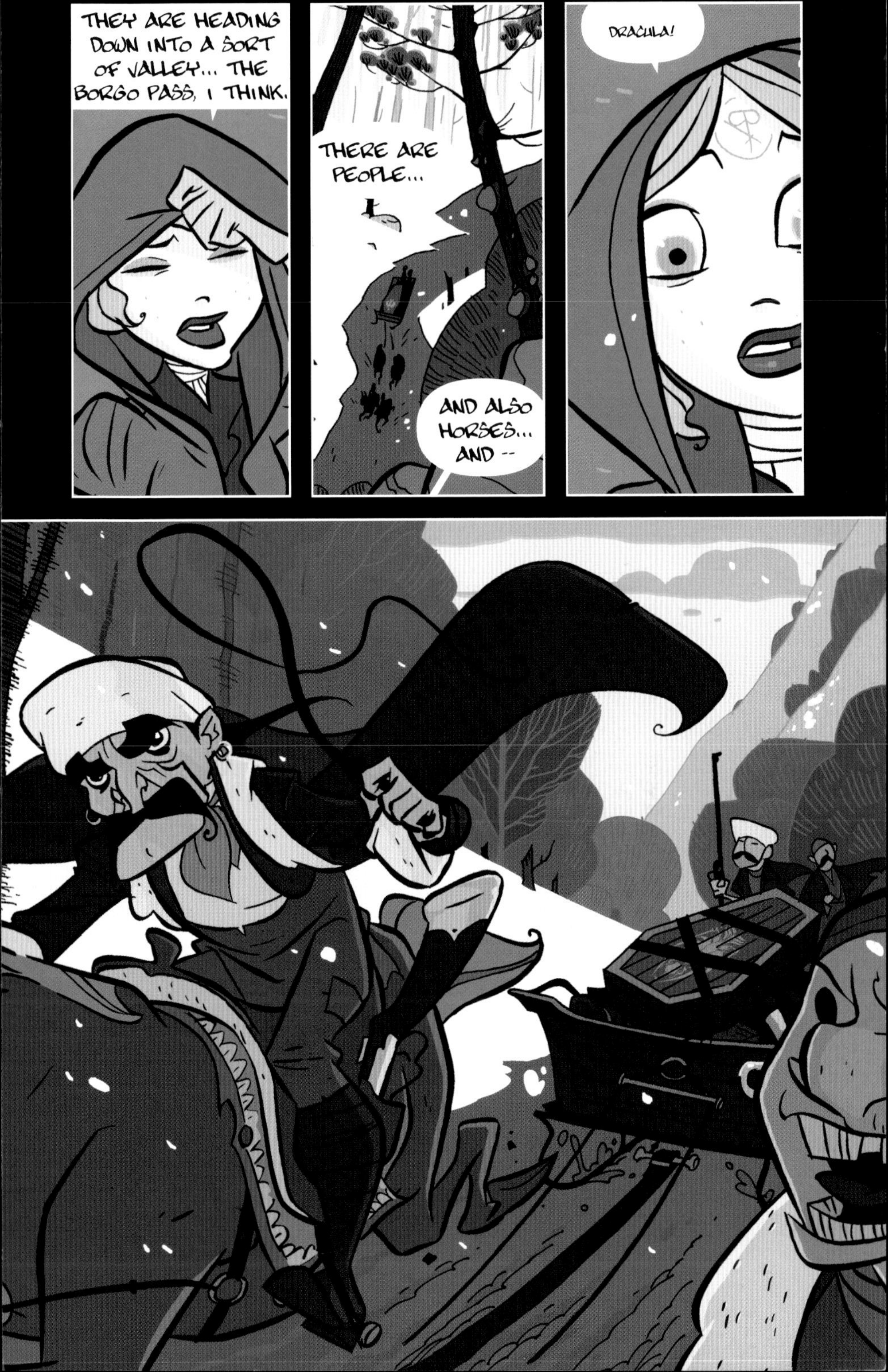
THEY ARE HEADING DOWN INTO A SORT OF VALLEY... THE BORGO PASS, I THINK.
THERE ARE PEOPLE...
AND ALSO HORSES... AND --
DRACULA!

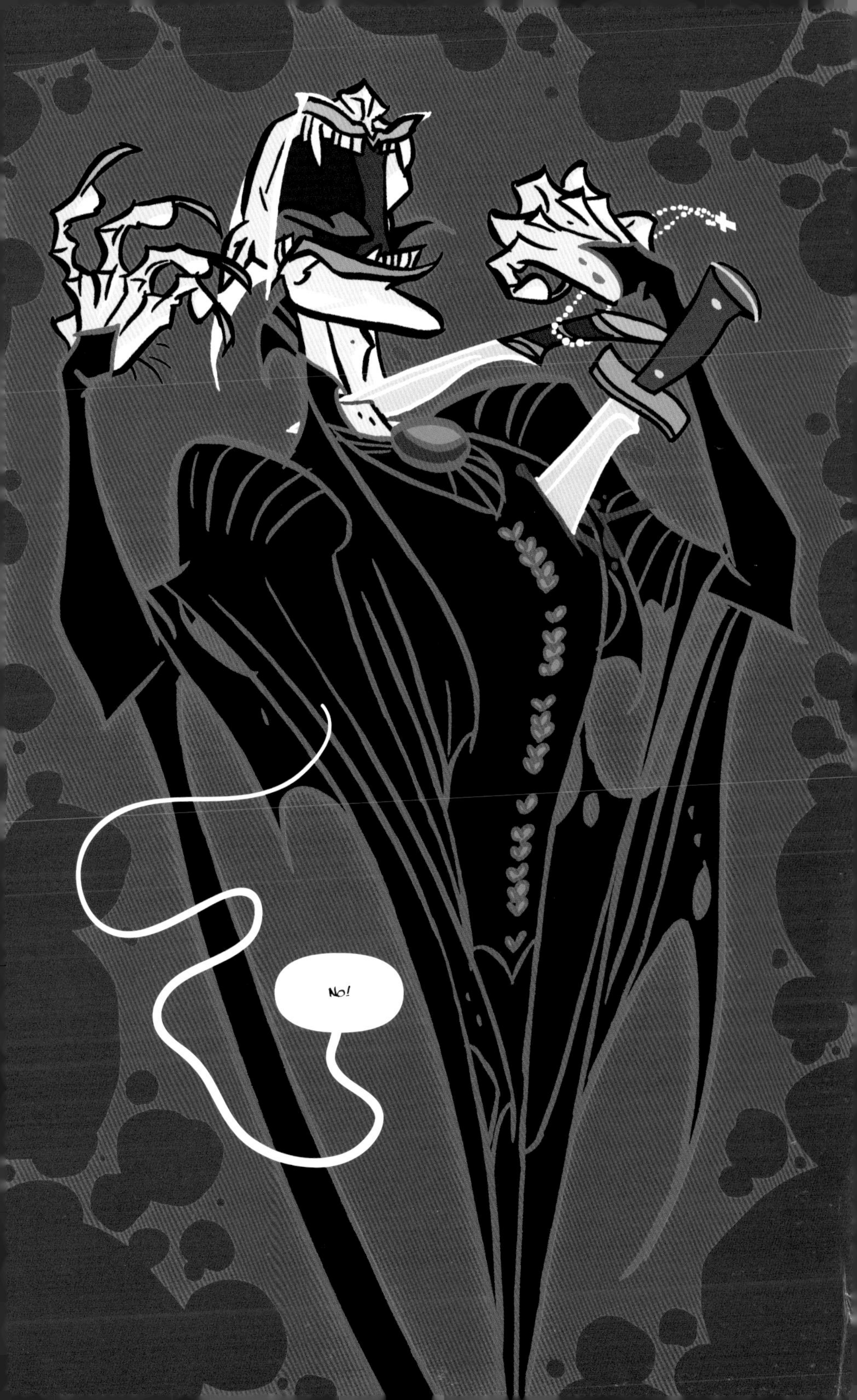
No!

FAREWELL, MR. MORRIS ...

6 NOVEMBER, BORGO PASS -- WE WANT NO PROOFS, WE ASK NO ONE TO BELIEVE US...

... IT IS ENOUGH THAT THE NIGHT-MARE IS ENDED...

... AND A NEW DAY BEGINS!

VLAD DRACULA TEPES (1431-1476) WAS A REAL PERSON. HE WAS NOT A COUNT -- IN FACT, HE WAS PRINCE OF WALLACHIA (A SMALL PRINCIPALITY IN MODERN ROMANIA), WHO OWED HIS CROWN TO THE KING OF HUNGARY.

IN THE FIFTEENTH CENTURY, THE TURKISH EMPIRE SWEPT THROUGH EASTERN EUROPE AND THREATENED MANY SMALL STATES LIKE WALLACHIA. AT THE SAME TIME, WALLACHIA ITSELF WAS TORN APART BY CIVIL WARS BETWEEN RIVALS IN THE ROYAL FAMILY. VLAD DRACUL WAS DRIVEN OUT OF THE COUNTRY, AND HIS SON DRACULA WAS BORN IN EXILE IN NEARBY TRANSYLVANIA.

IN THOSE TREACHEROUS TIMES, DRACULA BEGAN TO LEARN THE KNIGHTLY PROFESSION FROM WALLACHIAN BOYARS (ARISTOCRATS) AT THE AGE OF FIVE. HE WAS LATER SENT TO LIVE IN THE TURKISH SULTAN'S COURT AS A TEEN.

DRACULA FOUGHT MANY BLOODY WARS TO RECLAIM HIS FATHER'S THRONE. SOMETIMES HE WAS ALLIED WITH THE TURKS, SOMETIMES THE HUNGARIANS, BUT HIS ENEMIES WERE ALWAYS HIS ROYAL RELATIVES, AND THE BOYARS AND MERCHANTS WHO SUPPORTED THEM.

DRACULA WAS ONE OF THE CRUELEST MEN IN A CRUEL AGE. HE EARNED THE NICKNAME TEPES ("THE IMPALER") FROM HIS FAVORITE METHOD OF EXECUTION. IN THE 1450'S, HE WAS POWERFUL ENOUGH TO FIGHT FOR IN-DEPENDENCE AGAINST HIS TURKISH ALLIES.

BUT DRACULA'S EXTREME METHODS COULD NEVER COMPLETELY SECURE HIS RULE. HE WAS DRIVEN OUT OF WALLACHIA SEVERAL TIMES BY RIVALS AND REBELLIOUS BOYARS, FIGHTING HIS WAY BACK EVERY TIME. FINALLY, THE TURKS INVADED IN 1476, AND DRACULA WAS KILLED AT BUCHAREST.

VLAD DRACULA WAS NOTORIOUS THROUGHOUT EUROPE FOR HIS STRENGTH AND CRUELTY. BUT MODERN-DAY ROMANIANS REMEMBER HIM AS A NATIONAL HERO WHO FREED THEM FROM FOREIGN RULE.

ABRAHAM "BRAM" STOKER (1847-1912) WAS BORN IN DUBLIN, IRELAND. AFTER A SICKLY CHILDHOOD, STOKER ATTENDED TRINITY COLLEGE, THEN TOOK A JOB AS A CIVIL SERVANT.

BRAM STOKER WROTE NEWS ARTICLES AND SHORT STORIES IN HIS SPARE TIME, AND IN 1878 BECAME THE MANAGER OF THE LYCEUM THEATRE IN LONDON.

BUT WHILE STOKER WROTE MANY NOVELS AND PRODUCED MANY PLAYS, HIS MOST FAMOUS WORK WAS "DRACULA." BEGUN UNDER THE TITLE "THE UN-DEAD" IN 1894, IT WAS PUBLISHED IN 1897 AND BECAME AN INSTANT HIT. STOKER WENT ON TO WRITE AND PRODUCE A DRACULA PLAY, AND CONTINUED WITH OTHER HORROR AND ADVENTURE NOVELS INCLUDING "THE JEWEL OF THE SEVEN STARS," "LAIR OF THE WHITE WORM," AND SEVERAL SHORT DRACULA STORIES.

BRAM STOKER'S DRACULA IS THE MOST IMITATED MODERN HORROR STORY. IT HAS SPAWNED HUNDREDS OF FILM, BOOK, GAME, AND COMIC BOOK ADAPTATIONS, AND WAS THE INSPIRATION FOR OTHER HORROR CLASSICS LIKE THE GERMAN SILENT FILM "NOSFERATU."

VAMPIRE STORIES WERE POPULAR IN VICTORIAN ENGLAND (1837-1901). ORIGINALLY IMPORTED FROM EAST-ERN EUROPE, THESE GHOSTLY CHARACTERS BECAME THE STAPLE OF CHEAP "PENNY DREADFUL" MAGA-ZINES, WITH "VARNEY THE VAMPIRE" TERRORIZING ENGLISH READERS IN THE 1840S.

BUT WHILE "DRACULA" IS A VICTORIAN NOVEL, IT IS SET AT THE DAWN OF A NEW AGE. THE HEROES USE TELEGRAMS, ELECTRIC LAN-TERNS, TYPEWRITERS, AND DICTA-PHONES. THERE WERE ALREADY THOUSANDS OF AUTOMOBILES IN EUROPE AND AMERICA IN 1897, AND ELECTRIC LIGHTS WERE STARTING TO BRIGHTEN THE CITIES. MODERN MEDICINE, IN THE FORM OF HYPNOTISM (OR "MESMERISM") AND BLOOD TRANSFUSIONS, IS JUST ONE OF MANY MODERN TOOLS STOKER'S HEROES USE AGAINST THE ANCIENT SORCERY OF THE VAMPIRE KING.